The Danger Game

The Danger Game

Kalinda Ashton

Tindal
Street
Press

This edition published in 2012 by Tindal Street Press Ltd
First published in UK March 2011
by Tindal Street Press Ltd
217 The Custard Factory, Gibb Street,
Birmingham, B9 4AA
www.tindalstreet.co.uk

2 4 6 8 10 9 7 5 3 1

A CIP catalogue reference for this book is available
from the British Library

ISBN: 978 1 906994 28 0

Typeset by Alma Books Ltd
Printed and bound by
CPI Group (UK) Ltd, Croydon, CR0 4YY

For Keren, Danielle, Andrea, Allara and Julie
– with love and admiration

The Danger Game

They are playing the danger game.

Jeremy sits on a scarred wooden chair on the porch and watches his sisters run outside. Behind him, the screen door shudders closed, then flaps and bangs in the wind. In the garden, Alice frowns. Louise beams as she collects the old tea tin they use to keep the randoms in. She has to shake spider webs off the rusty container, which she keeps hidden inside the slouching rubber tyre that used to be part of a swing set. The tyre leans against the house on a bed of long grass. They haven't played the game for a long time.

Jeremy doesn't play the danger game. He lets his body fold in on itself. He keeps his eyes downcast. When his sisters start to choose randoms, he goes back in and sits in the hall.

He focuses on the fading blooms of the rose carpet and waits for his father.

Alice doesn't like the game and Louise rarely loses, but Alice plays just the same. His sisters have eaten dirt and fish food. They have swum into the deepest part of the river, where the current might take them. Louise cut her thigh with the rusted part of a razor. Sometimes Jeremy is the target of the danger game but it is hard for his sisters to think of anything worse than the injuries he already gets at school.

He came up with the name and Louise changed it into code with pig Latin. *Hetay angerday amegay.*

His twin sister needs the game. It makes her eyes shine. She becomes crafty, cut-throat, inventive.

Usually, Alice and Louise make the randoms by scribbling instructions down on bits of paper whenever they think of them and stuffing them into the tin with the others until they decide they are ready to play. But Alice has stopped creating dares. She's nearly thirteen and says she's too old. Louise forgets about the randoms, too, until the holidays, when she makes Jeremy help her decorate them with drawings of skull and crossbones or tiny warning signs. Alice tells her off for not putting in the right amount of free turns – where they don't have to put themselves at risk – and then they don't play for months.

The danger game has made Lou good at telling lies. Jeremy knows her real life but he still gets confused when Louise tells him about events that couldn't possibly have happened. She may not have done what she claims but it is likely that at some point she will. Her dares are astounding to him. He both believes and does not believe many of the crazy acts she has actually carried out.

Rain spatters on the roof. He waits in the hall. It's getting dark. He turns on the light switch but the bulb's burned out and no one has replaced it. He sits on the carpet and rocks, clasping his ankles with his hands. But he can still hear the game.

Alice is yelling: 'Cheater.'

'Am not.' He sees Louise kick at the old bricks, which have come loose from the paving. 'How come?'

'You looked.'

They are meant to pick a piece of paper from the tin, like a lucky dip. Most of the randoms are embarrassing or horrible but the rules say at least a third have to be nice things, happy ones – orders to ride your bike or get mixed lollies from the corner shop.

His sisters clatter inside. One of the elastic bands for Louise's pigtails has fallen out and she's lopsided, her hair bunching around her ear on one side, and falling forward over her shoulder on the other.

Louise looks at him. 'Why don't you play, dickhead?'

The territory of the danger game – the banned, the illegal and the horrifying – frightens Jeremy. He wants to go unnoticed. He wants to go down to the station and stand at the pedestrian crossing and watch the people get on and off the trains, or to read his science book.

Louise thrusts the tin into his hands. 'You choose for Alice.'

He reaches into the tin.

His older sister shakes her head. 'No. I don't want him to,' she says, and chews at her nails. 'I'm sick of this. I wanna go out and do something. I'm bored.'

'One more turn.' Louise yanks the randoms away. 'You have to jump out of the tree.'

'That's not fair. You just made that up. It wasn't even your go.'

His twin sister crosses her arms. '*Jump.*'

It's their birthday today, his and Louise's. They are nine. His mum gave him a book about Egyptian tombs and treasures but it's filled with fold-out illustrations of mummies in gold and black where the information should be. The paper looks flimsy and he doesn't want to open up the flaps in case they tear. The insides of his cheeks are sore from all the smiling he did to show how happy he was with the present and how much it was the right thing. Louise got a jewellery box that she had been nagging for. His dad is not home yet.

His stomach hurts from eating the cupcakes his mum brought back for them. 'They taste like soap,' Louise told her. He'd had to eat more so that his mother wouldn't go into her room and close the door. When they blew out all the candles together, she hugged them both at the same time and then she went to have a shower. She cooked chops and they got to drink lemon cordial. Louise spilt hers on the plastic table cover.

But it's eight o'clock and his father won't come home.

After his sisters have gone out the front to climb the oak tree, he buries his hands in the tin and pulls out different randoms. The slips of paper are mostly in Louise's handwriting and she can't spell. They say: *cross the road with your eyes closed, watch Freddy Krueger alone, stay in the underground tunel for an our, brake into school at night, kidnap a dog and write a ransom note, kiss a boy, do a handstand on the concreet, balance and walk along the top of a fence, flash your knickers to people on the street or in cars, have one of my birthday lollies, piss on the carpet* and *get lost on purpose.*

The list makes him dizzy. He saw Louise play the game all by herself once, walking on the balls of her feet along the barrier for the pedestrian bridge that goes across the freeway. She had wobbled on the rail and he had heard the shriek and crunch that never came, cars skidding on the wet road, the shower of glass like treasure on the ground.

You have to start the dare on the random within twenty seconds, or surrender. Louise keeps the points but she adds new rules all the time. She will decide that they can only play the game when it's dark, or when their dad's not home, or that Alice can't play without her. They talk in pig Latin and have to say 'enough' when they want to give up.

They played it a lot in the holidays last year, after his dad lost the job, Louise whispering to herself while she coloured in, 'I wish for danger': some invitation or promise Jeremy keeps well away from.

Often, when she forgets to answer questions at school, or doesn't check when she's crossing the road, he knows she's running through the plans for dares in her head.

Last summer is when Louise was held back at school, when his twin sister – his shining, buoyant sister – turned away from Jeremy. She stopped protecting him in the schoolyard. She stopped making up wondrous stories of many-headed monsters defeated by gypsy children and began telling lies instead. It's only after the bell rings at the end of the school day, when no one can see her, that she'll talk to him again.

Jeremy takes his schoolbag out the front so he will be the first to see his father arrive. He gets cold sitting on their low front wall but he can read ahead in his maths book beneath the street light, and he won't hear his mum stand up every time the house creaks or the wind blows and shakes the windows in their frames. Jeremy leans over the book on his knees. They are supposed to learn long division but his mum says, 'Use a bloody calculator: would you use leeches instead of penicillin just for practice?' so he doesn't like her to see him doing the working out. Mrs Daly asked him to do extra homework with fractions.

He glimpses Alice's leap from the tree on the nature strip. After she lands, Alice touches the raw, soft bark of the trunk and wipes at the blood from her split lip. Louise claps her hands. He hears Alice saying in her clear voice, 'I *win* the game.'

Louise tells one of her tremendous, enviable lies. 'The danger game is not a winning game.'

'Jeremy. Jeremy. Oi!' Louise puts her hand over his book so he can't read. 'Your random is to tell Dad to stop drinking when he gets back . . . and . . . and say he should fuck off.'

Alice pulls Louise's hand away. 'Shut up.'

Jeremy does not look at them. 'I don't want to.' He hears his voice, thin and whiny, as if he's speaking under water.

'Why not?'

'I give up.' Alice walks back towards the house.

Louise checks her watch, the one with the colourful band that their mum gave her when she learnt to tell the time. 'Look.' When he looks at her hand, he sees a tiny white spider crawling across her knuckles.

His skin becomes warm, electric. 'You have to get it off,' he tells her.

'It's cute. Want to hold it?' She is leaning in to kiss the spider.

He shakes his head. Louise flicks the spider away and he jumps up and almost falls, scraping his leg on the wall.

When his father does come home, he forgets to go and see Jeremy. His mum tells Jeremy, 'Bed now – he's drunk too much, Jem.' His mother's face shows nothing. His mother's love is drying up. It has to be pinched and prodded from her.

He shouldn't have waited. He can't get normal things right, even little ones, the kind of stuff Louise manages without even thinking, such as knowing which parts of the playground she's meant to stay in and where is out of bounds, or remembering to wear a costume on the proper day and not the next.

He likes to carry tiny stones with him that he picks up from around the streets but his favourite one looks too much like a tiny round eye: a marble or pea that watches. He has it in his pocket. It has been watching him for a long time. It has seen him pull apart the wing of a dying pigeon to see inside. It knows the way he places his feet on the footpath, the times he has been sick into the toilet – loose strands of spittle clinging fatly to his lips.

Louise's side of the room is covered in toys. Forgotten glasses of water wait on the floor near her bed. She throws her drawing projects down into the corner and doesn't care if they get squashed or torn. She nicks biscuits and hides them around the room and he has to be careful not to step on them with bare feet, because they are horribly soft and sticky.

He puts his maths book into his bag and climbs under the huddle of sheets and covers. The brown blanket scratches through the sheet. Jeremy reads his book of the planets, about Venus and the dense yellow clouds that encircle it, which are poisonous to humans.

His pillowslip crumples and makes a papery sound, a whispery crackle. Louise has left one of her notes. He's trying not to breathe at all. She's drawn him a map of everywhere they have been today, for their birthday. He knows where they've been. But the map means she's happy again, the map means she'll want to play with him.

As he is drifting off to sleep he imagines she is telling him that the danger game isn't real.

O n the morning I woke with Jon I looked out the window at the flat, scissored streets and grimy lanes of Brunswick. We were not meant to wake together. My flat was on the third floor and I watched a bottlebrush tree waving furiously in the wind. I had a student-teacher coming in to learn the cruelty of fifteen-year-old boys, and last night's wine hurt in my throat. When I saw Jon's shoes at the end of the bed, their shadows cast large in the glare of the morning sun, I put my hand over my mouth in an unintentional, ugly mimicry of a silent movie actress.

I met Jon almost a year ago, in one of those fierce, tearing nights at a Collingwood pub, when jugs of beer make you raw and earnest, and you believe everything you say. Jon wore sneakers and tweed pants and was recognizably hopeless. I saw his broad palms and narrow wrists, and the book he clutched to his side in soft protection. He put his hand on my back when we walked up Princes Street to another bar and then I knew.

I was used to being unloved and Jon had a wife – some slow, certain-faced woman I had seen getting out of a car one day – so I could already tell how much fear and distance was breathing between us. In Abbotsford, I teetered forward, waiting for him to ask me up, and he said, 'Shall we?' I thought he was brave then, even gallant.

I had climbed the cramped steps to what he called his studio – a tiny peach-coloured room, with a dusty easel and a barred window

– and paused in the doorway. There was no bed, just a greying armchair and thin plastic yoga mats laid across the floor.

It was a beginning and there was a blankness in me that was attracted to the pedestrian drama of an affair: the reassuring parameters of its disappointments, the ordinariness of its false starts.

Jon illustrated children's books. He hated politics; he liked to watch world news; he had read all the great Russian novelists; he usually came before I did; and he felt I was reminding him of something he had once lost. After we had been sleeping together for a few weeks he said, 'Mary's an absolute survivor and I admire her for that,' and I realized he was letting me know that the two of them would also survive me.

We didn't talk about the future. He spent three months in London with his wife and I tried not to sound pleased when he rang. We played at mundane domestic rituals. Once I made spaghetti with mussels but he was running late and ate so quickly that he burned his tongue. I wiped the sauce off his chin as he ran out the door – he was meant to have been watching football with an old friend. I would rub moisturizer into my skin in the evenings, seeking his reflection in my dressing table mirror, pressing my fingers firmly across my eyelids, then sweeping them down towards my chin, all the time hoping he was watching.

He read to me before he left at night. His voice was pleasing: smooth and light. I listened to the rhythms, the catches and pauses in his voice, and tried to predict when it would all end. I had feigned emotional immunity for so long it was difficult to recognize an honest feeling. We were losing pleasure in each other's bodies and pretending not to notice. I was a comfort for Jon and he was a distraction for me. It was an ugly but unabashed exchange, a deal.

We saw each other every week or two, during which there was desire but also terror. I shuffled him out of my flat in the early hours of the morning, looked the other way if I saw people we both knew at Coles, and wore secret bruises on my hips beneath my work clothes. I had thought I was better equipped for these useless jolts between terror and comfort, than for love.

I looked out through the window at one of Australia's ridiculous native plants shaking in the wind, with its rusty-red flowers bright splashes against the foliage, and let my gaze flicker over what I could see of the lanes and tarmac of Brunswick. Then I fixed my eyes on his shoes.

The phone rang. Jon's face was buried in one of his hands while he slept, a near picture-posed tableau of despair. The crumpled bedsheet had left tiny red lines, the imprint of a seam, on his arm. His fingers were lying loose off the side of the bed. My alarm clock glowed sullenly. Quarter past seven.

When our evasions were kinder, we had joked about finding organizational skills we'd never before summoned. He left for home on time, even if it meant doing the maths to establish whether there was time to have sex again before he left, or wiping himself clean with a face cloth in the bathroom so that the sharp smell of me was replaced by the tepid drift of rose-fragranced soap. I joked about watching the clock as he thrust inside me but this was too much: I was meant to accept his circumstances but not parody them, to wish for a different future without actually expressing it.

I picked up the phone, 'It's too early to ring someone,' and hoped I hadn't forgotten an excursion. Silence. When I swung my legs out of bed, my bare feet landed on the splayed back of *Anna Karenina*. The title page had fallen out and there were small pencil drawings across it: wombats with tea party paraphernalia looked perkily at a river. Jon's sketches.

'Hello.'

An automated voice message, the captured ghost-sound of a person, asked if I would accept the charges.

I knew who was ringing at almost exactly the same moment she began sobbing. 'Lou?'

'Alice. It's no good. It's all coming apart.' I heard traffic and the hoot and sway of a train pulling out in the background. I hadn't seen my younger sister, who lived in Sydney, in six months, since she'd borrowed eight hundred dollars for drug counselling and had nothing to show for it but her remaining purchases: a store of exotic goods, expensive cheeses and a flimsy metal scooter. She had told me on the phone that she went to the chemist every day with her methadone prescription but then she said a lot of things.

'What's no good?' Thick silence on the line. 'Where are you?'

Jon stirred. Through the gauzy piece of fabric that covered the side window I saw my neighbours in the flats opposite, lying on the carpet watching cartoons. Spoons idled in bowls of porridge on their fifties dining table.

'I had this dream. Dad was in it. And then on George Street I thought I saw someone.'

She was in her twenties but she still sounded like a child.

'What?' If I could see the neighbours, they could probably see me. I was naked, hunched forward, poised for combat. Ludicrous. I pulled a corner of the sheet across my breasts and huddled my back against the wall.

'Come on, this silence is expensive.' It was becoming hard to remember speaking to Louise without this shapeless fear descending – the dark fog of it settling around me, seeping into my skin and hair.

'Dad was talking to me, he knew who I was –'

'Of course he knew. It's Jeremy he forgets,' I told her. 'He knows who you are.'

'– and he said he had a surprise and that Jeremy was alive in an underground castle and we could visit him. And Dad had this red suit. In the dream.'

I should have put the phone down. I could sense the agitation beneath her careful lack of purpose. I swallowed. 'You're mixing things up with real life.'

Her crying was repetitive, strangely mechanical, unremitting and tinny like those toy dolls engineered to sound like babies that cry when they want to be fed. 'Who did you see?' I had a sudden longing, brief and mildly disingenuous, for Louise's chaos to be my own, even though I knew her confusion was also fraudulent.

'Mum.'

I watched through my neighbours' window, as the host for the cartoon channel clutched her stomach and pretended to laugh.

Behind her, on a smaller screen, a cat got hit hard on the head with an axe. There were tiny red hearts on her dress.

'I don't have time for this, Louise. What do you want?' I used my teaching voice, clipped and firm. She was going to ask me for money.

'I thought it was her. Probably not. On the street. Going into Chinatown. And I saw this TV show on . . . arsonists? Delinquents. But that was before.'

I tried to imagine our mother's face, the way she used to look, but the picture I summoned up was faded like old wallpaper in the sun. She had worn her fine blonde hair up, dragged into a ponytail, and she stooped her narrow shoulders when she was tired; she sang along to the radio on weekends. But my mother's distinguishing features were erased; her outline was suspiciously general, her expression robbed of purpose.

Since Louise had ended her love affair with heroin she saw, or pretended to see, a fleet of ghosts, long left-behind people from our childhood. Months ago she couldn't stop talking about one of the boys in my brother's class, when all I could remember of my brother's childhood torturer was the way he moved, thickly, with a gait too awkward to be a proper swagger: just a jumble of menace and desperation as if his body were not quite his own.

'Sleep it off,' I said.

'I'm not *high*.' I knew she was. 'Please don't be a cunt, Alice.' After I hung up, I unplugged the phone.

My alarm went off. I switched over to the radio. I preferred the incessant list of loss that was the news on Radio National to talkback, which made me despair of people. Jon and I argued about this. He said, 'Who are you to judge what's important for other people to talk about?' and I said, 'There's a war on and this woman is talking about her chickens, her fucking *chickens* for fuck's sake, and permits for coops in the outer suburbs.'

I opened a window to let the summer heat in.

Jon had always been more expansive, more magnanimous about other people's lives, because he didn't care what kind of mess they made of them.

In the glare of the sun, his eyes were puffy. His mouth drooped down.

I thought of letting him sleep so that the horror, when he got up, would be his own. I sprayed deodorant everywhere, stepped into yesterday's skirt and picked up my keys. My bedroom felt like a box: a small cell with a low ceiling. After I packed up my books and papers, I put my hand on Jon's shoulder and said, 'All right.' I ran the back of my hand along his cheek. He jerked awake.

'*God*, fuck, what time is it?'

Already, he was reaching for his watch, tripping as he grabbed his pants.

I ran down the stairs fast so that I wouldn't have to listen to him call his wife.

When I got to work, the school was teeming with kids and the sun burned heavily on the playground swings. Some of the plastic equipment was too warm to play on. I taught in a school that had a *reputation*, a bad name. I'd been at a professional development session last year on 'the gifted child and the learning-challenged child'. Integration and special needs staff cutbacks were being repackaged to us as a teaching opportunity. Another teacher, plump and cynical, had asked if I was from the school with 'all those commission kids' as if they were a mutant scientific aberration, some special strain of childhood.

I had grown up in a housing commission place just when the suburb was changing, and the Department of Housing sold some of its high-rises and let you buy out homes you had been renting. There was no community I remember belonging to back then, just parents who tended fussy gardens or built new window frames to hide the monolithic, clear structure, the architectural sameness that signified public housing. We'd got the kind they weren't building anymore by then, a fibro-cement townhouse, semi-detached, with a tacked-on brick porch out the front and a scrap of garden for a backyard. Our parents had stood on the patch of yellowing grass out front and clinked their beers together when they bought that home.

I realized recently that my mother's unerring instinct for the bottom line, as much a habit for her as the red elastic bands she kept round her wrists to tie back her hair, was caused not by being famously poor in a poor suburb but by having married a man who thought he was meant for greater things. Her realism, her grimly practical thinking, kept shame at bay while my father was inventing devices that he swore could make them thousands, or drawing renovation plans on bits of paper in between trips to ask for beer on tick at the local shop.

On my way into the staffroom, I nodded my head to the two brothers who were puffing on cigarettes just outside the gates, next to the not-so-temporary mobile classroom that had been erected three years ago, and wished I could join them. The Thomas boys were poor and rude. Chris was a punk and went straight to the principal's office with each new piercing. He wrote gentle sentences in sloping handwriting.

Hamish was fair and battered with bruises. To questions he'd often just hiss 'Cunt' and then look slightly surprised at himself. There was nothing like teaching high school to remind you of the pure, determined torture of children. When I started teaching I saw an earnest girl with intricate braids lean over to one of the shy girls who sat next to the door and say, 'I'm going to set you on fire.'

When I first taught history to Chris in Year 7 he thought the marches against the Vietnam War were not worth learning about.

'Miss,' he tried to explain to me, 'it's not *new* that everyone's got bombs. People don't wanna hear about it. We *know*. I get to explode people on the computer.'

History was about novelty and gore, video game gruesomeness, to Chris. He wanted to be astonished by something, to learn about ancient torture weapons or to gawk at the wretched bodies of landmine victims, to see the number of ways human beings could die, to be stilled and open-mouthed at the misery we can inflict on one another.

It was the same for lots of these boys: they hated the state, they loathed the cops and they couldn't care less what the government was doing, some kind of reciprocal adolescent rightness for the fact that the government wasn't too interested in them either.

*

By the time I collected my whiteboard marker and spare books, I was late. In the corridor outside the classroom, my students were lined up in jagged rows near the door.

When I'd taught the collapse of the Soviet Union, one of the Greek students said his grandfather wept on the anniversary of the Russian Revolution and thought that the failure of Communism meant history was over. The other students had tried to say the foreign words in heavy accents like the spies in early Bond films, dragging out *Glasnost* until it sounded like a Scottish toast.

'Perestroika's like the end of the world, right?'

'No, that's apocalypse.'

'Where everyone got nuclear rays.'

'Chernobyl?'

'Oh.'

Now, the neat girls at the front were folding paper into cubes to make 'Pick-a-Box' games and a few of the boys chucked a footy between the sections in the back row.

'Sit down. I *will* start naming people. Nicholas. Thanh.'

I handed back their creative responses to reading they'd done on the gold rush. I asked them to take out worksheets on the Cold War and tried to teach past their impervious faces – defining terms and wishing I'd thought to organize a DVD. I wrote 'Cuban Missile Crisis', 'Communism' and 'the West' on the board with a skittering hand.

Selena Papas, in the back row, waved her arm in the air until I could no longer ignore it.

'Miss, Miss. Why do we have to do this?'

'Do what, Selena?'

'Why do we have to do the Cold War?'

'Why not?'

Chris made a face. 'It wasn't even a real war.'

'Well, it's an important part of history.' That wouldn't do. I rubbed the back of my neck. 'With the Cold War . . .' I turned to ▓▓▓▓▓▓▓ board and then spun back. 'Who decides what becomes history? What counts?'

They waited patiently for me to provide the answer, curious and detached. I was confusing them. 'Okay, this is meant to be twentieth-century history. So how do you know what the big events are?'

Selena chomped on her gum. 'You tell us.'

'Yeah, but . . .' Out of my depth, I fell back on the textbook. 'With the USSR as it was then, and the United States, there were two major superpowers competing. We had the arms race, the space race. There was an escalation that many thought would end in nuclear war.'

'So?'

'So there was a lot of hope, in the wake of the Cold War, that arms spending would go down and that there'd be a more peaceful time.'

Selena tilted forward on the edge of her chair, her elbows on her desk. The other kids were enjoying her eagerness, her recent transformation from teacher's pet to anti-authoritarian. Her eyes were rimmed with blue mascara. They weren't meant to wear makeup but I wasn't going to send her to the toilets to wash it off.

'But it didn't.'

'Go on, Selena.'

'It's not more peaceful. Now America's on its own and there's still war.'

'That's because America's the best. They can,' Chris said.

I moved from the board into the small knot of kids clustered near the window.

'My country's the fucken best, not *America*.' The Greeks, the Turkish kids, the Vietnamese raised their voices. No one laid claim to Australia until Hamish began chanting, 'Ozzie, oi!' in a goofy voice.

I shouted. 'All right. Calm *down*. Obviously, some of the people who thought that the end of the Cold War would mean a less militarized world were wrong.' They ignored me. They defended their countries in the name of Eurovision, of sport, of food, and of triumph in armed conflict.

'Selena. Nicholas. Mustafa. Sit *down*. Chris says America can begin wars. Why can they?'

'They're the biggest,' Chris said, bewildered at the riot he had begun.

'They don't have the largest population or land mass. What else? Theo?'

'They won that war . . . the Cold War, and now everyone's afraid of them?'

'Possibly. Any other ideas?'

'They've got the biggest army.'

'There are different aspects to an army. America has more nuclear weapons and conventional weapons. Selena, do you agree? Why can America start wars?'

Chris had another go. 'They know they're right so their army *believes* what they're doing.' He waited. 'Morale.'

Selena looked at me. 'Because they have the most money.' The bell rang.

I met the student-teacher in the staffroom before the afternoon classes. She was nervous, with chipped nails and a small frame. She was dressed in a pinstriped suit and wore fashionable glasses with geometric black frames. There were streaks of blonde cut through her black hair and she had applied shiny grape lipstick, which was slightly smudged around her mouth. I was relieved she wasn't eighteen and petrified or wildly enthusiastic.

I introduced myself to her: 'Justine? I'm Alice.'

She looked around the spartan room with its litre jars of instant coffee and squat microwave oven, and I felt that she was disappointed. When she showed me her lesson plans – a study of apartheid South Africa for a unit on modern history – I asked how she was finding teaching.

'Good.' She looked down. 'I guess I'll get better at it. I want to tell them off but I don't know what to call them. How d'you remember all those names?'

The faint scent of the perfume she was wearing, along with the memory of Jon's visit, made me feel nauseous but my voice stayed brisk and confident. 'I can help with that.'

'Thanks.'

'When I started, they swapped names for the whole of first term. What brings you to this illustrious career?'

'I was in admin at a uni but I couldn't keep up with all the new databases for the fee structures. So here I am.'

I smiled. 'Year 10s can be difficult. For the first lesson they'll probably be painful but you'll survive.' I hated the boarding-school cheer in my voice.

'Everyone keeps telling me different things.'

'Like what?'

'One of the other teachers said, "Remember some of them are just horrible little shits" but Tom told me, "They're *great* kids. Use multimedia."'

I laughed. 'Tom thinks multimedia's always the solution. You can't use a DVD in the first class. They'll sense your fear.'

'Hopefully I'll get a nice easy private school next time.'

'Yeah, where daddy owns a racehorse and you can threaten them with corporal punishment.'

She didn't laugh.

'Are you going to apply here when you finish?'

'Teaching's kind of putting me off teaching.' She grinned, then looked aghast. 'And I've still got two rounds to go. Tom said there won't be anything because you might become a middle school next year.'

'I'm sorry?' Our enrolments had been dropping steadily. There had been rumours of funding cuts or streaming our older kids into one of the bigger schools in the next suburb since I started. But at open day, Tom, our principal, had just given a rousing speech to the parents about the unique community of the school.

'I've probably got it wrong. He said something like, "We won't be needing more staff. If anything —"' she broke off and imitated a gesture I knew must be Tom's, a patting of the air that suggested the desirable outcome would be fewer staff or no staff at all.

Our shoes squeaked on the floor of the corridor. The blue linoleum gleamed.

In the classroom I wrote her name on the board. Already the boys were switching chairs and throwing paper planes. I picked a note up off the floor. *You cunts are sluts.* Justine's hands shook as she picked up the whiteboard marker.

They settled. 'This is Miss Avery. She's going to be taking you for the next week so I trust you'll give her a taste of what teaching's all about.' There were a few uneasy giggles.

She looked over their heads. 'Good afternoon everyone.'

'Miss, have you got a boyfriend?'

'Are you a lesbian?'

'Why is your hair like that?'

Sam, one of my gentlest students, called out, 'Shut up youse.'

I stood up. 'Please behave or it's detentions all round.'

Sam frowned at me. 'How come? You never give detentions.'

Nam, who had been in Australia eighteen months, asked, 'What's "all round"?'

'For everyone. For each of you.' I smiled helplessly at Justine. 'Like drinks all round.'

I sat near the front of the classroom and watched her spend too long in the circle of safety around the whiteboard. Jon would have spoken to his wife by now. Justine picked up her notes.

She cleared her throat and stared back at the doleful eyes of the students. She wrote '*Population Registration Act*: 1991' on the board.

1991: the year the first Gulf War was waged under the first Bush presidency; the year the Soviet Union finally collapsed; the year the Birmingham Six were freed; Rodney King was beaten by police; Sonic the Hedgehog was created.

In 1991 Freddie Mercury dies of AIDS, Alexis Indris Sontana, who posed as a self-taught orphan from Utah and enrolled at Princeton University, is exposed as a fraud, Joh Bjelke-Petersen is tried for perjury, there is the Royal Commission into Aboriginal Deaths in Custody and New South Wales has a general strike. All history.

And in 1991 my brother died.

CHAPTER TWO
THEN: Jeremy - 1991, Monday, 7 a.m.

*I*n the morning, Jeremy wipes the sticky brine from his eyes and listens. Sleep has spread through his eyelashes like a web. There is a moment of panic when he tries to open his eyes and feels resistance. His heart thuds in his chest – are his eyelids stitched together? His dreamy fingers tug at the small shards of sleep that have gathered in the night and then he can see the poster his mum put on his bedroom wall. The poster is no good. It weeps at the edges; the corners fold forward where the Blu-Tack doesn't reach.

His dream was a tangle of wires and strings. If he moved, he was going to be electrocuted, step on some circuit that would send bolts through his body.

He listens to Louise sleeping across from him. Every time she breathes in, she snores. She breathes thickly, as if she's drowning or suffocating.

There are creaks and bumps as Alice thrashes in bed, on the other side of the partition. He knows she'll be switching her head from side to side and twitching her limbs, in a lolling, consciousless effort to get away from the sounds of Louise.

His older sister cried until their parents let her have her own room. She's painting her side of the wall with spray-paint and the fumes make Jeremy sick if he stands too close.

Water gushing in the gully trap mixes into the sound of his mother filling the kettle. She will shake tea into the old teapot, which used

27

to be a coppery pink – but now the polished skin is coming off in patches to reveal the dull metal deep below.

He listens as his mum pours water into the teapot. Jeremy cannot feel his dad in the house. Usually, of a morning, there is a sense of him. Nothing specific, not a pin in a map, but a low cloud, a heaviness in the air like a change of weather.

Just as his mum knocks on the door, Louise falls out of bed in a single wrench. Quite often, perhaps once a week, his sister wakes by falling. He hears her scramble and realign, feels the pause of her recognition: she is on the floor. It's morning.

His mother swings open their bedroom door. She looks tired. 'It's seven o' clock.' She zips up her jacket quickly: a fast movement as if she is striking a match. 'Jesus, Louise. Get off the floor.'

Louise's laugh catches in her throat, still half a snore.

'Jeremy.' His mum switches on the light. 'Get up. Don't forget about the test. Mrs Daly has to talk to you about it.'

Mrs Daly had visited their home on the weekend and drunk tea from a cracked cup. She held Jeremy's maths homework and talked about how he should take the exam for entry into a school for gifted students. His dad had been asleep under the newspaper in the kitchen.

His mum puts her hands on his feet and shakes them. Then she reaches over him and peels back the duvet. The cold air shocks him.

Jeremy sits up, woozy, and puts his feet on the pale yellow carpet. The fabric of his sheet makes his legs itch and there are red marks all the way down where he has scratched in the night. He reaches for his school clothes from the pile on the floor, but Louise snatches the top away. 'That's not yours, it's my one.' If his dad got offered labouring today, Jeremy would hear good sounds – toothpaste landing in the bathroom sink, the clomping tread of his dad's workboots on the stairs – but there isn't anything. He slides back into bed.

When he wakes again, Louise is already up, so he comes downstairs as slowly as he can, taking one step at a time. Alice pushes past him, already dressed. 'Hurry up.' She wears her school belt slung around her hips, and her sleeves rolled up. 'I reckon you should go somewhere after school. Don't come straight home.'

'Why?'

'Dad's fucked up. Can you go to McDonald's? No, go to the park.'

Jeremy nods. 'I have my test.' He waits in the hallway. He has to go to the toilet. He's desperate. But he can't get across the hall without seeing his dad. If he does, his dad will ruffle his hair and make some jokes. And then there will be appeals to boys being boys together and his dad will say, again, how his boy is special but does he really want to go to a toff school? And his mum will turn away.

So he tries to hold it in.

He pulls his shorts over his undies. It's a cold day but the boys make fun of his jeans. They all pretend to have owned and discarded the jeans and tell Jeremy that he must have got the jeans from the op shop. And then they pretend to admire the jeans, to like them, to want to know where they've come from. The jeans are too small anyway. They expose his pale, lumpy ankles to the wind. The jeans came from Dimmeys a few winters ago. They'd all gone to the store near the city and Louise had wanted to buy fairy wings but his mum had looked at the material and called it flimsy and said no way.

He stands in the kitchen doorway. Louise is in the shower. The pipes shriek. There is toast on the table, with the butter melted in.

His father is telling his mum, 'I thought you wouldn't do houses.'

'It's just one morning. There's not enough work at the offices. And it's too far to go every day for what they give me.'

'You don't even keep this place clean. Why should you be picking up other people's rubbish?'

'I'm not your slave, Shaun Reilly.'

His father hesitates, brushes his hands over the table.

His mum pulls on the thick gloves she wears when it's cold. 'You could pick up after yourself.'

His father spoons sugar into his tea and his hand shakes.

Jeremy's mother checks the clock. 'It won't be anyone round here.'

'I thought we agreed only offices.'

'You get a fucking job then.'

'Here we go.'

Jeremy wishes she would leave him alone. His dad's face is grey. His hair is black and curly, like a girl's, but it sticks up in clumps in the mornings. He pretends sometimes to check if Jeremy's hair curls too and then hugs him too close. But Jeremy's hair falls flat and straight and sticks to his forehead. The fringe gets in his eyes.

It's been so long since he took Jeremy out in the canoes you can hire near the river, or to play cricket on the street. Usually, his dad just wants to stay inside, until the sun goes down, and then he'll walk and walk for hours, planning what he'll do the next day. He tells Jeremy these plans. He wants them to live in Thailand where the weather's good and he'll have his own business, or he is going to win the fruit game at the slot machines, or the local drawing competition.

Jeremy tiptoes in to get his lunch out of the cupboard.

'There's something going at the meatworks.'

'The meatworks?' His mouth's a curl. 'You're funny, aren't you?'

'Jean told me. Not slaughtering. Packing. Her husband's there. You could get a lift. Only an hour up the freeway.'

Jeremy steers his sandwich towards his lunchbox.

'I was considered to be a *skilled technician* when I worked for AmpCore, did you know that?'

'I also know how much it costs to feed three children.'

'That company should've given us what we were owed.'

'All the other men, everybody else who got done over when they closed down, *found something else*. You're a great big healthy man so . . .'

Jeremy drops his sandwich on the ground and it lands on the dirty floor. When he picks it up, a thin sheet of onion skin – like cellophane – sticks to the jammy parts. He tugs it off and flicks it away with his fingers. His parents both look at him. His mother picks at toast crumbs on the table, collecting them in her cupped palm.

'Hi, Jez.' His dad calls out too loudly.

'Hi.'

His mum pushes the paper towards his dad. 'I saw a sign up at the supermarket. Working nights. Shelf stacking.'

'They want an eighteen-year-old, Chels. I'm nearly forty.'

'Jeremy, make yourself some cereal. Has Alice gone?'

'I think so.'

'Do you remember what you did last night?'

There's a bolt of terror like electricity through Jeremy's blood. He's forgotten what he's done.

But she's talking to his father.

'I had a bit too much.' His dad slurps the tea, and looks at the sport results in the paper.

'You stood over me until I gave you twenty dollars.'

'Jeremy, tell me, what are my winning numbers? For the lotto? You can pick them.'

Jeremy shrugs but they wait for him to answer. 'Five's good?'

His mum whispers to his dad, 'Fool yourself if you like, if you can, but don't try and fool me.'

'I don't want you picking up shit for fucking men whose wives are too lazy to do it themselves,' his father says then, but softly, to himself and the paper.

After Mrs Daly's visit, his parents had argued. Even though his father made Jeremy wait in the garden, Jeremy could not stop himself hearing. 'He's too gentle and they'll . . . those boys are stuck-up pricks . . . gets teased enough already . . . all that pressure.'

His mum let Jeremy back in while she put on her uniform for work and called after his dad, 'If you don't want him to do it, you tell him.' Then he and Louise had made their sandwiches for school the next day. The strawberry jam glistened like fake blood when he slopped it out of the jar on a knife, and Louise had stuffed two whole bits of white bread and butter into her mouth when his father wasn't looking.

Now, Louise comes into the kitchen. When she reaches for tea the plastic charm bracelets on her wrist click and knock together. 'Mum. I'm still hungry.' Louise doesn't worry about looking like the other kids. The other kids try to look like her. She can't pass maths, but he sees the way adults' gazes arc drawn to her on the street. She is admired.

His mum grabs Louise's wrist. 'Where did you get those?' The lines on his mum's face that run from her mouth to her chin – he thinks of them as her fury lines – deepen.

Lou looks back coolly. 'From Sarah.'

'Alice's friend Sarah?'

Louise speaks quietly. 'No, my friend Sarah. You don't know her.'

His mother shakes her head.

Louise pulls her wrist away from the inspection, and the pink and green bracelets send Jeremy's stomach lurching. They look like lollies, and he has to shit.

Jeremy saw Louise take them from the supermarket.

'Just don't get caught.' His mum shakes her head. 'Please.'

Lou smiles. She thinks she is invincible.

His father doesn't listen properly. 'You've got no shame, Louise Reilly. Taking charity from other people. Does her mum know you're getting pissy two-buck bits of jewellery from her?'

His dad doesn't know about the danger game.

'Was a present.' Lou always has the winning card. She remembers. She keeps track of time. 'For my birthday,' she adds. His father nods, bewildered. He leans back in his chair so far that the front legs leave the floor, and smiles over at Louise, pretending he knows what's going on.

Jeremy's mother's mouth is a straight line. Louise's birthday was months ago, same as his.

His father asserts what he does know. 'Big test today, eh?'

'Yeah.'

'Teacher says you're gonna ace it.'

'Dunno.' He has been guessing when he does his sums, lots of times, and Mrs Daly doesn't even notice. He forgets to show his working out and has to go backwards, trying to retrace getting to the answer. His hand gets stiff around the pencil and his elbow locks.

'Anyway, being clever is not the only important thing,' says his mum, catching up her bag.

'You should know.' His dad laughs.

Some of the shit Jeremy has been holding in squeezes out in liquid onto his shorts. He rushes back into his room. There is a stain about the size of a fifty-cent coin on his shorts. It's a dull brown colour. He picks up his jeans and goes into the bathroom. He sits on the toilet but now nothing comes. He will have to wear the jeans again today.

CHAPTER THREE
NOW: Alice

The next time I met Jon after he'd accidentally spent the night, was in a café in the middle of the day. I stopped at the park on my way: a small square of bright emerald grass with a dirty pond, sandwiched between high-rise flats, a garish nursery spilling peonies, agapanthus and ferns, and a service station that made a decent profit in porn. I hoped I wouldn't see anyone I knew but only a very thin elderly woman with calves small as a child's and a teenager with bloodshot eyes were in sight. The warm wind whipped against my skin. I felt released because none of the gutted strangers here would ask me what was wrong.

Why did I feel so bereft? I tried to remember if I even liked Jon anymore. I thought of my mother, delighted to have picked up a cutting phrase, telling me, 'You get what you settle for,' as she got ready to leave for work.

Louise had been ringing at strange hours with nonsense that poured out of her like joy. She said she could get me a cheap, flat-screen TV that wasn't hot and that most of the graffiti in Redfern, where she lived, was a kind of poetry. The week lurched on. In her last call she added that she had been breached by Centrelink and was in danger of losing her flat. She was collecting articles about house fires. She wanted to go looking for our mother. She asked how she could access files from Community Services. It was a madness and her hopefulness deflated me.

Looking at some five-cent coins, pale discs at the bottom of the pond, I caught a glimpse of my puzzled reflection and decided to go to Sydney. I could swap my classes with someone, go and see my sister who was adrift.

Jon was already waiting in the café, his choice, a place where people in business suits talked on their phones about the market like it was a natural disaster: unpredictable, dangerous but possible to get something out of. He was brown, as though he'd been on holiday. When he took my hand I had to grind my teeth hard. I concentrated on the coffee ring on the crisp tablecloth and promised myself I would do the washing when I got home. I couldn't work out if I was angry or just bored.

'It's not as if you love me.' He opened his arms in an arc – the sad gesture of a forty-year-old man who would like to be a dejected lover in a suave French film.

I didn't love him but I said, 'How would that make a difference? I don't have licence to.'

He frowned. 'It's not about licence. I'm not selling a car.'

'Are you sure? Because I need one. I'm going to see Lou tomorrow. There's another thing you don't know about me.'

'Don't bullshit me.'

'Aah, no, I actually am.'

'I mean, have some integrity, honesty, about this, Alice.'

We listened to the conversational hysterias and lulls around us. I remembered how white and vulnerable the flesh on his inner arm was, the way his little toenail curved inwards on itself. I didn't want this conversation to rely on the old grab bag of excuses and tidy phrases.

He pinched the bridge of his nose. 'Sydney's a stupid place to drive to.'

I shrugged. 'Probably I'll fly.' I rearranged the sugar sachets in their container. 'How's your week been?'

Jon said, 'She knows.'

I nodded.

He said, 'Listen, you're *fantastic*.'

I put my arms on the table and leaned over. 'I don't want to live with you. I don't want to make you tea because you're in a bad mood or help you choose photographs to draw from. I don't want calls at lunchtime saying you'll pick up the steak and do I know your unlikeable friend is coming over for dinner.'

He took back his hand and said, 'Is that what you expect?'

'That's what I'll get. Isn't that what you do with her?'

He recoiled and I was pleased. He said, 'You have no idea what I do with her.'

I said, 'Would you rather it if I was miserable?'

All the while I was ruining it – taking out my precious coins to pay for the coffee I didn't drink, flash-forwarding to the relief I'd feel when I told friends how sensible I'd been – I was also imagining him coming home with me, putting his hand on the back of my neck, touching my breasts.

After checking the cost of flights at such late notice, bent over the computer at my high desk in the corner of my flat, I realized there was no way I was going to find a seat. I thought of all those people cheerfully visiting relatives over the weekend, or flying for business, booking into hotels with stainless steel bathrooms and plumped up pillows.

In the end I borrowed a car from my oldest friend, Sarah. I was nearly thirty but forced myself to see the drive as the sort of zany road trip other people took in their early twenties, complete with truck-stop food and spontaneous detours.

Sarah and I had survived high school together. She resisted my humourlessness, and the assortment of tired regrets I had accumulated didn't interest her.

She lived in Spotswood in a weatherboard two-bedroom house with a low white fence and a trellis for roses. Her house was near the station, en route to Scienceworks. I had taken my class on an excursion there last term and the tired woman in her forties who was helping me find my way round leaned over and said, 'I hate children.' The kids I was supervising were flushed with excitement, madly dashing up and down, trying out the sports games, testing their times against one another, asking me if we were visiting the planetarium.

The sight of Sarah's washing pegged on the line, her open face as she rushed to meet me, was painful. I ran up the path clutching my bag, sunglasses slipping off my head, and stubbed my toe.

She tossed her keys from hand to hand. 'It'll probably conk out, and smoke as many cigarettes as you want but the ashtray doesn't open.'

After the fire I'd changed schools and stopped going over to her house. Years later, we bumped into each other again at an underage disco. We'd both squeezed out the back door to smoke cigarettes and get away from the music. We'd formed a punk rock band together at sixteen but she was married and divorced before I graduated from university. She went to live in the hills with her husband in a rented mudbrick house slouched low to the ground and sent me occasional, elegantly-written letters about nothing. For years we hardly spoke. A few weeks before she left him she wrote me a postcard. '*FUCK I'M BORED*'. The card had a kitsch photo of a housewife in a grainy-grey pinafore standing at the head of a table. Sarah had sketched in an anxious wrinkle and shaded a zombie pallor on the woman's face; a tiny thought balloon wafted above her high ponytail: *Was that the last of the Valium?*

At a dinner party when we had drunk too much gin, Sarah told me that she disliked most of my lovers. 'Dripping the existential angst of the middle classes. They grow up good-looking with parents who rarely touch them and think it's the greatest tragedy since Chernobyl. Private schools, quick minds, therapy, full employment, sensible investments. It's astonishing, this despair they have with life.'

Sarah's uncle died of lung disease because he worked in the mines but she remained undespairing. I lit a smoke and sat on the steps. The grass on her lawn was freshly cut. When I gestured to put the cigarette out she waved me away. 'What's life if you can't kill yourself, eh?'

Her gingham dress was hoicked up near her knees as she crouched down. Her flesh was tanned and firm, an advertisement for good health. There was a lightness to her that meant I often felt stricken by comparison, appalled by her capacity for forgiveness.

I nodded. 'Those roses are a terrible colour.'

'Climbing American Beauty. Same as the film.'

'It's too much. Vaguely pornographic. Why aren't you at work?' I stood up, hoping she wouldn't ask about Louise.

'Rostered day off.'

'Thanks, Sarah.'

'Are you still helping a certain middle-aged man break the marriage vows he made under God's watchful eye?'

I grinned. 'As best I can.'

'Is it all right?'

'Fuck knows.'

She scuffed her sandals against the brick path. 'What's Lou done this time?'

'She wants to find Mum.'

'Now?'

'She's got this theory that Mum knows something about Jeremy. So she *says*.' I felt dry-mouthed – a tethered shell. I avoided the invitation in Sarah's gaze.

The drone of a whipper snipper from the next house was giving me a headache.

'Be kind to yourself, Miss Alice.' She put her arms around me. I inhaled the smell of her skin, her coconut moisturizer.

I got into the car and cleared chewing gum wrappers and slips of paper off the sticky vinyl seat. Sarah tapped on the roof. 'Are you seeing your dad?'

I scrabbled around but the lever to unwind the window was broken. I shook my head.

She leant down. 'Don't crash, but if it dies quietly on the road I'll be secretly relieved.'

I waved jauntily and stalled. There was a sticker on the outside of the car that read: 'If you're not outraged you're not paying attention.' One of those slogans that had survived the seventies. It bothered me. I couldn't guess whether Sarah had put it there or if it was a benefaction from the car's previous owners. I stripped apart and reconstructed the phrase in my mind. Was it only that I was not paying attention or had I outlasted outrage?

I was already on Sydney Road when I turned the car around, went into one of those giant concrete shopping malls, bought some groceries and drove west. After I parked, I climbed the stairs and stood on the slice of concrete that inhabited the centre of my father's building. The only communal space in these flats was outdoors on the second floor, where beer bottles hugged close together and empty pot plants bred cigarettes. The door to the shared laundry had come off the hinges and mouldy towels hung in the shape of forgotten bodies on the silver hooks nailed at abattoir-height into the walls. Around me, plastic curtains hung in windows, although I caught a glimpse of a neighbour's kitchen through a jammed blind, stained with nicotine. A hotplate was plugged into the wall and there was a pornographic picture, faded by steam and time, the calendar set to the month of May. Each time I visited my father I looked for a new woman's spread legs and full breasts, but it had been May at this neighbour's house for a very long time.

When I went upstairs one of the tenants took my photo and explained he was collecting evidence and that he would call the police if it happened again. He was jittery and forgot I had met him before. I nodded calmly at his madness but I was still sweating and infected with his paranoia when I saw Diane, my father's neighbour, seated at a cheap plastic table and smoking Holidays. 'I've been to Singapore,' she told me, as if we were old friends.

'Right,' I said, edging forward.

'But I couldn't stay. Too many people. And they didn't like my dress.'

'Oh.' I almost said: *I'm sorry.*

'I've been having an affair,' she winked, 'but don't mention it to your father. He can be old-fashioned.' My father was afraid of Diane, because some days she'd bring him oatmeal biscuits and others she thought he was pinching her underwear out of the laundry room.

'Something in the air,' I said. I told her I was having an affair too and lit my own cigarette. I was only half-surprised by my revelation. Who would Diane have to tell about the tired intrigue of my sex life, and who would believe her if she did? The people in these bedsits

40

largely seemed not to exist. They became visible only occasionally in the papers as welfare cheats, bludgers or warnings to the working poor of how much lower it was possible to fall. Sometimes there was a lucky war veteran who got interviewed on *Today Tonight* and then there would be an appeal, because no serviceman of our country should have to live like that.

Diane leaned in. 'With a very wealthy man. He wants to marry me. He's going to give me a ring on the weekend. He said I could go shopping for it but I go, "you choose".'

I couldn't help it. I asked, 'Did he go to Singapore too?'

'No, I didn't need a man to rain on my parade there I can tell you.' Her face darkened. 'Men are useless. Give years of your life to them and then they put you inside.'

I could believe she had been in prison. There was something in her skin that looked used: discarded and put back on wrong. When she moved, she had the slow motions of a person used to counting time. Diane frightened me because she was what Louise could become. She had worked as a nurse; her boyfriend had shot her dog and left it on her doorstep; she was going to inherit a lot of money. Her leaden sentences fell like echoey voice-overs to a story I already knew. Her lies had no design, no ascertainable logic. They reeked of longing and fear, yet they were more compelling than truths, their intricacy and detail a kind of art.

'They want to stop smokers getting elective surgery,' I told her.

'Of course they do. Fucking do-gooders and Christians. I'd like to shit in their backyards.'

I tried. I said, 'What do you think about the nurses' strike?' but Diane scuffed loosely at the concrete and muttered, 'Oh well, nurses,' as if we were talking about witchcraft or gamblers, some social group that had its own impenetrable and unexpected logic. She began quietly singing.

The first time she told me she was getting married it was to the month-of-May man, and the fleshy folds of her neck reddened in excitement or irritation. You could imagine her young and dangerous, living an adolescence of cheap high-heeled shoes and skirt lengths that wouldn't pass the test in a church school.

She said the man knew there was an age gap but they could share a place and it would be cheaper. And, she told me, it's no good for people to be on their own.

I tried to count the cigarette butts loose in the puddle of water on the ground, but I couldn't hold back my laughter, which bubbled up out of mortification and anguish. Diane held her fleshy arms tight against the sides of her chair. When she left, her bare feet slapped against the wet concrete.

I was glad that she left because my giggles were on the borderline of sobs.

Jake – short as a jockey, tattooed and thick-waisted – who stood at Dad's open door last Christmas, giving boxing lessons to the air, hovering at the periphery of my ruined family, says that Diane really was a nurse and that she had a car accident that left her with one leg shorter than the other. At times her voice was clear and authoritative, and then I could imagine her in the emergency ward of casualty, proud in her uniform, no-nonsense to the drunks and the drug-fried. Now I conjured up the empathy for her, a sly substitution of the emotions I could not bring myself to feel for my father.

I knocked a few times and then called out. My father undid the chain on the door and dragged it open, his heavy body silhouetted in the light. I put my clinking shopping bags down and he pretended not to be interested in their contents.

I stepped inside. My father was in his fifties but I could see how the years of alcohol were turning him back into a child. His cheeks were soft and his stomach had become round and paunchy, although he had always been a gangling figure with long wiry limbs. He stooped to keep his six-foot frame in proportion to the meanness of his abode.

He hugged himself in the chilly room. 'You didn't say you were coming round.'

'I can't stay for long.' I put my keys on the table. A game of patience was laid out on the card table. I leaned in and flipped over some cards, resettling them in piles until I got stuck.

He was drinking again. His feverish skin and the piles of junk heaped around the flat seemed unequivocal. He had been sober all year. I picked up the faded wedding photograph that was lying face down on the floor. My parents were glowing with anticipation. The man in the photo was sun-tanned and wiry. Dust had accrued on my mother's face so I ran a finger across the glass, giving her a stripe of new life.

'You should get rid of this,' I told him.

'Alice . . . I haven't had a drink in . . . if you'd have come yesterday.'

What was the photograph for? Was it an elegy for the missing or some bizarre superstition, its presence intended to ward off any more black luck?

'It's up to you.' I yawned and waited for the disappointment to lift.

The flat smelled of craft glue and treated wood. My dad took his hands out of his pockets. 'I'm making a city.'

'Huh?'

'A miniature. To scale.'

'Which city?'

'I don't know.'

'Sounds good.'

'I'm inventing it. Designing my own.'

'What for?'

'I just wanted to make something.'

There was a silence.

'You got here all right then?'

I nodded. 'I've got a car.'

He shuffled the cards with thick fingers. 'Stay for a game?'

'I can't.' I unpacked some of the groceries I'd bought, feeling fond of the garish colours on the packets, the lime greens and fleshy pinks of the brand names.

'Bet you want a drink. It's quite a trip to get here.'

Checking his flushed face, I guessed he had forgotten which suburb I lived in. The painfully sentimental structures of his life once he had got custody of us – never drinking before Louise and

I were in bed, keeping the glasses rinsed, the bottles packed away, forcing himself through final assemblies and parent-teacher nights with shaking hands and fear so sober it was wretched – had been abandoned once we'd left home. He could luxuriate in the first drink of the day, sip it quietly without panic at 11 a.m., and nobody would mind. Then he gave it all up. There were dry months, years, but those two impulses, to care and to forget, struggled together like Siamese twins that could not shed each other. I said, 'It's not that far, really,' but I accepted a bottle of beer. He got two glasses with shaky hands and I wiped the grime off the rims before pouring.

He waited for me to sip before he began.

'Thought you might bring that sister of yours.' He kept his voice jovial, man-about-town, upbeat. His throat was quivering. His chin trembled.

'No you didn't.'

'She used to *beg* me to help her with maths.'

'She's in Sydney,' I told him but he didn't hear me. 'She's been there for ages.'

'Your mum couldn't add up to save her life.'

I promised myself I would only wait twenty minutes and I planned next week's lesson in the silence. Then my father showed me some of the buildings he was making in his tiny city. There was an expansive sweep to the skyline that made me pause.

He had made me a copy of a Barbie bus the year I turned twelve because he'd seen me looking at it in shop windows when I was little. He'd worked on it secretly in the evenings after work, treated it, painted it pink, installed campervan furniture inside. I'd only ever wanted the mass-produced Mattel real thing, a shop-bought present, and even that was too young for me, so I'd pretended to lose the Barbie bus, leaving it outside in winter to rot and fade.

'Louise is *beautiful*,' he told me, voice thick with ebullience. 'I bet the boys all want a piece of her.'

'That's great, Dad.' Irritation clattered through my body. I felt ugly, unwanted. On better days he missed Louise and wanted to see her. He would never tell us that he wished she was Jeremy, wished that it was he and not she who had survived. I wanted to tell him, *she can't bear you*, but I downed my beer instead and listened to the football results floating upstairs from someone carrying a portable radio on the street. He settled into the couch and kept his eyes on the beer. In five minutes he would be asleep.

He asked, 'Is she happy, though?' and I said, 'She's drug-fucked,' and then I waited but he started fumbling with his boots, untying the laces and easing his feet out slowly. I went into the kitchen and washed the dishes, slamming them hard against the sink.

'It wasn't that bad, was it? Living with me all those years?'

At the door I hesitated, my fingers wrapped around the door-handle. 'No.'

Before I left he asked, 'What about your brother?' as if for the first time. I couldn't believe he did not remember, that each time the news was fresh. I knew again, more bitterly, why I only came once a year, why Louise would not come at all: the sum of my father's wrecked life.

I said, at the door, 'Still dead,' and my father said, 'What?' and then, 'oh,' and I saw his eyes slip to the alcohol on the table and I watched the same memory flutter across his face and I promised myself this visit would be my last.

I drove fast, holding the steering wheel with one hand and resting my elbow out the window. I smoked cigarettes until my lips were cracked and my throat resisted. The reaching trees and shimmering road gave way to the old sore tooth of memory. There was Louise eating nothing but grass for a whole day when she wanted to be a horse. Jeremy and Louise copying Charlie Chaplin's walk. Louise pretending to swallow a piece of gravel for the danger game when we knew the tiny stone was tucked into her cheek. Her face was stiff and bunched.

I really had touched a lit cigarette to my tongue to win the game when I was twelve and Lou hadn't been able to hide her glee and horror. Jeremy had hidden in the big kitchen cupboard while I turned on the tap and let the water run over my stuck-out tongue, panting like a dog in summer.

I could feel myself flinching at shadows, veering into the next lane, so I found a turn-off. My dad was getting worse. Once, I would have brought his news clippings, carefully saved in a scrapbook from all those years ago, and lined them up for him to see. Now, I could recite the headlines without looking.

BOY, 10, DIES IN HOUSE FIRE

TRAGIC DEATH 'PREVENTABLE'

ACCELERANT FOUND: FORMAL INVESTIGATION INTO 'FIRETRAP HOUSE'

It was only at his most delusional and drunk that my dad could erase the past entirely.

The roadhouse I pulled into was crammed with truck drivers and had a dining room full of Elvis Presley memorabilia. There were Elvis pictures, Elvis cups. Mirrors where you could see your reflection imposed upon the painted background of Elvis's hair and glasses. It was disturbing. The place was called 'Nick's place'. The couple behind the counter were Chinese. Why did they choose a Greek name, or had they just inherited it with the business?

There was a story about volunteer firefighters on TV and we all watched unmoved. I rifled through the sexist rubbish stickers that tourists and long-distance drivers are meant to want. Behind baseball caps and coffee mugs, there was a dusty plastic box, a magic kit. I picked it up. Jeremy loved magic when he was little. He tried to make card tricks scientific, to expose the logic of the games we play. As a teenager Lou used to visit magic shops and look at the top hats, weighted coins and marked cards my brother had hungered for.

Jeremy owned a kit called 'do you want to be a detective?' complete with pencil stubs and illegible observation records on scraps of paper and a false moustache and wig, that my sister kept. For a while, every few months, Louise compared the contents of the rectangular cardboard box with their ragged instructions and counted the missing pieces in a belated, ritual inventory. I could imagine her peering through the cracked magnifying glass, narrowing her sight line to the telescoped tunnel of the toy, as if she could inhabit my brother's gaze. I remembered the magnifying glass as a cheap thing with shattered fault lines along its plastic lens, incapable of making any mystery clearer.

*H*e shifts in the pool of sweat on his chair and tries to breathe slowly, as if this rhythm can remove the stink of him, the crawling beads that weep onto his seat. He writes what he can remember in his activity book: the population of world cities, their latitude and longitude, the rules of long division.

Behind him, Michael Grieves, whose dad works in the butcher's shop where Jeremy's mother buys the cheapest meat at the end of the day, is whispering what he is going to do to Jeremy at lunchtime. Jeremy's neck prickles but he doesn't answer.

Mrs Daly gives out the worksheets and tells Jeremy to sit up front with her. Every week now, she calls him out of his seat for extension activities while the other kids scrawl and mutter and groan. When he writes he lets the shape of the letters calm him and keeps his head bowed and his gaze on the wood of the desk. He finishes but doesn't put up his hand like she has told him to. He goes over the letters many times in pencil, scoring them in. If he takes a while to put his books back in his bag after the bell rings then he may be able to travel to the library through empty corridors. Michael asks to go to the toilet and on the way out he feigns a trip on Jeremy's bag and kicks hard at Jeremy's leg.

Jeremy doesn't look up. He concentrates on not letting them see that his hands are shaking. He reads the swear words carved into the desk. He is meant to do his own problem to do with the theory of probability but he's muddled it up.

He jolts when the bell rings. He knows what Mrs Daly writes on his report each term: 'Jeremy has some difficulty in social interaction, which he is working on', 'Jeremy should try harder to relate to the other children', 'Jeremy's ability to interact with the class group could be improved'.

Sometimes Jeremy calculates the remaining days, months and years of school. Other times he tries to rationalize the misery: if his bag is thrown into the creek on Wednesday, then he will be left alone on Thursday; if the boys pull down his pants and laugh at his penis on Monday then Tuesday will pass by with only a few kicks and cruelties. He doesn't believe himself when he does this. He is learning about the law of probabilities and because the pain and humiliation seem utterly random he wonders if each and every day chance begins again or if it can be calculated, shaped into a pattern. There seems just as much likelihood he will be beaten as not beaten this time. Even if they hurt him recently.

Mrs Daly taps her pen on his desk. 'Hurry up slowpoke, the bell's gone.'

In the hall, Michael takes his hand, pretending to be his friend, and leads him out to the asphalt near the basketball ring.

'Hey, here's nothing,' Michael tells the boys in the circle. 'Watch this.' Michael kicks near Jeremy's groin and Jeremy doesn't speak.

'Are you nothing? Are you a fucking deaf man?' Michael stands on Jeremy's foot.

Through the blur, Jeremy sees an older girl coming, holding a skipping rope. He has known Kathryn Mackenzie since he was a toddler. She stops smiling. Her eyes go wide and she runs into the lunch room.

'So, right, his Dad is on our street last night and he fucken' pisses all down his pants. He's, like, calling out and he's crying, saying this guy's name. He thinks he's too good and he's covered in piss.'

Jeremy knows the challenge before the boys even think of it: can they make him piss his pants? Can they get him to cry?

He tries to think of the highest mountain in the world, the largest sea, all the pieces of information that stretch beyond this playground into the other side of the world, into another language – one foreign to these boys, who are weighted lead, drawn like magnets to the invisible circle of fear and uselessness that he carries with him.

It might take all lunchtime, they may go hungry, but they do it in the end by shoving possum shit and a snail shell into his mouth and forcing it down his throat.

Before the first period of the afternoon he walks out of school. Past the orange plastic seats lined near the tuckshop and the whir of a cricket ball in the playground, the smooth crack as the bat connects. Over the fresh tanbark at the base of the swings. The school was built next to the old tip and behind it, still, is the dump where the tip used to be, which has been levelled by bulldozers. And this is Jeremy's world.

He ducks through low shrubs and pushes aside the sticky vines that are beginning to take over so that the sky looks like a mossy carpet with specks of grey. He steps over the rotting logs that have fallen across the sagging fence that's meant to keep kids out of the bush track.

And then he's at the bombsite and he runs down the slope.

It's not really where a bomb went off, just a crater in the ground where the tip once was. You can still find old treasures and junk close to the surface if you dig, even with the new soil that the trucks brought and spread on top. It's a hollow the size of a swimming pool, about four feet deep. He's measured it. The hole has been there since he can remember. It's mysterious, all that remains from when a spaceship or a plane crash-landed. Or some long-forgotten trench from a war.

Louise made up a story about the creatures that live in the hole: they are green-skinned and have tiny pairs of wings, hundreds all over them. They come from a planet in the next galaxy where you eat fire to stay alive and you grow younger every day until you die as a baby.

Jeremy knows how far the world goes. He's nearly finished his project on the solar system. He wrote about black holes and the big bang theory and he's building a model suspended with string, almost to scale, with different sized rocks for planets. He didn't work for long on it because he knows he's not good enough to go to the other school, or pass the test, and the kids in his class, who are older than him, say he is a big TP, a suck, a teacher's pet. It's only after the day his Dad lost his job and got so angry and drunk he swore at everyone in the shops and called the customers 'smug fucking bastards', only since Mrs Daly has been making an example of him, asking him to read his work out loud, that they hate him. And since they've hated him, since he's felt the great wave of their hate building up, he can't move properly, or breathe. He watches the way he pours milk on his cereal or holds his pen.

The world goes on forever. Sometimes this fact is comforting, sometimes it terrifies him and he has to hold onto his breath and count the seconds to remain calm, as he has always planned to do if he gets caught in quicksand.

For Jeremy, this place is not about outer space but travel through time. He is building a time machine, searching for parts in the soft earth with his magnifying glass, tunnelling out like the men in *The Great Escape*. It's a kid's game: to pretend to go faster than the speed of light. Kathryn used to play with him. She likes to go back in time but he wants to be in the future. There he lives in a cave with lots of friends, underground, and catches the railroad beneath the earth to travel to other worlds. You can look like whatever you want, in this future, even if it's not a human shape, even if you appear as a great lake or a magician or a sunset or a ghost.

He takes out the magnifying glass and tries to catch the sun in it so the leaves underneath the glass begin to brown and frizzle. Jeremy's going forward two hundred years. There is a race of people who are living on an undiscovered planet after nuclear war. They grow fruit and vegetables in the mountains. Because of the altitude they are often dizzy but they have harnessed the way the brain changes under this pressure to destroy cruelty in themselves. They welcome Jeremy but they will not let him stay with them and he knows pretty soon he won't manage to hear them at all.

Jeremy burrows into the cool earth and talks to the people of the future.

Kathryn Mackenzie crashes through the thick trees into the clearing. 'What are you doing? Can I have a go?'

'Nothing.'

'We're not meant to go here.'

He digs with his hands and finds tree roots and bits of plastic.

'Don't tell on me.'

'You were talking to yourself.'

'To the beings.'

She whispers, her freckles like blotches against her white nose, her fingers stubby. 'What beings?'

'In two hundred years.'

'You wouldn't even be alive.'

'It's another kind of time.'

She wrinkles her nose, peels off her shoes and socks, and gets into the hole. 'Did you go in the time machine?'

Then Jeremy's hands strike against an object. The car is golden and has wheels that don't turn. It's bigger than his hands, a racing car with black trim round the sides and a bonnet that has the number one printed on it inside a star. The windows are permanently wound down.

Maybe it's a talisman, a protection, like his magnifying glass. 'Talisman' is one of the words he learnt from the magazines about war at the corner shop. The owner had let him stay and turn the pages without buying anything. The American soldiers wear crosses or keepsakes around their necks or carry photos in their pockets. Alice had snorted when she caught him looking. 'You'd be mincemeat in a war,' she said. 'You'd get blown to bits. Choppetty chop.' She had looked at the man behind the counter, who was skinny and had a tattoo on the back of his neck. 'He thinks it's the golf war.' He only thought that the first time he'd heard his dad talk about it, before he'd seen it written down in the paper, in an article on Kuwait and oil.

'Sports invasion,' the man behind the counter said and Jeremy had known he couldn't go back there again.

He scrapes the dirt off the car. 'Look.'

Kathryn shrugs. 'That's for babies.'

He hears a scramble in the bushes. It's Michael with some of the older boys.

'What makes you think you're allowed to be here?' They move from foot to foot in anticipation. 'This is where *we* go.'

Jeremy feels the panic of his heart in his chest, the racing lightness of the beats, the heavy bulk of his hands hanging like hams on his wrists.

'Want this?' He offers it to them in a small way, trying to make his movement inconspicuous and inoffensive. The car teeters on his upheld palm but the surface reveals itself as dull copper now, not gold.

'Giss a go.' Michael takes it.

Kathryn puts her shoes back on. 'I'm telling on you.'

They copy her, put their hands on their hips and jut their hips out, tilt their heads. 'Oooh-ooh. I'm tel–ling.'

She races back to school, her feet landing in the mud as she runs.

'He's got snot up his nose and it's all dried.' Michael peers right at Jeremy's face. 'Wipe your nose. You're filthy.'

Jeremy rubs the back of his hand over his nose and they laugh.

Michael chucks the car at a tree. 'I hope you didn't nick this because we'd have to set the coppers on ya.'

'Yeah, that's why it's so broken. His dad couldn't pay for it. Yeah, he just done and dug it up at the tip instead.'

'You get presents from the tip.'

Jeremy fixes his eyes on an empty icy pole packet teetering on the edge of the bunker. There are still rivulets of red on the sticky paper. He runs through the times tables in his head. Eight times, twelve times, five times. The people from the future wave goodbye very slowly. He doesn't remember how long it's been since he really believed in them, how long since they brought him comfort. There's a grinding. He's clutching the magnifying glass too tightly and it breaks in his hand so that there are thin lines running through the lens.

Kathryn's back with Louise following her. Louise does a handstand right near the big depression in the earth, arching her back, nearly tipping right over. When the boys look at her she says, 'What?'

'Do it again.'

She takes a pen from behind her ear and pretends to smoke it, puffing out air the way Alice would. 'Youse look like a bunch of poofters,' she tells them. 'Didn'tcha hear the bell?'

She brushes the dirt off Jeremy's magnifying glass and holds it for him. She waits until the boys have left.

He looks at his sister who is quiet now. 'You saved me, didn't you?'

Following the boys back to school, Lou flings berries at their backs. 'Stupid fucks,' she says. He doesn't know if he's included.

In the afternoon library hour Jeremy reads about Harry Houdini, who escaped from a glass box filled with water and from a straitjacket hanging upside down. He finds books about daring adventures and fantastic survivors.

When he looks up 'camouflage' in the catalogue he finds entries on the crab spider, which becomes the same colour as the flowers it lives on so that birds can't see it. The photos are creepy. Chameleon lizards, he finds out, don't have any ears, and some are very tiny. Their eyes can look in two different directions. They are common in Madagascar, Africa. Zoologists don't think they change colour to conceal themselves but for other reasons, maybe even to draw attention to themselves. The scientist in the book thinks it might be in response to changes in the light or their mood. Jeremy can't grasp this. Do lizards have moods?

He reads the proper Latin names for them until his head hurts. Class *Reptilia*, order *Squamata*, sub-order *Iguania*. Pig Latin, which is Louise's Latin, is nothing like this. He wouldn't know how to pronounce the italicized words if he had to read them aloud. The letters seem ugly, gathered in together.

His reading tells him that there must be a way for him to evaporate that is not fictitious or magical, a scientific conclusion that can make possible his disappearance.

CHAPTER FIVE
NOW: Louise

*I*f you dream of him at all then it will be in the morning, while you are still in the thick hold of sleep, the sway and grab of it. You remember him as a series of slides – not pictures or photographs, but projected images – colourful, unmoving, wide-screen still lifes of the dead.

You see him in the newsprint faces of the unloved that decorate your wall. You see him in the shuttered windows of the terrace across the road, his ungainly frame breathing near the flyscreen wire and lolling through your bedroom window. He sears and burns in camp fires, in the smell of wood heaters, in the burning rubbish bins that someone else lit to stay warm. He is six. He is keeping a notebook to record the possums he has watched and named. He is eight and giving away his lollies on the front step because the other kids tell him he has to. He is nine and he likes to pick up the baby mice at school. He is ten and there is a small cut on his cheek and he is smiling without teeth. He is ten.

You can feel your body returning to you, sweating and heavy, taking back its rightful shape against the star-bursting, rushing pulse of the drugs. Your feet are pushing against the point of your shoes. There's mascara spread like Vegemite across your palms and the earth is no longer sliding towards you. It's raining. Your skin prickles.

You feel habit-fried, stillborn. You count what you can remember with reverence. Your eyes were golden. You were fierce; you were forgotten; you were perfect. You feel over-large, swollen with milk and venom, toxic and glorious. You know the drug's glugged out of you, poured through your body back into the earth, like some mantra that won't stop, hissed back away, deflating you. You eye the shape your legs make in the dust when you stamp. You thought there was a crowd, a gigantic, moving mass. Not reassuring, this.

You are out the other end. You're sinking. You want coffee. Coffee in a tacky mug, squat and white, maybe even with 'caffè latte' or 'onion soup' written in brown, certain letters across one side.

You are leaking, haemorrhaging, split at the sides. You dreamt that men with brown skin and older faces loved you, that you cupped a foot, hot like a stone, in your hand and it was wonderful. You saw pillars of red take over the sky like bushfires, a bloody, rippling sunrise spreading its guts across the pallid morning mist. Astonishment, small gifts like peace.

You can see the arrangement of people, swarms or particles, heaving and shifting, streaked faces and torn clothes like car crash victims in the beginnings of the day.

The sun is up already, ungenerous. The Sydney skyline is flat and depthless, hanging like a show curtain, a second skin, on the horizon. Cars go by too fast. Bronzed figures are visible beyond the expressway, hands open, arms wide arcs. They hold gestures of welcome or surrender.

Your mother's closing the door again, your father puts his hands over his eyes. You know what they are telling you. You know it again. It's the dead one they remember. It's the dead one they love.

When you wake later it's to the hiss of tyres. Cars swing easily into the tunnel of the expressway. The lines on the road have been freshly repainted and glow yellow in neat dashes, a line of tiny stitches breaking up the lanes.

Sandstone is smooth and cool against your back. Damp creeps into your shoes. Low-rise buildings surround you, and the golden plaque next to you on the wall declares this to be the Kormac building. It houses two banks, an architecture firm, legal offices and the headquarters of a couple of corporations with anonymous-sounding titles: Knox Industries, Hailey-Morgan Proprietary Limited. When you were small you used to read the abbreviation 'Pty Ltd' as 'pity limited'. Not a bad suffix for big business. Underneath your jeans, your skin feels rubbery, chilled.

A woman walks into the square, which is blank and open: thick slabs of red stone bordered by cactuses growing in beds of white pebbles. She is wearing brown boots and carrying an umbrella, black with tiny brown spots, so muted and discreet they appear like a disease across the surface. She puts down her briefcase, takes her identification from the tag around her neck and swipes in. The security door beeps, and lights in the foyer flick on. You see a giddying glimpse of brown leather couches and a painting of a colonial house in a large paddock with grass the colour of piss. What time is it?

The stink of cheap detergent wafts towards you, the drift of bleach. The cleaner mops the mud away from the foyer area in slow, gentle strokes. He's a lean man in his fifties and you think he looks kind.

Glitter stings your cheeks. Make-up must be smeared all over your face. You have to move. Everything will be opening soon. You scrabble in your damp pocket, amongst tissue flecks and pale lolly wrappers. No dope.

'All right, love?' The cleaner's younger than you thought, blond not grey, and holding his cigarette gingerly in front of him.

You stare ahead at the dirty linen of the sky, the faint exhaust fumes ghosting the traffic, the pink rinse edging the clouds.

'Yeah.'

He chucks the cigarette onto the ground still burning. 'You can't stay. They've got their own security.'

'I'm waiting for someone.'

The shrug is negligible. When he turns away, you reach for the dog end of the cigarette. It's burning strangely, dampened by the puddle it landed in, but not ruined. You suck in the tobacco, feel its sour warmth.

The cleaner picks discarded takeaway containers and drink

bottles out of the low shrubs bordering the next office building. He snaps them with a pair of long pincers that remind you of the metal claws that reach for pink plush teddy bears or rabbits behind the glass in lucky dip games at arcades. When you visited the arcade with Alice once she cried because she wanted a giant pink plastic dog and only got some furry dice with stick-on white dots that soon fell off so that you could never roll more than three. When the man handed them over, you could see that this gift was a familiar disappointment for customers. His stoic grin was terse. He looked around for mothers. You stole a candy cane and chewed it until the sugary peppermint and the excitement made you vomit.

Now you shake out your hair, learning how to inhabit your body again. Last night, wasps were living there, burrowing against your scalp. Later your hair was golden and fell behind you like a silk coat. The memories nestle into you shamefully; they make themselves at home beneath your skin. It's cold. You don't have any money. It's Monday.

You could walk home away from the great Sydney fakery: the harbour and the bridge, the opera house, the Domain, the gardens. But the thought of enforcement orders piling up in your mailbox in crisp envelopes – the accumulation of small steps before eviction – makes you ill.

As you stand and brush off your lap, you see two men hurrying from the parking lot. They trigger central locking on their cars in swift identical gestures. You see them swing back and aim, holding their keys high with diffident certainty.

The older man is wearing an old-fashioned suit in dark grey, with a red and blue waistcoat with gold buttons. You imagine him drawing a fat fob watch out of his pocket, skittering about like the tardy white rabbit. You don't want to think about this story. Or Alice. You make Alice into a jigsaw puzzle, a mosaic. You remove the frozen features of your sister, knowing and fitful, and redraw them: a mouth of wonder, eyes that glitter.

'I think you've missed something, Vince,' the older man calls out.

The cleaner's turn is agonizingly slow. He puts down his tools and plastic sack of rubbish.

The man in the waistcoat gestures at you. 'The trash that lands on our doorstep.' He unclips his phone from his belt.

You stand, dizzy. 'Fuck off.'

His companion puts down his thin black briefcase and raises a soft palm. 'I'll handle this, James. Go on up.' He is in his mid-thirties, with smooth plastery skin. He has a polished, inhuman quality, as if he were made and not born. There's a silver band on his left hand.

The older executive shrugs as he strolls off. And strangely your heart moves for him, clearly the junior of the two, perhaps even a clerk.

'Oh dear.' A grin. 'I'm David. And you're a PR nightmare. We can't keep you.' He smiles. 'But, then again, removing you might be difficult.' He speaks in the singsong patter of a sitcom, even pausing regularly as if to allow enough time for the track laughter. 'A conundrum.'

Your throat is dry. He's trying too hard. He has the thirst to talk of a man wholly alone, impelled with the uninhibited zeal of a Jehovah's Witness.

'You look like you could do with a cup of coffee.'

Angerday. Danger.

You stare down at the black night of his shoes.

The first dare in the danger game was when Alice asked you to write your name in the wet cement in the driveway of the new shopping centre. You did it in special handwriting, cursive not printing, so that they wouldn't find you.

'See, we're not all monsters. Just the overwhelming majority.' His lips are plump, pale.

'I'm going.' You move towards the road. He follows.

He speaks to you as if you are on a tour of the building. 'We do small stuff here. Investments – ours and managing other people's. Large personal loans. Onselling debt. Sharemarket's all about speculation, which is –'

'I know what that is.' Stocks, bonds, commodities, currencies, derivatives. You clasp your hands into fists inside your pockets. 'It's gambling with better odds and more money than the slot machines or scratch tickets, predicting what other investors will do, what the market will support. It's a bet on other people's hopes. Except for short-selling, which stakes itself on failure.'

'So you see why you are a problem.' He has taken hold of your arm now. 'You don't inspire,' he flicks his fingers in imitation of quotation marks, 'credit confidence.' He lets go of you and pulls out a card. 'Security. Integrity. Dynamism. Our logo. I never thought marketing got that right. Dynamism makes us sound like risk-takers, which we are, of course, any dummy knows that. But we don't advertise it. Dynamism sounds too much like dynamite – it could blow up in your face. My vote was for "forward thinking".'

He's a nutter. You realize you have been dreaming of Jeremy, and the memory of the dream hooks and tears at your skin. Jeremy was drowning in the sea, his pale arms, short and plump as a baby's, flailing and churning in the dark water. You had been too busy, trying to catch the inky seahorses that floated past, to notice him. And when you did you knew it was play, a joke, right up until he changed colour and became transparent: a huge child jellyfish melting into the water. In your dreams, Jeremy is always young. Why can't you dream him older, instead of younger, this brother of yours who knows that you are culpable?

David cocks his head to the side. 'I bet you can do all sorts of things.'

You think: *Hetay angerday amegay.*

Sometimes the only way to manage the daily percolating drip of fear, the corrosive dread of debt and humiliation, is to embrace another sort of terror, to put oneself in danger.

He puts his hand on your shoulder, clamps it too tight. 'Come on, there's a café round the corner.'

You go with him because it is stupid and he is appalling and there is nowhere else to go.

The place he's chosen is unexpected, with zany wallpaper and airy, thin staff. The windowsills are pale candy-pink. Geraniums sit in large wicker pots in the courtyard. You flip through a newspaper someone has left behind.

The waitress is wearing a short black skirt, white ballet shoes and a striped tie. The man waits until she has put the coffees down.

'Can I?' He puts his hand on your back. 'Do you mind? What's your name?'

When you edge away he begins whispering, 'I want you to let me touch your back. Just your back.' His voice is a high murmur, a dull toneless hum. The sound of him is the calming noise of whitegoods.

You sit on a metal chair, the wind blowing against your shirt through the gappy back, and the seat leaving tiny heart-shaped impressions against the skin of your legs. The black coffee is bitter, burnt.

'Don't you have a job to go to?' You are bolder now that there are other people around.

The lines down his palm curve like rivers on a map. You imagine them pushing over their borders and washing away his skin.

He says, 'And then I am going to touch your legs. And put my hand into your pants.' The table is rippled glass, with a ceramic sugar bowl in the centre. He grasps your wrist. You watch your own legs drowsily through the glass, their loose soft-focus drift, the way the swirls and gathers of glass make them alien and ghostly, as though you were looking at them underwater. His skin is facelift smooth. He breathes quickly.

'Are you on the game?' His fingers flutter as he again makes quotation marks in the air in some lacklustre attempt at irony. 'As they say.' He watches you closely, his mouth slightly open.

The cover of the *Sydney Morning Herald* is about police corruption. You tell him, 'Not really.' You consider being motherless in more conventional terms, perhaps in a more fashionable way. He might give you some money. He strokes the inside of your arm.

'My mum's sick.'

'Oh?'

'Bone cancer.'

He stops stroking. 'Sshh.'

You lift your skirt to show him the pink mass of scars across your thighs and down behind your knees, the slash and pulp of it. He takes his hand off your wrist.

'Christ.'

'They tried transfusions, some of my tissue. Bone marrow.' He is not listening, which is important. If he pays attention he'll see the lack of sense in it, the gaps in your story.

'Yeah? *Shit*.' He turns the pages of the paper rapidly, then ruffles inside his wallet. He finds motions that distance himself from you, that render you strangers at the same table. He doesn't want to fuck you.

You pull the paper towards you. It is then you see the photograph of a heavy man who looks just like your brother, or what he might have become if he'd lived. The caption reads: *Ornton's new protein analysis represents a break with existing scientific models.*

Sometimes you think nothing else happened: your brother's death comes back to that moment when you found him with Michael Grieves and the other boys, when he saw all those years of school still stretching in front of him. And there you are, Louise, walking away again, leaving him behind once more.

On these days, when you think he wanted to die, it's easier to unwind, to unravel all the way back to the beginning like a spool of wool or a ball of string. Other times, it is a bowerbird's nest of random scraps, hopelessly entangled borrowings so deeply embedded in other stories they won't ever be undone.

After a few minutes of silence, you have almost forgotten the man sitting opposite you. Then he tries to put his hand inside your underwear. His fingers are cold.

You say, 'She's dying.'

He scrapes his chair against the brick paving and puts his hand in your lap. '*God*.'

His fingers bruise against your thigh. 'I'm just after a screw, you filthy bitch.'

You read the sheet of newsprint on your way home. It's not much of a story, buried amongst the soft news just before celebrity gossip and horoscopes. But you keep seeing Jeremy, his hand cramping around his magnifying glass.

The scientist in the photo looks unhappy about having his picture taken. His smile looks prearranged: his cheeks bunch uncertainly; his eyes slide towards someone out of the frame of the camera.

It has been both your abiding fantasy and nightmare to know the truth about the day Jeremy died. To find answers that are whole and sharp and shameful, which would hum in the right key: recognition. You fold away the face of the man in the paper.

'I'm sorry, I don't understand.' The woman at the government office is pudgy. She has bobbed, shaggy brown hair and pale green eyes. There's a touch of the kindergarten teacher about her, with her deep blue knitted cardigan and pleated skirt, but her mouth is tugged down with melancholy. Underneath the smooth paint of the lemon walls you see cracked brown tile.

'I want to see the records from after my brother died. I want a copy.'

You've been waiting in the hush of the white corridor looking at the thick carpet and the framed photographs of flower arrangements and green plants for too long.

'Louise Reilly, right? Let's look you up, shall we?' She clatters into a computer, smile fading at the entries.

'Okay. Your benefits have been suspended. Failure to attend a scheduled activity. It's a breach.' She leans back in the cool leather of her chair and swings in towards the pine desk. On it is a photo of her with a nondescript husband and another woman, perhaps a sister, who seems ominously beautiful, with slanted cheekbones and thin wrists.

You thought you'd remember everything about that day but you don't. Mostly you remember how the wet grass felt against your feet in the backyard as you walked back into the house, and then the way your dress stuck to you in melting layers, clinging like a plastic bandage to your burning skin. The smell. Your dad rolled you over and over in the dirt to put out the flames. You remember a stretcher with a sheet pulled over a shape; they opened the doors to the ambulance you were in and then someone said, 'No, the girl's in there.' You were crying and still you thought you could hear Jeremy.

The woman opens a drawer and removes some pamphlets. 'This isn't my area. You'll need to go to the regular office and wait in line for an appointment.'

'Miranda.' You like to use their names, it puts them off balance, and hers is on a bulky name tag pinned on her shirt as well as on the door. 'I don't want to talk to you about my benefits. I want to get the notes from the interview after my mother left, after the fire. I want to see the social worker's report from then.'

'I don't know what this is about. Let me see. I've got a disability entry and a methadone PBS record and, oh, a sheriff's enforcement notice – and your housing situation we don't deal with here, that's already in the Tribunal now.'

You try to speak in simple sentences. 'This is not about *now*. The social worker's name was Janice Overton. I want the paperwork. I am trying to find my mother.'

Miranda looks sadly at her feet. You see pretty, strappy leather sandals and peeling pink nail polish.

She speaks gently. 'Is this your birth mother? We have a process for that, there's new legislation.' She squints slowly at the computer screen. 'Um . . . there's nothing in your file.'

Your file probably says you're a junkie and in debt. Your file says you got a warning for assault and for shoplifting.

You got glass in your feet the day he died and that hurt more than the burns at first. You thought you could hear him inside the house. Twins are meant to be connected. You used to tie yourselves together with strips from old pillowcases and pretend to be Siamese twins doing shows in the circus, landing in a grotesque tumble of hands and feet.

'It's from 1991,' you tell her.

'A lot of people we see here think social workers are the enemy. But I'm someone you can trust if you want to talk.' Her eyes flick past the face of her watch. 'We could have a cup of tea.'

'The file is from 1991, which is when my mother left. I'm not adopted. She left. Chelsea Reilly. There was a house fire and they interviewed us to see if we were allowed to stay with our dad. That's what I want.'

Miranda sighs. Outside, Sydney hums: the terraces of Surry Hills glow. You can see flowerpots on balconies, and narrow windows shaded by bamboo blinds. The streets are cramped and elegant;

European tables, laid with white linen cloths and shining wine glasses, are out on the footpath.

'I think we were still on paper in ninety-one.'

Blackness rushes towards you. She's a patronizing filthy cunt.

'Can I get that?'

'What?'

'Can I have the fucking paper file then?'

'It won't be kept here at the Sydney local office. Why did you think it would be here?'

There are bees under your skin. You want to fall onto the carpet and breathe in the thick fibres, the synthetic false smell, inhale the institutional vapour of old times.

'I thought you could tell me where it might be.'

She shrugs, pleased. 'If a file's not active it might have been shredded. Confidentiality. I think you'd be better off concentrating on the housing issues.' Her cuffs are dirty and her pale lipstick has smudged across her teeth.

'I think you'd be better off concentrating on not being a useless bitch.'

She breathes in sharply. 'Calm down.'

'Fuck calm.' But you're crying. 'I want the file.' The box of tissues she hands you is covered in a lurid pattern made up of bright bunches of flowers. You blow your nose. 'Can you try again? Please?'

When she leans forward you try to see the password she punches back into her keyboard but she's too fast. Her fingers skim across the keys quickly.

Before you leave you memorize the employee number on her security pass just in case.

In movies, when people leave there are careful rituals and portentous glances for those left behind to chew over. Mothers hold their kids too long and say, 'I love you'. They behave atypically, a little off-centre, just enough to be noticed later. Or they agonize: they stare at photographs and look for signs.

Your mother left four days after the fire, during the autopsy, before the funeral, before the investigation. She didn't organize anything, she didn't see anyone except for the police and Community Services staff. She made a complaint against her boss at the cleaning service and she smashed a vase in one of the offices and your father had to pay for the damage, which he did mutely, not used to being the one asked to take responsibility and cowed by it.

You know she once smelled of sorbolene cream and she used to sing songs by Peter, Paul and Mary and Joan Baez when she peeled potatoes, scraping the peeler down rapidly as if she was brushing off a rug. She said that the TV on in a cold house was like an old friend, and that you were all her favourites.

At school you said that she was a spy and had to go into deep cover. Later you said she had killed herself.

You'd like to know what she's become.

The lemon tree on the corner of your street is diseased. When you run your hands along the branches, they are swollen like arthritic arms. They bulge, brimful with growths under the skin: alien embryos, steroid muscles. You stroke the twiggy limbs. Imagine you're holding onto a banister, touching someone's arm, but the tree holds a chill, there is some coolness in its core.

When you do get back, someone's waiting out the front. 'Louise!' Ted waves at you. 'Beginning to think you'd forgotten about us.' He's in his flannelette shirt and stiff new jeans, hugging a wrapped package to his chest.

You're watching a glass shatter beneath your feet, a window breaking. You've done it again, Louise. You've wrecked something else.

'I got held up.' How long has he been waiting? When were you meant to be there?

He reaches for your hand, pulls you into a hug. His shirt smells of stale tobacco but it's soft against your cheek. The package crackles, pressed between both your bodies. Pins and needles rush up and down your arms. You're giddy. Ted was your publicly funded drug counsellor when you got caught shoplifting years ago. He's relentless, though he's long since chucked in the job. He'll turn up at the flat, ask to see your drawings, fiddle around making coffee and whingeing about pollution and how crap the new bands are, as if he isn't forty and just about to get married.

'Nat was here too but she couldn't wait.'

It's Monday. Your head pounds as you realize you were meant to meet both of them.

'Are we going up?' He slouches back. 'You look sick, bella. You don't have to cook. We can get burgers and sit in the park.'

You rub at your arm with your nails until the scratches run white and then red. 'That's okay. I'm good.' You climb the stairs slowly because the landing light is out. Ted looks dreamy. His hair is rumpled and he taps a drumbeat out on his thighs with flat palms. There's a warrant-order for recovery of moneys owing under the door. You turn the light switch but nothing happens. The electricity's off. He can't see you blushing in the dark and he can't see the stack of dishes. There's a rush of vertigo as if you were leaning out the penthouse of a skyscraper, and the barrier gave way, tilting you towards the edge and into falling. You steady yourself against the spinning. If you pretended to faint, would he catch you?

'Oh, sorry. Lights out. D'you want toast?' You rustle in the cupboard for instant coffee, reel back from the ants crawling into the opened bag of Coles chocolate biscuits. But when you look up, he's prowling the cupboards, kicking at the few cockroaches that lurk in the corners of the kitchen when it gets warm enough for them to make an appearance.

'You forgot, didn't you?' You had promised to make dinner for them the night you'd all been smoking a joint together in their airy flat in Leichhardt.

'No,' you summon mock outrage, 'I just got the times messed up. I'll go to the shop. I can roast something. Potatoes. You want potatoes?' You're rehearsing in your mind how you'll do it, using the card to pay and then, if it doesn't go through, acting surprised and penitent and then admitting that you've been cut off by Centrelink, peeling away one layer of easy confession.

'It's too hot for a roast.'

You can taste metal in your mouth: the toxic flood of fear. You've tried not to take shortcuts with Ted, not to blur promises, and to slide into performances as little as possible, because his hopes for you are a warm real thing, a kind of love. If you look too closely, if you see yourself in his hopes, you'll be stopped silent at how much he already knows. He told you once to stop speaking about things as if they were how you wished they would be.

'Come on, babe.' He picks up a jacket and holds it out.

'I'm not babe.' You stuff your arms in the sleeves.

He shrugs his shoulders. 'Okay. I'll buy you a counter meal.'

'When you say babe I think of the little pink pig.'

'Oink. Oink.' He flaps his hands as if they are small pig hooves and then he's moving out the door and into the corridor.

'I can't. I've gotta ring my sister.'

He comes back into the doorway. 'How about if I bring you back something?'

'Sorry about this. Sorry.' Your shoes are still a bit wet and your legs are shaking. 'I was going to impress both of you with my clean flat and a four course meal.'

'Next time. What're you listening to these days?'

'Not much . . . lots of crosswords.'

'What, no music to slash your wrists to? Where's Joy Division and other cheery friends?' Even when he was meant to be focusing on rehabilitation, Ted used to chide you about your grim taste in music.

'I don't have a CD player anymore.'

'Stay off the bloody ice.'

You see bloody ice in your mind: a car smash, red fluid trickling across dirty snow. It's only when the panic subsides that you recognize he's talking about drugs.

'Yeah.'

'I'll bring you over some stuff that's hip with the kids.' His voice is deep and low. 'Are you painting?' He puts the package down near the door.

'Yes. I'm doing my dreams.'

'That'll make a pretty picture.'

Your nightmares hover in the shadows. He brings out his wallet. 'Let me give you some cash.'

You hesitate and then, when you reach out your hand, you think you have never been more abject, more alive with shame.

His fingertips are warm. You don't look at him.

'You can always come by ours for a game of Scrabble, Louise, no matter what state you're in. Better for me if you're a bit fucked up. Enhances my chances of winning.'

The door clicks shut so softly after him that you want to let your legs collapse and fall straight to the floor. Inside the brown wrapping of the present that he's left are reams of folded canvas, paints and brushes. You think you'll paint bloody ice, the collision. The moment after.

They've switched off the electricity and gas so you wait in the dark with your limbs chilled. Even now in summer, it is a cool night. They'll freeze you out. You lie on the mattress under the sleeping bag smoking the rollie you've made from the ends of other cigarettes. It smells synthetic, mildly toxic. Mrs T who lives across the hall said the Sheriff's Office came today with enforcement orders to recover your property. It's worth enjoying. What would they take? She had Susie in her arms and the boy grabbing onto her legs. She must be on prescription painkillers because she's always smiling. She sweeps the shared corridor of your floor in the building, and hums.

You'd like to get through the night without ringing Alice. You edge into the faded circle of light cast by the streetlight and go through what they've left. There's a pale blue letter, typed with your full name and a court date, a leaflet with a list of your rights as a tenant and an offer of a one-off consultation with a financial advisor.

You put a pair of socks on and eat cereal dry from the packet, unsticking it from the roof of your mouth and your gums with a finger. You take out the cask wine bladder and suck out the remaining thimble-full of alcohol. You should have gone back to the restaurant after the trial and asked for another chance. You shouldn't have had a taste the other night.

You find an old newspaper lining the kitchen drawer and do the crossword in it because you are afraid to sleep like this, with the vomit hesitating in your throat.

Once, when you and Alice and Jeremy had to walk five kilometres in the rain because the bus was cancelled, your mother played a game with you and now it's become a habit. You passed the walk by listing all the things you would eat and drink and do when you got back. The list climbed into the impossible: you'd have a bucket of popcorn and seventeen Calippo icy poles; Jeremy wanted a microscope for his experiments but you all said that wasn't part of the game. Even what he hungered for was wrong.

So you still list all the things you'd have if you were rich. Central heating. A spa. Cheese sandwiches, cocaine and a small sports car.

And then you dream of numbers on a page, growing rapidly, expanding like a stain on paper. It isn't until the deluge lifts that you remember what one of the leaflets said. You have a right to see the information that government departments hold about you. Freedom of information. If those files with the interviews still exist, you can get them. They have to give them to you.

The phone box is four blocks away and you run from the light cast by one streetlight to the next, just like you used to when you were a kid. You feed the coins into the slot and you're dialling Charlie's number from memory, your fingers fast as habit on the silver buttons. When he was your boyfriend, he agreed to try a seance with you so that you could speak to Jeremy, but the glass wouldn't move. Charlie gave up heroin before you did and then he gave up you. 'Yup?' He answers and you don't speak. 'Hello?' You're afraid to breathe. 'Louise, hang up,' he tells you. The coins click and settle into place when you put down the phone.

These are Valium phone calls – weekly rituals that deaden your nerves, keep you calm. Sometimes it's the parents of the boy who frightened Jeremy at school, or your old friend, Katrina. 'Obsessive and compulsive,' Alice would say, and she'd be right.

When you do call Alice, Jeremy's magnifying glass is in the pocket of your jeans, pressed close to your skin. It feels electric, alive. You pat your pocket. Be kind. Your neck aches and the thud of blood in your head beats out remorse.

You huddle into the phone box and snarl back at the fat dog behind the wire fence while the phone rings.

'We have high hopes for you, Jeremy,' Mrs Daly announces. He sees them ascending into the sky, brightly coloured kites, invisibly tethered to the earth, propelled by gusts of wind. He sees washing flapping loose on the line, other people's ideas ballooning on the horizon.

The hopes are not his; they belong to someone else.

Mrs Daly hovers over him after the last class. He must take the exam for the school down the road. Jeremy sometimes sees the boys in their uniforms at the shopping complex, buying milkshakes and making jokes. The boys seem huge to him: oversized. Even their wrists and ankles are thick. They hold their schoolbags by a single handle looped around an elbow so the bags slouch off their hips and take up too much space. He is terrified of passing the exam, of being accepted. These boys have parents who are accountants and lawyers, who drive smooth cars when they drop their children off in the morning. He will be unbearable to them. The rubbish gathering on his front porch and the step littered with broken glass will repulse them. He will get a name. He knows this just as well as he knows his times tables, the spelling of long words.

Mrs Daly says, 'If you don't take the exam, how will you ever get out of here?' She elbows him as if it's a good joke they have together. Her smile is fake.

He bows his head. He wants to leave. He dreams about being an explorer, about seeing all the countries on the earth, about the languages he could speak and the journeys he would make. But Mrs Daly makes it seem as though he is on some tiny island, placing a foot forward on a bridge that leads into the future, to a place he can't see. If he leaves, she suggests, he will not be able to come back.

He hears his father's voice, strained and flat, 'I wouldn't get a big head. You're just as good as the next kid. No better, no worse.' And he is. Sometimes he cheats and copies the answers from the back. He used to like doing the working out. He could cleave the numbers apart and then build them back together. He did it without straining, without showing off – just found the patterns and followed them.

Now there are maths problems written in words and he can't get hold of the puzzle. It's like trying to grab onto slimy weeds in water, or to separate the jump ropes for Phys. Ed., once they're all caught up together in knots and tangles.

His father still thinks he is worth more, deserves more, ought not to be where he is. He tells Jeremy about the research he's doing into exotic fish at the library, and he circles good buys in the *Trading Post*.

. His mother wants him to go to the new school. 'Might as well give it a go. It's a free kick.'

If he gets accepted, the boys at his old school will call him a snob and his new classmates will make fun of his house, his second-hand uniform, his puny body.

But if he fails, if they don't want him, he is worse than they thought and it's six years in the high school Alice goes to.

Mrs Daly sighs and shifts her heavy frame to a chair. 'You are a very bright boy, Jeremy. You could do something with that mind.'

'I just remember things.'

'Well, hurry up. You want to get there with plenty of time to spare.' She stands and gathers the class textbooks and locks them in the cupboard. He waits.

'What is it? Have you got a pen? Who's taking you there?'

Something flickers in Jeremy's memory. His dad is meant to meet him, to walk him there and wait for him outside. 'I'm walking.'

Mrs Daly pulls at her sweaty T-shirt and turns off the lights and the fan in the room.

He bends to tie his shoelace, which comes off in his hands, leaving abrupt stumps instead. He knots the shortened ends tightly. He takes the broken laces, which are damp and speckled with soil, and hides them in his palm.

'The other boys will have their parents there.' She opens the door for him. 'But don't let that put you off. They don't go in.' Mrs Daly advances towards him. Jeremy realizes that she is going to shake his hand and he will not be able to hide the broken laces. She presses her fat hand against his and nods decisively.

'All right. Don't get panicked and don't forget to *read* the questions.'

He steps into the empty playground. The fading light at the end of the day makes the school seem softer, looser. He leans over the drinking fountain and turns the tap on. He recognizes Michael Grieves, who is in the boys' toilets. He ducks his head and accidentally thumps it against the wall. Jeremy drinks furtively and gulps the water until it makes him feel sick. Michael Grieves is bent forward touching his penis. He is jerking off with the door open. Jeremy straightens up but not quickly enough. Michael rushes forward with a flushed, worried face.

'You're a fucking pervert watching me.' Michael doesn't seem that strong without his group of friends. He has peeling skin on his knees – old scabs – and his school clothes smell faintly of the butcher's shop the whole family lives behind. He raises his fists in an anger that does not seem entirely real.

Jeremy turns away.

'You're nothing and you didn't see nothing. Right?' Michael dances after him.

Jeremy says, 'I don't know what you're talking about,' firmly, because this is important, because he cannot imagine what Michael might do to keep the piece of information Jeremy now knows from getting out.

'Yeah?' Michael's zip is half undone and his face is red as he yanks it up. Jeremy moves quickly. He sees Louise at the edge of the school fence. He breaks into a trot.

'Psycho.' Michael yells but Jeremy feels out of his force field, feels lighter, feels good to be moving away.

Louise is waiting at the front gate. 'What was he doing?'

'Not sure.'

'Wanking?'

'Shut up, Louise.'

'He *is* a wanker.'

'How come you're still here?'

'I'm taking you. I'll walk with you, okay? But I'm not waiting.'

He says, 'Yup.'

Jeremy's chest expands. He is going to the exam with his sister Lou, who no longer plays with him now that he is in the grade above, who does not wish to be his double, his mirror, his twin.

Lou tugs her chocolate-coloured hair back into a rubber band and starts to walk off. She looks up and down the street.

'Did Dad forget to get me?'

'Dunno.'

He remembers that Louise has still got his talisman and that he should bring it into the exam. 'Can I've my magnifying glass?'

'You have to play the danger game to earn it back.' She jumps over the cracks on the footpath. 'Play the danger game, Jeremy. Lie down on the pedestrian crossing.' Jeremy checks in his pocket for the sharpened pencils Mrs Daly has given him. He smells honeysuckle in the air. He shakes his head limply.

They walk up to the freeway, Louise plucking leaves and flowers and tearing them into small pieces as they go. She skips. She takes newspapers out of people's letterboxes and puts them back in the red postbox. She tries to test him on maths but interrupts saying he's got the wrong answer before he finishes.

Jeremy trails behind her, trying to rehearse solutions to problems in his mind. Halfway to the new school, Lou tells him that their dad is really mad today, that he will not leave the couch.

'Alice says she wants to kill him.'

'Who, Mum?'

'Alice says he's wasted years of Mum's life.'

'Are you gonna go home?'

Louise pauses. '*I* could kill him.'

Jeremy remembers the magazines in the library that contain details of real crimes and defendants who got off on technicalities in their court cases.

'How?'

'He sleeps all day, doesn't he?'

'Not always.' Jeremy falls behind again. 'You'd get caught.'

'I wagged this afternoon and Mum goes,' Louise draws herself up, prepares her body for the mimicry that she does so well, 'This time I've had it. I've *had* it.' Jeremy laughs at Lou's imitation of their broken mother's voice.

'Yeah. That's what she always says.' His mother is full of warnings, of final chances and last times. The same moments keep happening.

'Alice is a bitch, anyway.' They walk in silence over the bridge, watching the cars flash by underneath. 'We're better.' Louise spits down at the road.

Jeremy would like to touch his sister – to move closer towards this new intimacy of hers, this kindness that could expire by the time he returns home.

She says, 'What about poison?'

'Nah.'

'Or, "bang", a bullet just like that?'

'You don't have a gun. You don't know how to use one.'

'I could learn.' Louise is losing interest. She sees the wrought-iron gates of the school and stiffens her posture. She scowls down the hill.

'Yeah.'

Since they accelerated him a grade and he left her behind, Louise sometimes goes to the park or the fish and chip shop instead of class. At home, she draws instead of filling in her worksheets. Jeremy tells her she'd have to suffocate their dad because then there would be no way of proving she did it.

His heart hammers as they arrive. He still has the shoelaces tucked in his palm. He stuffs them in his pocket.

There are lights on at the school. Rose bushes sit in circular patches of earth on the grounds. They have an oval with a running track and some of the buildings are three storeys high. He should want to go here, because Mrs Daly thinks there is a great science lab, but the school looks false to him, with its green clipped lawns and swept paths; it's like a trick photograph. In the pale sunlight it seems papery and flat like the background scenery of a television set; it's not a place he can go every day. Lou stops at the tall gates. 'Dare you to call out the answers in the middle of the test.'

'Nah.'

'I don't know why they think you're so clever. You're quite dumb.'

Jeremy turns towards her. He thinks she is afraid to go in with him. Her bare feet are grubby and her nails are black.

She speaks quietly. 'You don't want to go there. You don't want to get in.'

There are other boys spilling out of cars, all different ages. There are parents drinking cups of tea in a huge room with pale green couches and paintings on the walls.

She unzips the front pocket of her backpack and holds out his magnifying glass. 'Ta da.'

She is not smiling. He tells her she can keep it for the evening and puts down his own bag but keeps hold of a pencil and a blue pen.

Louise brushes sand off the handle. 'I'll hide it for you somewhere and write clues. Or a map.'

'Do I go in now?'

'Follow the others. I'll tell Dad to get you at the gate.'

Sweat pours down his legs. His jeans feel too tight at the waist. Louise leaves. He cannot know what it might mean to succeed at this test.

If he passes, and this school wants him, with its stiff blazers and lawns where sprinklers tick and turn like clocks in steady time, he cannot guess whether his parents will be pleased or afraid.

When he is sure she has gone, he walks away.

CHAPTER SEVEN
NOW: Alice

*A*fter drinking a cup of takeaway coffee that tasted of burnt milk and polystyrene, I waited for my sister, scanning the crowds of Central Station. I was on a bench outside the station, and watched pale tourists get on and off buses promising tours of Sydney landmarks. A toddler still in nappies heaved around near my feet, merrily peeling a banana and then throwing chunks of it as close to my toes as he dared. Louise was late.

I had circled Chinatown and parked behind the University of Technology. The students walking into the university looked colourful and brazen, wearing skirts with uneven hemlines, and dangling bold costume jewellery around their necks. In a glass display case, built into the brick of a wall, were a woman's bleached bones in front of a canvas of ghostly, luminous spheres, huge pale oranges of light. I tried to save the images from this tiny pocket of art in my mind.

I wanted something tangible to focus on, a phantom I could see, not the haunting that was dissolving my sister, hollowing her out, taking her apart cell by cell. Louise slipped between the past and the future but the present was wafer-thin for her, compressed to a sliver by the twin blocks of before and sometime.

As a toddler, she'd taken a long time before she started to speak, pointing with fat hands instead of asking, lurching after Jeremy. At first I'd wished she was my baby, while at the same time wishing that she was no one's, and now it felt as if both of these were true.

The air felt too warm. My armpits were sweaty and my shirt stuck to my back. Buses drove on to Canberra and Brisbane. I hated the disguise of Sydney, the gleaming glare of it; the heady holidayers staring at the shimmering harbour from plastic Circular Quay; the modern art museum with images on blazing white walls; the prim botanical gardens; and the opera house shaped like a pristine shell, or a dropped white handkerchief fluttering to the ground, buoyed into extraordinary shapes by the breeze. Still, I liked watching the muscular brown bodies of the surf girls at Manly and the teeming swarm of Bondi, orange peel and chip wrappers tangled together on the streets in accidental intimacy.

Lou had been living here for four years. I tried calling her flat but her home phone was disconnected. When I turned my mobile on there were increasingly shrill messages from Jon on it. I deleted them rapidly, but not before I caught the start of one where he was saying, 'I am beginning to get really annoyed with you,' in a falsely friendly voice. I had worn the wrong shoes and my feet were throbbing. If I went looking for Lou she would accuse me of being suspicious.

I ran back to feed the meter and realized I had left my backpack on the bench. It was gone when I returned. I asked at the office and a fat train worker pointed to the sign above him that said I shouldn't leave my property unattended.

'This is Sydney,' he told me. 'You've got to be more careful.' I nodded my head and tried to look as if I came from some tiny town where the neighbours all left their cars and front doors unlocked.

He handed me the bag and inclined his head. 'Okay, silly girl, what do you say?'

I grabbed the straps firmly and shovelled the backpack towards me. 'Fuck off.' He blinked and looked over his shoulder for a witness – someone to be outraged with. I walked down the street singing 'fuck off fuck off fuck off' and felt better.

I thought I would drive to Lou's place, but there was too much traffic and Sarah's car began juddering and letting out blasts of dirty steam through the exhaust pipe so I left it parked awkwardly in a lot rimmed with barbed wire and shadowed on either side by buildings: one a mustard yellow postmodern collision with silver struts and protruding red sills that made me think of children's furniture and the aura of a fast food restaurant; the other, a squat Art Deco.

Walking to Louise's flat I gave two bucks to a busker because the song's melody was jubilant and there was no school and no Jon and my body sang back.

As I veered through Newtown I passed a Thai takeaway and a fruit store selling magnificently expensive mangos, their skins cool and fleshy when I picked them up. The local pub had been renovated and some men in suits were gathered in the afternoon sun at the tables outside, toasting each other with dripping glasses of beer.

The public housing flat bordering Redfern and Darlington that Louise rented at subsidized rates was in a cramped greyish building of subdued repetition. I'd been here a year ago, seen food rotting in her kitchen, and abandoned, half-finished jumpers left slung over the backs of chairs, some with knitting needles still dangling from the woollen rows.

The security door was closed and a sign taped across cracked glass read: THIS IS A RESIDENTIAL DWELLING. ONLY INVITED GUESTS WILL BE TOLERATED. LOITERERS WILL BE PROSECUTED. WE WILL PURSUE WRONGDOERS TO THE FULL EXTENT OF THE LAW. I tried to remember which floor her place was on.

I knocked at the first door at the top of the stairs but no one answered.

On the way back I walked through the Block, then past the Aboriginal Legal Service and three divvy vans. One of the constables wound down his window and put his radio in his lap. 'Hold onto your purse, Lady.'

In the park nearby, a stringy white man prowled and sold drugs. Two teenage Aboriginal boys loped after a battered can of Sprite, kicking it forwards across the concrete.

The papers had been full of letters about how the Redfern terraces and high-rises were an eyesore, a breeding ground – though the authors never said for what, just left it ominously implied, as if they were talking about animals or bacterial disease. Successive governments promised to 'clean up' the Block as if it were a spilled drink. The Block was prime real estate now and developers nursed their interests and plans for luxury dwellings.

I'd taught a unit on architecture and history to the Year 11s when I was first doing my teaching rounds. The Redfern district was on the list of essay topics. I thought I was trying to show the relationship between control of space and physical marginalisation. Their keywords were: community, belonging, exclusion and boundaries. I had lesson plans based on struggles for land rights and the vote. I'd drawn up a timeline tracking the campaign for Aboriginal control and ownership in the 1970s, to the downturn and the heroin boom of the 1990s, right up to recent history, the Redfern riots and deaths in custody.

But the students went for the first question and the easiest. I got thirteen essays on laneways in Melbourne, several of them nearly identical, perhaps copied from the same source.

A man had been shot dead in his sleep the year my brother died. He was a black man who lived in public housing. He was not the suspect the police had been looking for.

I bought a drink from the supermarket. One of the giant murals stretching across the wall near the train station read: *100,000 years is a long, long time. 100,000 years is on my mind.*

There were still traces here of the bicentenary protests, the rage against Expo 88, and, before that, the freedom rides of the 1960s. Signs of a time when surviving meant resisting.

I collected the car and risked driving to look for her. I found myself at the squat where Louise used to live. It could be abandoned, except for the lingering smell of cooked meat. Stained newspaper littered the verandah. The windows were boarded up. I climbed the steps and knocked.

A man in his fifties stuck his eye in the crack of the door, then swung it open. He was enormously fat, his eyes bloodshot. There were crumbs on his faded purple sarong. The house smelled of dope. The carpet emanated a damp rotting smell, which filled the corridor.

'Is Lou around?'

'Eh?'

I cleared my throat. 'Louise?'

'Nup.'

'She stayed here last year.'

His eyes glared dully. 'No fucking LOU-EESE here.'

In the darkness behind him a woman shifted in choppy, short movements. I had a blurred impression of a purple fringe, a cheerful freckled face, before she called out, 'Hurry up and shut the door, Gary.'

I smoked a cigarette outside, holding the tobacco in my lungs for as long as I could, thinking about where to look for her.

Near Glebe Point Road I stopped at the house Louise lived in when she arrived in Sydney: the junk house. The letterbox was still painted red. I could remember a tumble of people hanging around, Lou vomiting onto the pale pink tendrils of her bedspread, the smell of sour milk in the kitchen. Her bedroom had been at the back of the house, filled with light that poured through a small, high window. A rusting Hills Hoist had stretched out bare in the garden like a reprisal, reminding us how far we'd strayed from the suburban Australian dream.

Louise would lie on the sea-green mattress in her room and refuse to come out while I sat stupidly in the lounge with the others, who seemed anonymous and interchangeable: women called Skye who made laksa and stitched needlepoints of pictures they claimed came to them in their dreams, tangle-haired boys who quoted Bob Dylan to each other – '*Eeeverybody* must get stoned' – and slept without taking off their boots. I would put money in the cracked china apple that accumulated dust and insects in the laundry and slam the metal back gate behind me, relieved.

I crushed some of the limp magnolias hanging over the low fence and concentrated on the stickiness in my palm.

I heard a baby wail inside. The front door was open. A voice called out 'hello' down the echoing corridor. I wiped off my hands, tossed the fading stems back into the garden.

'What are you doing?' The woman frowned at me. I knew her, even without the black bat's eye-makeup and the sullen, drifting addict's gaze. Her name was Katrina and she helped Lou get into the methadone program and let her paste up collages of broken glass and strange objects across the back fence.

I couldn't remember if Katrina and Lou were friends anymore, if they still smoked together in the afternoons or if she was another casualty of Lou's silent misery, the dark she trailed with her.

Katrina was heavier than I remembered. She had firm wrinkles in the corners of her eyes and her breasts were leaking milk onto the floral smock she was wearing. Behind her a man cradled a baby. She seemed vague and sweet-faced and very tired.

'Sorry, Katrina. I was meant to be meeting Louise at Central.' Silence. She didn't appear to be looking at me. 'I'm Alice, Lou's sister.'

'Oh, hi.' She frowned.

'I don't know if you see her anymore.'

She waved away the man in the darkness behind her. 'Did she tell you she was here?'

'No, I was walking past. I've lost her number.' I lied without thinking.

Katrina flattened her mouth knowingly. 'Lou wouldn't come here. Maybe Abercrombie Street?' Katrina turned back and held out her arms for the baby. Over her shoulder she said, 'Give her my love.' She paused. 'That'll piss her off. She's probably angry with me.'

'I'm not sure.'

'We're clean here. Your sister's a bit of a fool.'

I swung the gate closed after me.

When I got back to the car, I realized that the needle on the petrol gauge was low. I picked at the vinyl upholstery and poked through the glove box. When my mobile rang I picked it up without thinking.

'For God's sake, Alice. Fucking hell. I have been ringing you all fucking day.' Jon sounded wrong when he swore. He was from Adelaide money and his accent was too proper. He used to be in advertising and he sounded as if he was trying to speak in the language of a teenage boy. I straightened out the contents of the glove box in my lap and sorted through bits of paper. Sarah had written: 'good cheese, soap, CDs' on a scrap of envelope.

'I'm in Sydney. And you have *given up on me*, remember?'

When we last spoke on the phone, he had asked, 'Is there anything at all going on in this numb soul of yours?' and told me to find someone else to self destruct with. I still wanted to see the dreamy flicker of his eyelids as he slept and bury my face in the warmth of his neck but I couldn't be certain it wasn't the promise of pain that pulled me back in. The truth sliced into me: he loved someone else. Our moments together – the drinking of tea, lying in bed smoking cigarettes, his rambling accounts of the lives of Russian authors – were not the main game for him.

'We were having a good time, weren't we?' he asked.

I said, 'My numb soul can't tell. Too numb.'

He sighed heavily into the phone.

'Don't you ever wonder, Alice, why you enjoy – no, *thrive* – when things are confused? And then as soon, as *soon* as it's difficult, a decision has to be made, or it's . . . I don't know, meaningful or needs some . . .' he trailed off.

'She's your wife,' I told him.

'I am aware of that, yes.'

I said, 'I think you're unhappy with me because you believe if I loved you unreservedly then it would be easier to decide.' Even to me it sounded like a Mills and Boon line. *She realized she loved him unreservedly.*

'I've decided. I'd always decided. It's not that.'

I put my feet up on the dashboard. 'Well then.'

'I miss you. I don't want to give it up.'

'Do you think if you keep going she won't find out?'

'She doesn't know what she wants. Well, she doesn't know it's a thing. We should talk properly. I can't do it like this. Shit. Other phone's ringing.' He hung up and I stuffed Sarah's junk back in the glove box and slammed it shut.

When Louise finally called me it was late afternoon. I had been dozing with my head on the steering wheel and I woke to the taste of onion and processed cheese in my mouth from the takeaway sandwich I'd eaten earlier. Her voice sounded giddy and embarrassed. The excuses accumulated. She was staying out of the city and was too scared to get on the train because she hated sniffer dogs. It was daylight saving or it wasn't – she couldn't remember. She had lost her place in the Centrelink queue because she didn't have enough identity points. She said she would meet me at the Sandringham.

The streets of Newtown were slick and taut with unease. Footpaths and gutters streamed with summer rain that trickled on the verandahs of shops and the tin roof of the local high school. I sucked in deep breaths through my nostrils and lifted my chin. Clusters of homeless men near the train station watched their cardboard signs soak, impassive.

On King Street I drove past espresso bars, and cafés with glass-framed art house movie posters and violet walls. Small circles of teenagers were distributed along the footpath. Juice bar chalkboards advertised combinations of watermelon, pineapple and peppermint for energy and recovery.

There was little residue of the old Newtown – once inner-city slums housing the working poor, who were sold the *Tribune* door-to-door in the 1950s. As I waited at the lights, a transvestite clacked past in wedge heels. Afro hairdressers' open windows released gusty smells of hair oil and the scent of old men.

Schoolgirls walked home with achingly certain steps, their dresses faded and short, their faces open and knowing.

I waited for Lou in the Sandringham, listening to the ping and chortle of slot machines out the back. There was a couple at the table next to me. The woman was dressed like a housewife but she also wore gumboots. Her companion had suit pants and a jacket but no shirt. His jacket was pinned together across his midriff with a set of badges. The combination of badges seemed peculiarly open-minded: one for the Anzacs, one with a great marijuana leaf and another that appeared to be a rainbow. I took another sip of beer.

The woman said, 'And I said to her, I said, "listen, love: I don't think you can do it. I just don't. I said, nothing to go crying about, I'm not giving you the rat's arse, it's just I don't think you can."'

The man nodded slowly. The woman added, 'I told her: "you've had your fun and when will it be time for mine?"'

After a whispered conversation, the woman said urgently, 'Sex? You've got to be joking. What would *I* want with sex?' Her voice rose.

From the darkened corner a man muttered to himself, 'Who'd wanna fuck *that*?'

I heard footsteps and then Lou was seated opposite me. She was lean and brown, except for the paler ribbons of scar tissue that crossed her arms under the plastic glitter bangles she shook around. All her black hair was gone, mowed loose and short. It was shaved at the sides but she had kept her long floppy fringe. Her T-shirt was dotted with tiny strawberries with intricately drawn seeds and green tops. Her nails were jagged and dirty. She jiggled her feet on the blackened floor. I leaned across the table and hugged her. She pulled papers out of a plastic bag.

'What's all this? A plan to beat the casino?'

'I did have one of those books. Do you remember? Some mathematician. Crock of shit. If you can beat the casino legally why do you need the royalties from publishing the fucker? Nah. Centrelink stuff. Get me a drink?'

'Where have you been? I've been stuck in the city for hours.'

'Is this a fucking interrogation? Yes, I was late. I've been waiting in queues all day. You're here just to fuck me up.'

'Yes, Louise, I drove for thirteen hours just to fuck you up.'

She stretched. The bangles clattered. 'Sorry. *Sorry*. I need a drink.'

While I lined up, I thought about Lou as a little kid, rubbing at her eyes as she tried to practise her reading, picking flowers from the next-door neighbours' garden to give back to them as a present. I stuffed my hands in my pockets and arranged my expression in the mirror behind the bar.

I brought back schooners and accidentally slopped amber liquid over the table. She grinned. 'Alice, you are my lovely saviour.'

'Lovely me. Do you have a place to live?'

'I'm trying to get the paperwork sorted and I need you to sign.' She slid the last page across the table. There were boxes for me to fill in my date of birth, tax number, address and occupation. The header and footer listed the Department of Community Services.

'Where's the rest of it?'

'That's all you need to do.'

'I'm not signing a form that doesn't say what it's for.'

She shrugged. 'Fine. I'll find it.'

'Yeah.'

I got us more drinks, wine this time. Louise slid my packet of cigarettes towards her across the table and took one. She played with her lighter, removing the childproof catch, experimenting with different fuel strengths and flicking the flame on and off. 'Do you ever miss the danger game?'

I put my hand over my eyes and rubbed viciously. My head hurt. 'No, I'm an adult.' The danger game had been Louise's obsession for a while in the old house, before Jeremy died, before our mother left. Once, she'd found a tunnel leading into the underground drains and hidden there for a whole school day, peering up at the footpath through the metal grates and losing herself in the tangled corridors until a pipe burst and water flooded right up to her knees. We had each walked barefoot over broken glass in the empty leather factory five blocks from home. I had wanted to dare her to swallow the glass but I thought she might.

'*I* still do it.'

'Are you broke, Louise?'

Her lips were stained purple from the red wine.

'What were the rules?'

'I don't care.'

'The rules were that you had to do it in twenty seconds and you had to do it on your own. You couldn't tell anyone. And it ended with the code word in pig Latin.' Her neck was so straight it looked held in place by an invisible brace. 'In the danger game I had a choice about what happened in my life.'

Her glass thudded on the table.

'You used to say it was about throwing yourself open to chance.' She had slept around without any contraception. She hitchhiked out of the city. For all I knew, she had shared needles, telling herself she was playing a game of luck with dirty syringes. 'Now it's control?'

'I did it . . . the first time I made up the game was to stop being scared . . . because you never cried when Dad screamed at us and I'd be so pathetic. I'd be shaking and freaking out. I was practising doing things I was afraid of.'

'Your whole life's like that. You don't need any more practice.' I started ticking things off on my fingers. 'Heroin. Running away. Borrowing money . . .'

'You did it too, Alice, even when you went to high school.'

'What does that have to do with anything? Please don't do this again.' I could have put my arms around her but I was flooded with suspicion. I was waiting for her to tell me what she really wanted.

'I was just thinking about it. There's this job going, where you walk on stilts to advertise the festival. Sort of like the circus. It was on the job board. I could do that.'

'Can you walk on stilts?'

'I could *learn*.'

'Uh-huh. Why am I here?'

She leaned forward, a few stray strands of long hair twisting towards her drink, and then she looked up at me. 'You're helping me.' She used a baby voice, flirtatious, ashamed.

She kept playing with her bangles. At the top of her pile of papers was a picture of a sculpture, a cheap glossy postcard. The background was electric-blue framing a woman's torso made from glass or plastic. The woman was facing forward, but, like a half-peeled orange, or a bandaid flapping in water, this woman was unravelling. Above her breasts there was only one arm, her other arm invisible, undeclared. There was a diagonal curve, a clean line, instead of a neck. She had no head.

We shared another cigarette, fingertips touching as we passed it back and forth between us. Louise rolled up her sleeves and pushed back her bangles when a man at the bar stared at the scars around her arms.

'Stop this compulsive stuff and tell me what's going on.'

'And the truth will set me free and drugs are dirty and for losers, and honesty is the best policy ... Is that what you tell your students?' She ground out the cigarette and ran her hands over her face.

'You said you saw Mum.'

'Maybe.'

'What would you have said if it had been her?'

Her face crumpled a bit. She gathered up the change on the table and counted it out to buy another round of drinks.

'No more for me, I'm driving.' I tried to see if there were needle marks on her arms but she was cunning.

She leaned forward. 'Where did Jeremy go the night he disappeared?'

The carpet was green with psychedelic black swirls that seemed to spin and mutate if you stared at them for too long. I slid the car keys into my pocket and shouldered my bag. She hoped it could perform a kind of exorcism for her, running back over the old, sunken grooves of memory, slipping into the sickening, familiar contours of back then. It felt like drowning to me.

I said, 'He went to the river. He went back to school. He went to the station. What difference does it make?' but I knew. She thought the answer might free her of burden, the way confession is meant to – that this knowledge would make her well and whole.

'It makes a difference to *me*. How he died. You know, if he meant it.' She held a cigarette and roasted it in the flame of the cigarette lighter. She dug out some dope from her bag.

And I have thought this too. Did he want to die? Was he making himself a cup of tea, lighting the stove? Did he think there would just be some supercool explosion, like a rocket blasting? Did he believe Mum would save him or that I would? How did he get inside without anyone knowing?

'How about I lend you fifty bucks and then we go to Centrelink?' She kicked my shin. 'Don't fake it with me.'

'None of this seems to be making you happy.'

'Coming from you, Alice, that diagnosis means very little. *You* are unhappiness at home in its lounge room.'

'What do you want?'

'I want to come to Melbourne. Sydney's shit.'

'And, what, live with me?'

Her eyes gleamed blackly. She was my sister but I didn't know her at this moment. She could have been intoxicated with joy or reeling with fear and I wouldn't see it.

I said, 'Are you using?'

She looked at the table, forlorn. It was a terrific performance. 'Not really.'

I drank the lukewarm beer in front of me and stood up.

She put her papers down fussily, 'Settle, settle, settle.'

I thought of the collages she used to make with broken glass. 'I saw your friend Katrina. She had a kid.'

'So?'

'So, nothing.'

'What if I looked for Mum?'

I laughed. 'Where? For what?'

'You look like shit, Alice. You're a hunched-over old woman with a sour little face.'

I told her, 'She's probably not even in Melbourne.'

'She smashed up shit at work before she left. That was the last thing. Not us.'

'She didn't do anything like that.'

'She fucking well did.'

'You're a fantasist, Louise.' We sat back in the sullen silence. A few tables down, the older women had put down their stubby complimentary pencils and lotto forms and were watching us.

'Let's go.'

She smiled, resigned. 'I am, alas, evicted.'

A boy came towards our table. He was about sixteen, with a blue baseball cap and a rash of pimples across his chin. 'Got any grass, mate?'

Louise ignored him and I sat back.

His whisper was gravelly and adolescent. 'Give us some and I'll get it back to ya.' Louise sat gracefully, silently, her throat exposed and her eyes averted. The boy turned to go. He jolted back and tipped her glass onto the table. 'Right, fuck off then.'

When the barman walked towards us, the boy backed out calling, 'I know her. She sells. She fucked me brother. Cocksucking bitch.'

The barman looked back at Louise. From his angle he couldn't see the tissue of scar that ran down the back of her neck to her shoulder. When we stood outside in the light I could imagine her circling around the Cross eating leftovers from the bins and cleaning syringes with homemade solution; I could see it in detail, as if it were already happening.

'Fine. Get in the car.'

She touched the skin on her forearms absentmindedly, soothingly, and rolled her joint.

The thing about Lou was that she was burnt.

Before we left I drove to one of the faster Centrelinks, in a wealthy suburb of Sydney, where it wouldn't take all day for her to speak to someone. I waited in line with her. We hardly spoke, shuffling our feet across the pale blue of the carpet, stretching our ankles the way runners might before a big race. We were like gamblers – time had no meaning for us – we would wait in the queue until someone saw us or we were sent home. I watched Lou's profile in the darkened window. She was in pieces, because the blinds broke up her reflection and the tinted glass distorted us. Like people behind the windows of government cars or limousines, it made us seem more important than we were. One piece of Louise in the window took off her brightly coloured sunglasses, ran her finger across her eyebrows, then put them back on.

A gaunt man kicked a glass bottle on the footpath outside. Although he was in his forties, he walked with the gait of my dead brother: hands clasped behind his back, head tilted towards the mysteries of the ground. The sky escaped him. The wind didn't move him. His legs swung to a rhythm that bled inside his head.

The dust on the venetian blinds bothered me. I sometimes helped my mother take a wet cloth to the blinds of the institutions she cleaned. Before I learned better I would request lollies or demand drinks from the few dedicated or desperate corporate execs hanging around in the evenings at the offices we vacuumed. I shamed them too, and just as well, since they drank hard and worked hard to be kept away from scrawny mothers with little girls scraping through their wastebins and wearing their poverty like a badly stitched second skin.

I studied the faint imprint of fingers on the venetian blinds here. They were only a few feet from the floor, which made me wonder if they had been left by a child, yet the fingerprint marks were fat enough to belong to a wide-palmed adult. I was pleased to have found a tiny gap in the flat, certain world of Centrelink, but the fingerprints also bothered me. How did they get there?

Louise placed her hands in the pockets of the pants that sagged limply off her hips. Yesterday's clothes clung softly to her. She had failed activity tests; she had not kept up the client end of the bargain. Welfare offices, like the school I taught at, thrived on euphemisms. Mutual Obligation. Job Networks. Jobsearch Training.

Lou scanned the faces behind the desk. There was a tired man with silver hair and a wide-lipped woman with glasses who typed quickly and frowned, then smiled as though her day was comprised of endless expectations and disappointments.

A woman I once taught with – we were friends in a way, she had a guttural laugh and the kids never knew what to do with her – had worked at Centrelink in a previous life. She had said, 'If first year psychology was rats and stats, unemployment was all junkies and job snobs,' and I had said nothing, but then avoided her calls and invented reasons to eat my lunch on the run rather than in the staffroom.

My sister was twenty-four and regretted more than she could remember.

She talked to me in a rapid monologue about the mad circularity of her predicament. She couldn't prove she lived where she did, because she'd been evicted, but she needed an address for correspondence and she couldn't be paid because she'd been evicted for having no money, but she had been cut off because her circumstances had changed and she hadn't notified anyone and she couldn't collect rent assistance without a current legal lease. Her voice grew higher. She began to sound cheerful. I wondered what Louise might have wished for when we were children. She would have wanted to be beautiful when she grew up, the way girls are encouraged to, and now she almost was. She might have wanted to be clever, because cleverness seemed the certain way out of all that had come before.

She'd been a late reader, and her whole adult life she'd never been able to do simple arithmetic because she'd been held down so much in school and missed so many classes, but she loved word games.

When she still lived in Melbourne she was working at a bottle shop where the manager pinched her arse. Once I came in and the manager, assuming I was a customer, hissed, 'Serve that woman even though she looks like she spits instead of swallows,' and I had seen Lou not knowing whether to be indifferent or embarrassed and which would keep her the job.

The thought of what my sister might have wanted for herself was almost unbearable. I fixed my eyes on the bright, hard white of the Centrelink wall.

The 'Work for the Dole' poster on the wall showed a young woman beaming in an army uniform with the word 'opportunity' lettered across her chest.

While Louise showed her forms to a thin young man at the counter, we heard shouting. Someone at the end of the line with a wretched face smoothly toppled the rubber plant next to the window where the fingerprints hung in the dust. The plant landed quietly, and earth and stones tipped soundlessly onto the carpet. The gesture was filmic. A security guard rushed out but the man had already made his exit.

'Computer's frozen. Just be a few ticks.' The thin man chewed on his pencil and turned a page in the newspaper he kept behind the counter. Louise leaned in.

'Ruin,' she said.

He shifted in irritation. 'What?'

'You're missing five down. The cryptic crossword.' We all stared at the clue. *Damaged urn in disrepair.* 'Ruin.'

*A*t the railway line he counts the number of goods trains passing through. He watches the disguised signals – the lights – that tell the train drivers it is safe to keep going. He wonders if these signals are centrally controlled through a computer system, or triggered automatically when trains are on the tracks, and what happens if the drivers are running late or there's a crash. The railway crossing is overgrown. His dad says men used to open and close the gates but now they ding down automatically. It occurs to Jeremy that his father may be very, very angry when he returns home.

He sits near the tracks and presses forward to try to get a sense of the passengers in the train as it rushes by. It is difficult. His own landscape is pressed onto them in the dark reflections of the window, and the faces he can distinguish bob and float in the embankment where he sits. He is ten. He cannot think of being thirty-eight. He cannot conceive of himself at his father's age. Another goods train passes and hoots into the empty dark because it will hurtle through the station without stopping. The train rocks on the rails in an even hum. The boom gates lift and the bells stop ringing. Jeremy creeps onto the railway tracks and feels the warm rails. He sees Paddle Pop sticks and plastic bags wedged in the tracks. He takes off his shoes and stands on the railway sleepers, right in the centre. If another train comes, he will hear the boom gate and bell.

He touches the black rocks that line the railway track. They are smooth and dull. He feels a cold wind through his school jumper. He chucks a rock into the air and fails to catch it. He has seen some of the boys in Alice's class come down here. They graffiti their tags onto the trains in giant, incomprehensible letters.

His father may have come to collect him. The school would ripple with his father's awkwardness. Would they have read out his name on a roll?

He can remember sedimentary, igneous and metamorphic rocks. But the train rocks are not like the rocks geologists look at.

The magazines in the library say you can suffocate someone by putting a pillow over their face or a plastic bag over their head, but Louise does not know this. There is smoke rising from the factory behind the railway yard and sparrows pick in the long grass on the other side of the tracks. Jeremy wonders if drivers own special rail maps that show the routes of trains all around the suburb and the state. When you are on a train you can trick yourself into thinking that you are static and the world – rather than the train – is moving. Jeremy looks at the clouds in the sky and tries to balance his vision so that the clouds are still and the moon, the whole sky, is lurching around them.

He picks up some black rocks and takes them to the side of the tracks. He lays them out in order of size. There is one rock that is white underneath. He fingers it. The white isn't chalk, isn't bird shit. It is on the wrong side of the rock to be paint. He throws the rock away and it bounces high and skitters back onto the railway tracks. He looks away and tries to find the rock when he looks again, but it has blended in.

He thinks of being at the beach with Louise. Sand is broken down rock. Glass will become smooth in the sea, its edges lose their sharpness, but syringes stay the same and his mother will not let him pick them up from the shore.

If he could get onto the train then he wouldn't return home. He would be vanished. He wouldn't see the set of his mother's face or the disguised relief of his father who is going to be so disappointed by him. He doesn't have a ticket. He doesn't have any money. He is ten and when you are ten you cannot be a magician.

The boom gates begin screaming again and he hears the murmur of a train in the distance. It is very difficult to stop a train suddenly, even if you slam on the brakes. He wants Louise to tell her old stories about silver trains that move so fast you cannot see them, that travel underwater, under land, and crash into countries and islands that haven't been found before. Trains like liquid that change shape and have passengers that can see the future and the past all at the same time. He steps onto the tracks as the train turns the curve.

Jeremy leaps back again.

He gathers his rocks – there are nine of them; the tenth is lost now – into his arms and cradles their slight warmth, and he heaves them back up the embankment towards home.

I walked to the tram stop in the rain, taking choppy steps on the slippery footpaths. I held my umbrella low to avoid making eye contact with the others rushing to work.

I'd left twenty dollars and a spare key next to the bed for Louise, who had stayed up late sorting through her notes, rustling like a small animal. She was now on a rubbery lilo on my living room floor, her face buried in the pillow, only the short, uneven clumps of her hair, glossy and thick, spilling out from under the blue-spotted cotton sheet. Her wrists were so thin. There was a stale packet of green tea and a box of cornflakes on the bench but no milk in the fridge. My heart fluttered when I left the money but twenty dollars wouldn't buy much of anything Lou might hunger for.

We'd arrived in Melbourne in the early hours of the morning. She'd spent the trip singing along with the radio and chewing through Sarah's ancient box of mints that had been rattling around on the floor near the back seat. With a couple of shots of gin at a stopover in Albury, Louise had told me how it was all possible: she was going to get a great job, she could just tell, she felt the time was right, she could be different in another city. And still my heart leapt for her, though I thought I knew better. Still I thought she might be on the verge of some discovery.

Meeting this woman that she hadn't touched or spoken to since she was ten was meant to tell Louise where our brother went when he was missing, and how he found his way back into our house where he died. Discovering our mother was meant to close the wound. Louise felt sure that she would stop collecting news stories about house fires and could stop having nightmares if she found her. This certainty unnerved me. She believed herself. I told myself I wasn't involved.

Before I woke, I had been dreaming about the installation I'd seen in Sydney, the yellowed bones and fleshless body. My brother had become a ventriloquist's doll in a coffin, mouthing advice to me that I couldn't interpret. His face was plastic with deep-set eyes with fake lashes and a sudden gash for a mouth.

When Louise and Jeremy were born, Mum let me take the sugar lumps from her tea tray at the hospital and eat them, one after the other. Louise came first. Jeremy was born much smaller than her. Often one twin dominates, even in the womb, and absorbs more of the nutrients. The hospital smelled of antiseptic and floor cleaner. My father, who was driving a forklift back then, sat on the hospital bench in grey overalls, begging a God he didn't believe in for things to go right and then shouting at him for being a fraud. I had recognized the Lord's Prayer from my grandmother's training. She'd minded me Saturdays, a stiff white-haired woman who'd taught me to cross my ankles like a lady and to sip the huge mugs of Irish Breakfast tea holding the handle and not the cup. I wasn't meant to be learning the prayer because Mum hated the church, but my dad's mother let me play with the china Jesus and use her best crayons if I recited the words with her.

I thought if Louise did find our mother somewhere I would have to feel sorry for her, and I didn't want to. She might simply refuse to see us or sit quietly without expression as my sister begged, bullied and bared her teeth.

At work I marked essays through lunch and took the Geography teacher's Social Studies classes because he'd stood in for me while I'd been away. I had a fax on the desk about updating the teaching materials on values. The poster that hung behind the door listed tolerance, diversity, initiative, caring, trying, and giving everyone a 'fair go' as good values, and provided examples. There was also a report in my pigeonhole attached to a union notice titled: 'Some comments on viability and flexibility in under-performing, low-retention secondary school programs with diminishing enrolments.' It was awash with jargon, an early draft by some public servant that I guessed someone had leaked, and the author's initials were pencilled quite small at the top of the page.

The Year 8s were meant to be discussing stereotypes. Twenty-five faces watched me sullenly. My student-teacher was working with the older kids. I caught a glimpse of her walking along the corridor, shoulders hunched as if against a strong wind.

Nick talked about Aborigines and told the class with the sure tone of one who knew he spoke the truth: 'All they do, Miss – *all* they do – is *drink.*'

'They sell drugs,' a new girl added. 'And riot.' The rest of the class stirred. They were keen on riots and thought they were fantastic. They assured me that the kids who had burned down their schools were fantastic too.

'Who knows what a stereotype is?' I didn't tell them I'd been to Redfern and seen a wall of cops at the train station, hands on their batons. I asked them about police violence and Aboriginal deaths in custody and racism in Australia. We had four Aboriginal students in the school.

I pulled several of the tables together. 'Push your chairs back carefully. We're going to play a game.' I pointed to the four corners of the room. 'Each of these corners is an area. I want you to run to the first corner if you can say *yes* to the following statement.' They huddled together in the centre of the room. 'If you are wearing white.' They all shifted into the first area; white was part of the school uniform. 'And move on to section two if you are a girl.' Half of them ran on. 'And go to the next corner if you have ever felt unfairly treated.' They pressed forward together. 'Move on if you have ever been picked on.' It was mostly the female students that walked forward. They stared at each other and told the boys who were whispering, 'oh, boo hoo, poor you,' to shut up. 'If you wish you weren't in school right now' – only a handful had the courage to change corners. 'If someone has told lies about you.' Most of the class shifted awkwardly, shoes squeaking against the linoleum floor.

Hamish hung back. 'Why aren't you playing, Miss?'

'Because I'm the teacher.' It carried the shadow of a phrase I had promised myself I wouldn't utter in class: *because I said so. Just because.* 'But I'd be in that corner if I played.' I pointed randomly at the far side of the room and watched Hamish try to figure out what I was admitting.

'Keep going quickly; try not to stop and think. Go to the next station if you think that you have experienced racism.' They waited. A group of girls walked forward, trying not to acknowledge each other. Although sections of this neighbourhood were almost entirely multilingual, I had also heard people on excursions speak to the Vietnamese and Arabic kids in loud, exaggerated voices, using simple words, even monosyllables to ensure they understood the presentations. Hamish himself had chanted *chink, chink* to impervious Asian students on his first day of school, although he wouldn't do that now.

If groups of Sudanese teenagers bought chips at the milk bar on the other side of the suburb, they were watched by the shop owners who clasped baseball bats under their counters, or only permitted them entry one at a time. They would be followed around as they compared prices and brands of bubblegum.

I had phrased it in the wrong way. Admitting you had been discriminated against wasn't tough. It suggested victimhood, hypersensitivity, the inability to get and take a joke. They were beginning to look bored.

'Or you think you have been racist.' A few slouched against the walls. Others came to a dead stop as if they were playing freeze.

Becca put up her hand. 'But, like, maybe if you were racist, you wouldn't know, so why would you go to the next corner?'

Hamish strolled across the room. A cluster of students pretended to cheer him.

'Can things be a stereotype even if they're true?' Nick asked.

'We'll talk about this after. Go to the next corner if you think you or your family or your culture has been stereotyped.'

In the flurry of running feet, Becca, who had crooked teeth and dirty white-blonde hair down her back, tripped over.

'Oops. Are you hurt?'

She got back on her feet. 'I'm okay, Miss Reilly.'

I put my hands to my cheeks to cool them. As the bell rang Nick said to me, 'Can we do that every Social Studies?'

'Not a chance.' I was smiling even though it felt like I had conducted a daggy exercise from one of those ancient textbooks on group dynamics, written by social workers or aimed at building rapport amongst executives.

After the bell rang I read some of their exercises on empathy. Becca had written: 'I understand the Aborigines because now I live in houses like them. Dad takes –' She has crossed 'junk' out and written, 'drugs'. 'I watched TV and then the Services took me away and now my sister isn't with me but where I stay is the same as theirs and maybe they could come and have a riot too in the place where I am.'

I picked up another response. Unsigned, in cramped boys' handwriting, it read: 'They are fucked. They should get used to it.'

I waited behind in the classroom. Did my anonymous student think Aboriginal people should get used to it because things weren't going to be any different or because they deserved it?

The realism, the blank resignation, of the sentiment appalled me. But was I any different? I thought it was a rigged game, a shitty system. But I lacked the courage or the hopefulness to imagine any alternative. I stuck doggedly, out of habit and history, to the few expectations I had left. The seventies slogan from the sticker on Sarah's car taunted me. I wasn't outraged or paying attention. For all Louise's slipperiness, her evasions and her brittleness, at least she remained defiant.

Usually the trick with yard duty was to ignore your peripheral vision and keep your eyes firmly to the front so that whatever the kids were doing had stopped or been hidden by the time you arrived.

Our principal was cranky because a couple of people were away on stress leave and our emergency teacher had already left for the day. I walked past walls covered in graffitied posters for safe sex, and complex concept maps with ballooning circles that intersected to show the multiple career choices that were meant to be available to my students. I hadn't eaten and my skin felt tight.

We'd had complaints that some of our ex-students were chroming by the school gate. The eighteen- or nineteen-year-olds who sniffed in old car parks or closed youth centres were harmless – hollowed out by boredom. These were the same boys who cut down a bunch of trees in the primary school last summer. I swung between a searing sorrow for them and rigid irritation. Why was their despair at the system so passive, so self-hating? Why did they stop themselves like magnets at the gateway to our school to draw in the ones who might still get by, who might finish, might get out?

I didn't ask myself what I thought getting out meant.

The playground was flat, punctuated by a few tea trees and some patches of scrubby grass. The younger girls swung on the bars, and fed and soothed their pet Tamagotchis. The older ones talked under the shelter of the trees and sent text messages swiftly, surreptitiously. The boys played basketball on the asphalt and leapt into the air when they got an unlikely shot through the askew ring, or sat in the woodwork room, with their backs to the door, where they were not allowed between classes.

There were a couple of aerosol cans near the gate but no chromers. Year 7s jumped faded hopscotch lines. The Thomas boys crouched at the edge of the school, leaning into the wire cage fence with their heads nestled together, sharing a single set of earphones.

Sam, a big, easy boy repeating Year 10, was in the woodwork room when I walked in. His parents had moved into the area from a tiny country town a few years ago, but his father was killed in a car crash a couple of months later. Parents who couldn't buy a sports uniform or new editions of textbooks poured in money to buy flowers for the funeral. I hadn't seen his mother at the parent-teacher interviews this year.

'You're not allowed in here after the bell's gone.'

'I'm not doing nothing.' He was sanding a coffee table, the same project they all got given year after year. His maroon and grey jumper looked faintly ridiculous on a sixteen-year-old. His hair ran over his collar, dyed black and green.

In my head I said, 'anything'. I crossed my arms. 'It's a school rule.' I started again. 'If I make exceptions I'll have half your class in here, some of them stoned, playing with saws and sanders.'

Sam kept his hands on the table. He was trying to be happy: building things he hoped would stay solid. I realized that it was moments like these when I hated teaching – the pettiness of it, the arbitrary rules.

'Why don't you lock the fucking room then?'

I felt a stab of anxiety. I remembered that Max who took Woodwork and the apprenticeship stream for the final-year students probably *was* meant to lock the door at lunch.

Sam turned his back to me.

'What's going on? Is there a problem with the other kids in your class?'

'I want to make my table. Mum's gonna use it.'

'You've done a good job.'

'You reckon?'

I had no idea. 'Can't you finish it next week?'

'Might be leaving, Miss.'

In the time I'd taught Sam I'd seen him with a broken nose from trying to fight a group of kids at the bus stop who'd been calling out 'go back to where you came from' to some Somali girls from his class. He read science fiction at the local library and handed in stories about mind control and cloning instead of history essays.

'Where will you go? You've only got a few years left.' I sat on the bench and looked at the curled wood shavings on the ground, which turned in on themselves like apple skins.

He looked at me as if I was absolutely vacant.

'Just work. Mum's really sick. Same thing I'd do anyway.'

I chewed my nails. I'd seen it before – a handful of boys always left at the end of Year 10. I told myself I was used to it. And why should they stay? Most of the time I didn't do much for any of them but give them bits of history – tastes of old struggles. But I wanted Sam to be different.

'You don't have to leave right now,' I said. 'Why don't you hang on?'

'Yeah.' He meant *no*. 'I'm sick of school. I don't wanna finish just so I can get a job and tell people what to do all day.'

He must have thought that was what I did. 'How's your brother?'

'Living with some really rich guy. Daytona at home in the living room and a *glass* basin in the bathroom. He says she's putting it on, Mum is, and that she just wants another man to come and rescue her.'

Even to me, Daytona and yuppie renovations didn't seem a bad deal. 'See how you go. But talk to me about it before you decide.'

'Yeah, Miss.'

It was the end of the day when Tom, the principal, called out to me. He rubbed at his eyes behind his glasses. Tom was a careful man in his early sixties. He was slender, with a clipped beard, a love of pinstriped suits and a habit of getting uproariously drunk at the Christmas party each year. When he hired me, it was just after his application to be the head teacher at a private school proved unsuccessful, and there were private bets among the teachers on how soon he'd retire.

'Alice? Were you supervising at lunch?'

'I was only on duty for the second half.'

'Where were you?'

'I checked the gates. It was fine. I guess the chromers had a day off.'

'One of the girls fell off the step and hit her face. Her mother came down to the school. We couldn't find you.'

'I was in the woodwork room. One of my students is about to drop out.'

'Even if we can't prevent accidents, Alice, the point of duty is to make sure someone's there. You're supposed to keep moving when you're supervising.'

He was right. I had spent too long with Sam. I'd only been at the school four years. I had trouble controlling my classes. I told Tom I couldn't be everywhere at once.

'Was it a male student in the woodwork room?'

'Oh come off it. He was upset.'

'I don't like it any more than you do but we have to cover ourselves. It's a really bad idea to be with a male student alone.'

'It's ridiculous to think –'

'It's not about what I think, it's about how it looks.'

'I'm sorry.'

'That's the way the department sees things. It's for your own protection.'

'Yeah.' I felt thick, rebuffed.

When I got home, I found some drawings taped up in newspaper under the junk mail. Jon's jerky piecemeal handwriting gave him away. I sorted through notices that houses in my area had sold for record prices, and pictures of three-inch angry termites in an extermination company's brochure. There was an ad for steam cleaning that questioned, 'Does your carpet look like this?' above a photo of a spoiled square of off-white pile.

I gathered up the leaflets with their coaxing and admonishing, their alternate engendering of ambition and fear in potential purchasers, and I took the collection of drawings upstairs. Last week's news blurred away as the headlines smudged my hands with black ink.

There was white wine left in the bottle so I sat on the balcony and poured a glass. The sky was pale blue. The light was golden, drowsy. I smelled sausages in the air. Bees circled the potted lavender and loops of jasmine. I wanted to be the sort of person who would make lavender jam, or marinate their own olives in jars and grow tomatoes, or design their own cards at Christmas. I was seized briefly with the urge to immerse myself in domesticity. If I succumbed to frivolity at least I would be productive, not just bored. I felt a giddy lightness, a sense of falling into happiness, with the sun on my skin, and my empty flat.

I read the report from school before I opened the package from Jon. The options were carefully worded, listed in a neutral order, but this was from the office of the Minister for Education. The least viable option was for our school to retain a full program and staff and continue fully funded. I was on a contract, the most expendable teacher if staff were cut. Someone – probably Anastassia, the union rep at school – had scribbled questions across the page. There wasn't any detail about what would happen to us if funding was reduced. Louise didn't know that I had recently begun paying our father's rent. My savings were disappearing.

I knew Louise was already changing, or changing back. I didn't think our mother would ever be found. She'd have changed her name, erased her history. Our family was in debt when she left and she hadn't even come to the funeral, which had been delayed for the autopsy. I'd begun to wonder, without telling Lou, if she had already been planning to leave before Jeremy died. It was the absences that made room for the conspiracies. Louise and I had been tangled together against the world, but often the world had divided us against each other, too.

Still, I loved Louise. I wanted to believe in her.

Through the glass doors I could see the cardboard edges of a school project my brother made about the solar system, jammed behind an expensive hardcover book on architecture I'd never read.

I tore open the bundle from Jon and out fell the drawings and his note: 'sorry, yes, I fucked things up', scribbled over and over. I was half expecting more of his usual fare: he was commissioned to draw limp watercolours with intricate borders and attractive, unthreatening woodland creatures for some authors; and bold, impudent, cartoony kids with mismatched socks and crooked smiles for others.

Jon had asked me once to test out some of his sketches for a Young Adult book on my students and I kept pretending to forget because I could hear the glee in their voices – 'these pictures are gay', 'fuck the spaceships, where's the guns?' – as they demolished his eager, nostalgic representations of what it meant to be young.

But the first drawing was charcoal. There I was: seated, looking out the window, one hand supporting my chin. My eyes were blank. My eyebrows frowned fiercely. I leaned forward and my toes were squat and splayed on the ground. Something about my jaw suggested I was preparing for an attack.

I listened to the clock on my wall, each tick a tiny death, and smoothed out the creased paper wrapping.

Jon had disappointed me. His gift was hardly an insight and his conclusions insubstantial – I was unhappy. I should do yoga. The beauty of the natural world didn't please me. Any bright six-year-old could tell you that.

Then I realized that Louise was clutching onto my back in the picture. She was the size of a tiny, tame monkey but her features were intricately rendered: Louise's come-fuck-me stare the monkey's backward glance. Her clinging hands had broken nails. A syringe and a bookmark were tucked into her back pocket. Finding Louise in the picture winded me. The recognition that Jon had cruelty and menace, a conscious streak of unkindness, was a relief after so many nights of being injured by the accidental, the incidental, the breathless remark.

He'd never seen Lou. He must have got the face from the snapshot tucked into the edge of my mirror, taken when Louise was seventeen.

When I went to turn the page, something else caught my eye. As if providing an in-joke amongst cartoonists at a snappy magazine, Jon had written himself into the picture. His hand waved or trailed behind him like an afterthought at the edge of the page: Jon, out of the frame, on his way elsewhere.

Until this moment, this image, I had not thought Jon clever.

I took the remainder of the drawings into the bathroom, where the tiles were cool under my feet. I sat with my back against the wall and focused on the gold of my taps and the ring of grease that coated the pink surface of the bath. I'd painted the walls pale green and Jon had helped with the sills and window frames. We'd laughed at the colour names on the tins: waterberry, luminosity.

The remaining pictures were drafted like proofs for a children's book: Peter and Jane in style, naïve. Jon and I were children. We walked. We ran. We even played with the neighbourhood dog. In this narrative I was the sulky older sister, tethered to a whimsical, childlike brother who was always looking the other way. I supposed there were worse ways to tell the story.

I left a message for Sarah to tell her that her car was back. I stuffed the drawing of Louise and me down the side of the bed, then I tore up the rest of Jon's sketches and used the scraps to wrap up the dead flies that hovered along the skirting boards, before I threw them in the bin. I ate dinner quickly at the kitchen table. The oily leftover pasta was cold but I chewed it, wiping the grease from my hands on my pants, and then I filled the percolator with strong Italian coffee.

I hoped it was Lou ringing but Jon said, 'Don't hang up on me.'

'Fancy that,' I said, and then, 'I'm not the hanging-up type.'

'Don't be so unambitious. Everyone can be the hanging-up type, given the right circumstances. Besides, you've done it before.'

He had been drinking. He sounded afraid.

'Are we siblings?'

'What? *Are* we?'

'In the drawings?'

'Not sure. Not sure.' He waited. 'Let me come around.'

'Lou's here,' I lied.

'She came back with you?'

'It's what they like to call a long story.'

'How are the drawings?' he asked.

'They're very well. Serving two masters. Nice coffin padding for some recently deceased flies.'

He cleared his throat.

I lit up a cigarette. 'Are we finished?'

'I shouldn't have stayed the night. I promised myself when we started.'

'Well, you shouldn't have come if that's where it was going to end up.'

His voice rose. 'Where did you think it was going to end up?'

I asked him what his wife said when she found out.

'She just said I'm a fuckwit man and that I'm blundering and obvious.'

'You are.' My voice lifted suddenly. 'That's it. You are a man, a fuckwit man.' The elation ebbed away. If I asked him where he was calling from, he wouldn't tell me. The reassurances he must have given his wife remained unacknowledged between us.

'It's not the sex that upsets her. She *says*. It's all the lying. She thinks I'm foolish.'

'And what do you think?'

'I don't know. A marriage is a messy thing.'

I didn't want to know about his marriage. He was lecturing me from the inside of an institution he assumed I knew nothing about. Why couldn't I let him go?

'What did you promise her?'

'She says she's thinking about whether she wants to try and fix things with me . . . if she can be bothered. Fuck, she works all the time and then she says she wants to have a baby. Next week she doesn't want to have a baby. She wants to rent an apartment in Paris and take photos. I thought men were meant to have the midlife crisis.'

'Oh but you are, dear one. What else am I?'

'Look Alice –'

'*I* can't be bothered. I just can't be fucked.'

'I guess you think I've treated you pretty badly. And I'm a shit. But there was something there. We had something. Even if it was raw and difficult, it was real. At least give me that. Right?'

He'd slipped into the past tense beautifully, without a breath's pause.

'Yes it was *real*. What sort of criteria is that? Global warming's real. And rats and nuclear weapons. Leprechauns aren't.'

We laughed. He said, 'I'm coming over.'

'Where's Mary tonight then?'

He breathed in. 'You are gentle and lovely and soft and warm and you know the blackest parts of me, won't you let me come round and talk to you. Just tonight?'

It sounded like a song. I tried to make it into a tune in my head: *you knooow the blackest parts/of me/Won't you let me come round/ just tonight?*

'Hang on – the coffee.' The coffee percolator hummed a warning and I jumped up with the phone but it had already exploded coffee all over the stove.

Jon said, 'You should get a new one' and I answered flatly, 'A new what?' and then we were quiet.

*

When he knocked on the door he was carrying a paperback copy of Bulgakov's *Master and Margarita* to read to me. We embraced in the hallway. I looked at his face: the smooth brown skin, the break across the bridge of his nose, the wicked tilt of his eyelashes, the faint creases beneath his eyes.

'I thought I'd meet your sister.'

'I'm not sure where she is now.' I glanced at the clock. 9.30 in the evening: early if you were twenty-four and jobless. 'I don't really want her here. You'd think she's magical and stunning and she'll tell you she can play the drums and she had a speaking part in a famous TV show or that we had a dog called Alexander that was hit by a car and you'll be nodding along until you realize it's utter invention.'

He brushed at his hair, nervy. 'Right.'

'I wish she wasn't staying with me.'

He laughed. It was a throaty, earnest sound. 'Now tell me what you really think of her.'

He was being ironic but I considered the question. After a long time I said, 'I admire her.'

We got slowly under the covers and I felt the tug of sleep approaching. His skin was warm and dry. We kissed but it felt performative, self-conscious, as if we were rehearsing. It was too much: the faint stubble grazing his chin, the smell of pencil on his hands, my dread at the announcement I was sure he would make. I worried that I could never feel the right thing at the right moment.

He read quietly, in a gentle voice that belonged to a younger man. He licked a finger before turning the pages and he waited for a number of beats between sections. He was the only man who'd ever read to me as an adult. He put the novel aside and stroked my hair.

He began drawing on my foot, a path leading to an open door. It was too much like being branded, so I tugged away. 'Freud would go to town on you.'

'Why?'

'Next you'll draw a train in a tunnel.'

His laugh was rough and nervous.

I realized that when Jon was illustrating, a pencil worn down to a stub in his hand, I knew him least. I asked him what it felt like when he knew he'd got an image right, how he could tell the good drawings from the bad.

'When I get it right it feels familiar, like something that's already happened to me. I remember it, even though it hasn't happened yet.'

He sat up. 'Why do you admire your sister?'

I'd put on some blues music. There was something generic, clichéd, about our poses. For the first time since the affair had begun I felt almost squalid.

'She hasn't given up on the idea of justice. Economic equality. Rights for the homeless. She thinks fairness is possible. She doesn't live in the real world.'

I wanted to avoid his having to tell me that it was finished. I looked at the pest control brochure crumpled on the floor.

'Does this sort of stuff work on anyone?'

'What?' He shifted in the bed towards me.

'Advertising like this?'

He shrugged. 'Depends.'

'Come on, ad man.'

'Well, that's pretty crude. Crappy design. There's nothing that would make you remember the company. But the principles are the same. It's about images, repetition and association. You have a product and you get people to aspire to own it or you get them to fear something else and you sell the solution to it – governments do that all the time.'

'But people . . . *consumers* . . . see through that.'

'But that might not stop them buying. What do you have in your bathroom cabinet?'

'Disprin and home-brand plastic strips, aka band-aids.'

'Mmm, and cream that promises to reverse the signs of ageing. You don't really think you'll look twenty forever. It's the hopefulness you're paying for, not the result. You're purchasing the aspiration – not the reality.'

'Surely I look twenty now?'

But he wasn't flirting. 'You train people to want something and forget what they need, or create needs that they didn't know they had.'

'Assuming they're greedy and stupid.'

'Advertising's much more creative now than it was when I started. Especially television; it's far more oblique ads, like pop video clips. The industry attracts a huge amount of talent.'

'Did you make lots of money?'

He frowned. 'A bit. I was pretty bad at it. We had guys who'd breeze in after 10 a.m. cocktails with storyboards and slogans or they'd leave it till the hour before they were meeting the client to get the adrenaline to do the work for them. Never lasted long but they were sexy. I was an A-grade plodder.'

I ran my hands across the smooth skin of his back and watched a line of goose pimples appear.

'The hidden life of Jonathan Foley.'

'Think of pharmaceutical companies. They make their own markets. No one's ever heard of ADHD or knows they suffer from "social phobia" until the drug companies repackage it as a disease. Then they sell the answer. Run articles in medical journals and newspapers, ads next to the stories, samples in the doctor's drawer.'

'Why'd you stop then, oh guru of the market?'

'Because advertising is a shitty, shitty business.'

'Really?'

'No. They mostly quit me. And Mary wanted . . . well, you know.'

I kept count of the amount of times he'd said her name in our conversations so that when he told me he was leaving me I could embarrass him.

I asked when he knew what job he wanted – how he could tell what it was he wanted to be.

He got up off the bed and went to pour himself a glass of water. 'This is not what I wanted to be,' he said, and though I explained I meant an illustrator, not an adulterer, the moment was already lost.

*

The first time I had thought about being something was in the office of Community Services after the fire. Louise and I sat on plastic chairs while the social worker talked to us about grieving, and ceiling fans stuttered loud in the hot room. She asked us for thoughts on expressing grief. We didn't want to talk about expressing grief but rather to know whether we'd have to live with strangers. I watched an ant climbing onto the woman's table, surging forward into the warm sun.

The social worker told us: 'You can say anything here.' We knew that we couldn't. She said, 'Tell me about Jeremy.'

Lou said, 'Tell me about your fat cunt,' and I said nothing.

The woman shifted in her seat and placed her hands on the table. We listened to the uneven pace of the fan and Louise made the ant climb her finger. Then the woman touched Lou's bandages very softly and asked, 'How do you feel about this?'

Lou stared directly at her face and said, 'About what?'

Towards the conclusion of the interview she seemed to give up and talked about her own life and movies we might have seen and making weak jokes. We sat brimming with hostility, silent anger sparking off our skins, while she talked about trauma and self-protection. In the end the social worker said, 'So, what support can I offer you? Girls, what do you want for yourselves?' and my mind had jolted. Later, Louise admitted she thought we were going to be given presents or clothes; she had planned what she might order for herself. I was fourteen – I hoped we were being asked to choose who we could live with.

The social worker was young and nervous. We knew she wasn't on our side.

'Or, what are your goals? What do you want to be?'

They hadn't been much into being anything at our school. It hadn't really occurred to me that you might be something other than what you were. We were too old to think we would be TV stars, or brides of rich men, or train drivers, which was what Jeremy had hoped to be back when he was in kindergarten. We would be what our parents were, or what we needed to be. The social worker must have known more than I did, though, because a few months after the interview I chose my subjects for Year 11 and thought I would become a teacher.

Still, Lou said, 'A rock star' and the woman leaned forward, approving. Lou explained that she sang in the school choir. We didn't have a school choir and Lou didn't listen to music much.

They let us go home rather than into crisis care that day. We exited through the glass doors. I remember thinking about how pretty the social worker was, and how expensive her dress looked. But when I went back in to get a drink of water, she was whispering to the receptionist, 'Those girls are *unmanageable*.' I had understood then that the project of school, of social services, of the government handouts my father would collect, was the beginning of a lifelong project of making me into a manageable person.

I told Jon: 'I thought I wanted to be a teacher and *make a difference*.' Our laughter was low and musical, extensive with disappointment and joy at the hopes of our younger selves.

He peeled off his pants, revealing Bonds Y-fronts with black elastic at the waist. Their bleached whiteness was moon-like against his brown legs. I couldn't imagine him washing or ironing. These, then, were the signs of his wife, who had a career of her own: domestic thoroughness and attention to detail.

'There's some report floating round from the Education Minister. They might close our school.'

He shifted back on the bed, up onto his side, and stroked my legs. 'Would that be a bad thing?'

'I'd lose my job.'

'But you hate it.'

'I still think the school should exist. We deal with some kids no other school in the area would even take. Otherwise it's just a merciless replication of privilege. You condemn them. If you're a migrant or have unemployed parents you'll get crowded classes and be quietly encouraged to drop out at Year 10.' My cheeks were hot, my voice rising.

Jon smiled, puzzled. 'You make it sound like old-fashioned class war.'

I was trembling.

He put his hand on my arm. 'If the kids are clever they'll still find a way through. Look at you.'

'We don't get the funding so we don't get the students so we don't . . . It's fine for the schools in Camberwell with the best teachers and pretty, red-brick buildings with athletics fields the size of Pluto.'

He scrunched his face. 'How big is Pluto?'

'*They* don't worry about closing. Didn't you go to one of those?'

He gasped in horror. 'A *state* school. I don't think so. Grammar boy all the way, thanks very much.' He reached down and started kneading at the inside of my thighs. 'Can't you tell by my manners?' He was dipping his fingers into me. 'Ladies first.'

'Get off. I'm talking.'

He took his hand away, unsure about whether to be offended or penitent. 'Sorry, love. Honestly, Mary writes those sorts of things all the time and mostly it's just covering their arses. They've had a ministerial question or a shitty resident or an Opposition promise and some committee's asked to do a summary.'

'I didn't know she was in the public service. Function on tonight then?'

His erection was still there and he moved awkwardly onto his belly.

'Let me give you a little clue for your next affair,' I told him. 'Bringing up your wife in bed is not sexy.'

We fucked anyway. He stroked my face when he entered me, both of us standing and trembling, my back pushed against the wall. The last time we made love he had been weeping and the tears fell saltily on me. Now I licked his shoulder, ran my hands over his ribs, then pressed the soft flesh of his arse. I felt transported, even though he was impatient and we were both hurrying through doubt.

He came too fast, and without much effort, urgently, groaning deeply. He rested his head on my shoulder. I thought of his gentleness then and his loyalty. After he got his breath back he dropped to his knees and went down on me. My knees started quivering and I pressed my hand against the wall to keep my balance; then I was coming, as I heard footsteps on the staircase outside.

He checked his neck for evidence in the mirror above the pale couch, cooling his cheeks with his hands. I breathed in the smell of sweat and sex.

I was pulling a shirt over my head when Lou opened the door.

'Nice cock,' she said, watching Jon, who was pulling his underwear back on.

'Can't you knock?' I must have left the deadlock on the front door snibbed back.

Jon reacted slowly. 'Thanks. Fuck.' He found his pants on the floor and zipped them up.

Lou waited in the doorway, her head tilted to the side, her body lounging against the doorframe.

He gave a small bow. 'Hi. I'm Jon.'

She nodded with the exaggerated patience of those who deal with emergencies or children: ambulance drivers, primary school teachers.

'But, Alice, there was a key. I thought that was why you left it. So I could use it. How else would I get back in?'

Jon talked quickly, the blush spreading down to his chest and collarbone. 'So . . . it's late for me anyway.'

I pulled my sticky underwear back on and crawled under the covers of my bed. Louise walked into the living room and plumped herself on the couch, put her boots up on the table. He looked down at her lean brown legs and glanced away again quickly.

'Alice, I won't be able to call for a bit.' He struggled out the door with his bag slipping off his shoulder.

'Can I have a smoke?'

I threw her the pack.

'He seems like a bit of a joke.' She puffed heavily into the silence.

I put the electric kettle on without thinking, calming my hands on the plastic handle. 'In what way?'

'Just a general man way.' She looked away. 'Do you like him, Ally Al?'

'I feel like he's my second half, the missing part.' Lou looked sadly at me. 'Yeah, I like him. Today I probably even love him.'

She began to hum a pop song out of tune. 'Would you get married?'

'That post is taken.'

'Is she sexy? His wife?' Lou was up and dancing now, her face rubbery and animated and half in shadow, as she twisted and gyrated away from the light cast by the lamp.

It was not a question I could answer. When I had seen her, she'd seemed very graceful, with a severe posture and loose limbs; older than me. I had been struck by the narrowness of her feet, and her tiny hands, when I'd seen the two of them walking once, arms linked. There had been crow's feet around her eyes, and seeing those fine lines on her fair skin had touched me in some way that I didn't fully understand. 'I don't know. She's kind of elegant.'

Louise nodded. 'Probably at Yogalates as we speak.'

'Yeah.'

'Bitch.' She was snapping her fingers constantly, as if we were advertising executives brainstorming a product.

'I'm the one that's fucking her husband.'

And we left it at that. I poured Lou some tea and she made a sandwich and slathered the butter on thickly, singing quietly.

The air was thick with cigarette smoke and the smell of a perfume of mine that Louise had apparently dug out and sprayed liberally on herself. I rarely used it but it had come in a package labelled with a preposterous name I could imagine would appeal to Lou: *Goddess* or *Vixen*. She danced to the music for a little while but I could see the strain on her face, despite the sparkly glitter she was wearing on her cheeks.

Louise sat on the couch with her knees tucked under her. 'Are we getting better?' She took small bites of her sandwich, holding it carefully over the plate.

'How do you mean?' I knew what she meant. I chewed the ends of my hair.

'Don't,' she said, without looking. 'This would never have happened if Jeremy hadn't run off.'

'I'm sick of talking about it.' I thought of my brother taking home the school mouse the week before he died, too scared to let it out of its cage in case it escaped, but poking his fingers between the bars, carrying the cage into the backyard when our parents fought. 'What started you on this again?'

She swallowed. 'Mum might have found out things after. Where he had been. Or . . .'

I said the same thing I always said when Louise agonized and wished she had collected Jeremy after the test. 'There's nothing left to know.'

She lit a cigarette and handed it to me. 'It wouldn't have happened if Dad hadn't spilled kerosene everywhere.' She laughed without any joy, mocking the bluntness of her conclusions. 'That's why the house burned so quickly.'

I had found out that the kitchen was bathed in accelerant during a police interview with a thick-fingered constable who clutched a paper cup of tea in his big hands and sighed too often. 'Where were your parents?' he had asked, many times. 'Why did you and your sister go to the park in the dark on your own?' We did not know or we did not say.

To the police our parents thus became morons, the sort of people who left chemicals on low shelves in unlocked cupboards and never taught their kids to stay away from fire.

My dad's escalating threats began after he could not find work. He tried to extort money, and sometimes love, from our mother. The promised acts had grown more menacing, more ridiculous, in direct proportion to the size of my father's desperation. My impressions of this time were muddy, without fixed shape. I had stayed in my bedroom, reading magazines and cutting out photos during these episodes where alcohol turned 'please' into 'you must', and 'help' into 'fix me'.

Now I stayed on the other side of the room to my sister and stared at the floor: the polished boards of my flat, the fraying Egyptian rug. I looked directly at her. 'Mum should have had more courage.' I shook my head. 'Or been more scared.'

Louise lined up her crusts on the plate and drew on her cigarette. 'You think Jeremy didn't realize? Too scared to smell the fumes . . . too freaked out to notice . . .'

It was as if she were watching an old videotape, waiting for some secret meaning to reveal itself in the paused expressions of the figures on the screen: pressing 'rewind' so that people took back their steps, withdrew their actions, and then made the same mistakes over and over.

I cleared my throat and looked out at the lights of the city, which were low pinpricks in the dark sky. They cheered me, these scattered pinpoints of colour in a grey city, and the warm fluorescent squares from office blocks and upstairs bars. 'Were you working as a prostitute in Sydney?' I asked her.

She smiled tightly. 'No. Are you prostituting yourself now?'

I feigned consideration of the question. 'Maybe. Maybe I am prostituting myself for the read-out-loud pleasure of a few Russian novels and some kind words.'

She was calmer now. I walked over and put my arm around her. To distract her I told her, 'There's some funding crisis at my school.'

'How come?'

'Poor area. Under-performing in exams. Drugs. It's just a whole lot of shit; they've been dying to close it.'

She got up, excited. 'You should run a campaign. How about sitting in? Well, not exactly a sit-in like for civil rights but barricade yourselves in and say you won't leave until they agree to fully fund it. You should leak it to the media now, say you're outraged, say –'

'I have to see what the union says, see what happens.'

'I can help you.'

I went into the bathroom and started to get ready for bed. I changed into a loose top and my pyjama pants. It felt safe to bring up Louise's latest plan. 'How's the project going?'

'If you were going to change your name, what would you change it to?'

I was incredulous, appalled. 'You thought you could just look her up?'

She shifted gear. 'I'd change mine to the same as someone famous so I could get stuff for free and good seats.'

I nodded, not believing any of it.

'You should look with me. We should hire someone to search. Why won't you help me?' She ashed with tiny taps into the glass bowl I'd been using as an ashtray.

I sat across from her in the elegant green armchair I'd never quite managed to sit comfortably in. I'd bought it under duress from Kirsty, another teacher at school, whose fiancé was the manager of a designer furniture store. The back of the seat arched unkindly away from my own back and I felt a draft creep up my spine. I looked out the window at clouds tinged with mauve. 'What if she won't see you?'

Louise rubbed her eyes. 'I'll make her.'

'How?'

She shrugged and her black sweater fell forwards, revealing her narrow bones beneath the fabric. 'I'll pretend to be someone else.'

'Are you going to try and get a job?'

She turned to face me. 'I'm not *staying* here.'

'You'll be disappointed if you find her, Lou. Nothing will change.' She put out the smoke. My throat was dry but I had to ask her. 'Why did you try to go back into the house? We thought Jeremy was missing.' Louise had flung herself through the gate, forced her way in the back door, even though the smoke was pouring out by then and I could hear the fire crackling.

'Maybe I could hear him.'

'That's not what the firefighters said.' We had been searching five minutes from where he died. Louise had called his name at the park, which was three blocks away from our house. 'They reckoned smoke inhalation would have got him before we saw the place was burning. He was dead when you heard him.'

She watched me, thoughtless and deadpan, her eyes glassy and indifferent, like those of a snake. 'Come with me to talk to Dad,' she said.

CHAPTER TEN
NOW: Louise

*I*t's the sounds that shake you out of bed: wood splintering and falling, the heavy lick of flame hissing as it grasps your nylon dress in the dark dust of morning.

You wake with your face pressed into your own snot on the pillow, tears rinsing your cheeks like splashes of creek water.

The sun's too high in the sky, an egg-yolk shimmer. No Alice.

Collecting things, you find some novel Alice's boyfriend has left behind. Jon doesn't seem real to you: he's a minor character in a movie, an actor whose important moments happen offstage. But he's real enough to her, and so is this: the flat; the friends; the job; the busy clutter of right now. She's struggled her way through to it, and how she clings with brittle nails to what she's made.

You eat peanut butter straight out of the container, sticking your finger back in the jar and then licking it off.

There's Jeremy's old detective kit packed into a plastic bag, alongside the freedom of information submission you wrote out in Sydney Centrelink.

You know that you are slowly destroying the kit with touch: the sheen has worn off the cardboard box and the corners are soft and battered. The players' tokens are gritty with the dirt of another time and the magnifying glass is an obliterating eye, shatter lines spreading across it like fine spider webs.

Touch the kit and it will sing an old tune.

If your brother was planning to die then he should have left signs. He'd buried the kit months before, which might have meant he was saving it, or that he was bored by it. Is the kit itself a clue? You take out the instruction leaflet but it says the same things it always has and nothing else.

Jeremy wouldn't play your game – the danger game. Alice didn't like it much, but she used to play anyway, calling plaintively 'enough', the word for stopping, sometimes before she'd even tried, wanting it to be over. The game is how you were able to go back into the house when it was burning. That's why you are all scars and second skin.

You pick up Alice's key and the identification you took from her wallet. Tip out the mess of papers and stare at the art postcard of the half-woman. The woman being undone. For you have wanted to peel off your own skin, unwind your flesh like cloth bandages.

Looking under Alice's bed you find a dusty packet of Peter Jackson cigarettes that you shove into the pocket of your jeans. A used condom, smelling of rubber and old fucking, lies between the bottom of the mattress and the wall, and behind that a crumpled bit of paper. You unpeel the shreds of a drawing: a broader, more substantial Alice staring into the distance. There's a figure you can't make out in the background because the torn paper is creased and withered. You could look at this for a long time and not know whether it was meant to show love or hate, intimacy or repulsion.

Alice's bathroom is painted peppermint and berry. Artificial flavour and bloody fruit. Black-and-white tiles on the floor – too-small hexagons that hurt your eyes. You brush your teeth, spit into the sink, avoid your face in the mirror.

There are pale flickers, the ghosts of fireflies, behind your eyes.

On the tram you watch for ticket inspectors. Alice's licence and teacher's ID have photos taken a few years ago. She's got her hair back in both, but the teaching one is better: there are more distractions. She is wearing too much blush and a floppy collar.

You practise her signature a few times. The A and R at the start of the words loop hugely and the letters are slanted back on each other.

Melbourne skids past, buildings low to the ground, the Yarra River a dirty slick.

The man at the pharmacist lets you photocopy Alice's cards with photo ID and he certifies them, taking his time because you aren't buying anything.

When you arrive at the banks of offices where various bureaucratic headquarters congregate, you pause. First you need to see how things are done.

A large, sweeping desk curves across most of the room, three women all wearing headsets seated behind it. They hardly look at you when they direct you to the Freedom of Information Officer. Good. He's in a smaller glass office at the right-hand side of the building, visible through the open door.

You hand over your ID to be photocopied and sit at the leather armchair while the solicitor scans the letter you've written.

'This is going to be a lot of information.'

You shrug.

His posture is alert. 'Because if you are looking for something in particular it might be worth being specific.'

'Anything that has my name on it. Any kind of document.'

He puts down the paper and looks hard at you. 'You'll receive a written response outlining what we've found or if any of the information falls into an exemption category or if there are extra charges for time it will take to locate this volume of documents. Respondent agencies can ask for more time, too.' He settles into the firm brown leather of the chair.

'My sister's going to make an application too. Should she come and see you this afternoon?'

'We shut at five and I'm out at four-thirty today but Tessa will be here then,' he nods towards a bleach-blonde woman. She smells of coconut oil and is wearing pink lipstick. Wrinkles run like faint ripples across her skin, even through the orangey foundation. Malibu Barbie hits the antipodes. And you want to laugh.

Your hands fly up to your face. 'Oh, she can't get here until half-past five. It's exactly the same as mine, only in her name, obviously . . .' a tremor of a laugh.

'She has to make the application herself. You could ask to access documents that name her but then there may well be some privacy concerns outweighing the public interest in disclosure.' His words are crisp. He's said all this before.

'Of course. Yeah. No, she's a doctor on shift work. Well, an intern.'

'I don't need to be here myself if she includes her payment and identification. She'll get her acknowledgement via email in the morning.'

'Who should she leave them with?'

'Try the girls at the front desk, but they don't like doing it. Not really their responsibility. Otherwise she can organize for you to bring them in. Or she can post them or fax her ID, scan it if you like, and send them electronically.'

'It doesn't have to be in person?' You think of your carefully chosen clothes, the pink powder on your cheeks, the cards nicked from Alice.

'No. She can send it in.' He takes a card and scribbles across it in pencil. On the way out you post the application in Alice's name and buy some hot chips. Lick the grease off your fingers; chuck the paper cup into a rubbish bin.

The local library is six blocks from Alice's flat, out the back of the dishevelled, grand Town Hall building and across from the public pool which is bright aqua in a bed of hot asphalt. If you had bathers you'd sneak in and lie in the cool lapping of the water, hoping to dissolve.

There are *White Pages* for the states and territories in a high book-shelf in the reference section. Your mother's oldest friend Jean must have remarried or you don't know how to spell her Polish surname, because she does not appear on the phone lists. You write down all the Reillys in Victoria and New South Wales but your mother will have another name now. Maybe she's in Perth or New Zealand or in a cemetery halfway round the world.

To have that power, her power, to simply walk away, would be intoxicating, dreadful, deadening.

'Excuse me, can I help you look for something?' The librarian's holding out her hands for the phone books.

'I'm fine.'

She clucks. 'Other people have to use these,' she says firmly and it's only then that you see the wet mess of paper, the way your tears have sloughed down onto the page.

'My mother just died,' you tell her, but she's already frowning at your sticky face and thin arms, backing away to serve a man at the counter waiting to borrow magazines about boats.

You wait before you type in the words to search online. Somehow you think if you write her name, it means she'll be dead. So you find the address for the records office of births, deaths and marriages instead.

The big public hospital is opposite graceful old gardens, where psychiatric patients walk warily on day release. They remind you of addicts: half in this world, half elsewhere. The head administrator just keeps shaking her head. 'I can take your letter but there's no guarantee we'll release the records to you.'

'How can they be confidential from me? They're mine.'

She snatches your paperwork, puts it on her desk. 'This is a well-established privilege. You do not have an automatic right to patient records. We can withhold them. *Particularly* if the medical assessment is that such information could be damaging or confusing. If you want to know more, get some legal advice.'

'Just the medical reports about my burns when I was a kid.'

She looks at you carefully. 'We have a counsellor here, and a liaison solicitor for the hospital.'

Stop. Begin again.

The flats overlook a tobacconist's and you crouch next to where the bins are kept. When your father leaves he walks down the staircase out the front of the building, whistling an old disco tune. The last time you saw your father was before you got off dope, before you got a job and lost a job and had an abortion and stole Katrina's money and emptied her account.

You follow him to the milk bar where he buys soft white bread, spearmint leaves sparkling with sugar and counted into a brown paper bag, some tins and the newspaper. The assistant counts the change into his palm and he locks his fingers around it with the eager grip of a child. He squints into the light and loops the plastic bag of shopping over his wrist. Then he pauses. You turn quickly back and begin walking up the street to the train station, pulling the black hood over your hair.

'Jeremy?' He is following. 'God. Jeremy.' He clears his throat and begins to run. Breath rasps, his chase is shambolic. You sprint and then trip on a raised concrete section of footpath. You turn to face him. He touches your shoulder, breathing in little gulps, mouth gaping open-shut like the gills of a fish.

'It's me,' you say. 'The other one.' His eyes gleam. 'It's only me.' You grin in misplaced relief.

'Oh.' It's a huge, gentle sigh. His knees give a little and he sags forward, low in the knees, like an unsupported toddler or a hand puppet.

Where is your courage, Louise? You only had a small taste back in Sydney, coasting through the E in the early hours of the morning. You don't let yourself think about the wanting but surely how you'd love to be back in the falling, the pillowed warmth, the thick water holding you with kindness.

Sydney shatters through your thoughts, a waterfall of glass shards. There is the lumbering office building, the taste of waves smashing your chest in the ocean, the rot of the flats, the faded orange and red checked tablecloths hung for curtains across the windows of the Abercrombie Street terrace, the cramped corners and low bluestone of the Rocks. Men wheeling down Oxford Street on a Friday night, spilling takeaway south Indian food on their designer jeans. Your father's never been to Sydney. He grew up in Brisbane with his religious mother in a gaping house raised on stilts that smelled of bilge water and lilies. Sydney was a place where he didn't exist.

You slide your hands into the comfort of scratchy pockets.

Your father says, 'I thought you were . . . Where were you . . .' He breaks off. 'Is Alice here?'

You do a little skip on the sidewalk. 'You thought I was the dead one.' There is a slight gathering of fat around his waist and he doesn't wear it well. You grab a spearmint leaf lolly out of the bag and begin to lick off the sugar. 'The dead-and-gone son.'

He's let the bag fall to the ground now, amazed by his own expectations, left off balance by the gap between what he'd hoped for and what he's got.

You swallow the lolly and it jams in your throat before going down.

'Louie.' He clasps his hands. 'One of my old girls.' His hair has more grey in it now but it is still thick and so curly it's almost in ringlets; and his face is burned brown, his nose slightly crooked. His brown eyes have a soft cast of sadness in them but the rest of his expression is disconcertingly cheerful.

You fidget with beads around your neck.

'You were in Townsville. I didn't think I'd see you.'

'Sydney.'

'Yeah. Sorry. Sorry about the . . . mistake, sorry, sorry.' He looks at his feet.

Does he mean the city or the morbid mistaken identity?

'I'm not feeling well. It's the weather. Makes me . . .' Your dad's sentences are small lurches. He used to have a stutter and you can hear the ghostly silent sounds of the unrepeated letters in his pauses.

'Are you in trouble, Lou?'

And there it is: the old generous impulse, the helpless helpfulness that your father's always had, his instinct to put things right for his two daughters, nearly worn thin now.

'Why didn't you try to get Jeremy out of the house?'

'What?' He stops, and perhaps for a moment he's even considering it, the white expanse of forgetfulness, but he knows his son is dead: today, he does.

'When it was burning. The day he died. Do you remember?' You duck your head, shaking off the misery of it, and you walk together down to the muddy creek, his shopping bag left behind on the street, right in the centre of the footpath like a hazard warning – an orange witches' hat – for a danger that is as yet unknown.

He tells you: 'He was *missing*. He wasn't – we thought he wasn't – in the house. He didn't take the exam . . . just disappeared, L.'

'But when you saw that it was burning . . .' you say dully, even though this is an old conversation, one where fangs and knives have already been worn back to stumps and stubs.

'At first we didn't realize it was the house. There was just a weird smell, something smouldering. We went outside to search for him, hoping he was hiding nearby. I said I'd look for him; we rang the cops, go back up to the school. Then the smell of smoke got really strong. Chelsea was calling out to you and Alice. I was following. She went to the front step. That's when we knew it was burning. I already told you. She's telling me, "you did this," but how could I have? I was right there with her. She goes to the front door but she couldn't find her key and she fell over.'

'On the front porch?'

He shrugs. 'Tripped on the stones. I touched the door; it was hot. I went next door to ring the fire brigade but they'd already called.'

'How did he get inside?'

He shakes his head. 'You know why they didn't take you from me? Chelsea knew she was going, even then when the cops asked her about it. She said that we'd had a kero bottle with a missing lid hidden where you and Jeremy used to play games. At the hospital, before we went to the station, she cooked up what to tell them. That you were little shits, really. Not our fault. Then they couldn't take you away from me. You wouldn't be put into state care.'

He has never mentioned this before. You lean in. Is he lying? 'She thought she was going to be investigated?' You grin. 'People might say she wasn't a fit parent.' You imagine a sense of fit, jigsaw pieces snapping together in easy symmetry. 'Fitness for purpose' is the technical test for any description of defective goods sold by retailers. Your family is more like an epileptic fit: convulsive, biting down on itself.

'Louise, love, after they found him she would not speak to me.'

'Did she tell you she was going?' you ask.

He pauses at the shoulder of the creek bank, stares down at the bald, black patch of earth in front of him as if the flecks of dirt will tell him what the right course of action is. 'She talked about it before. Always with taking you kids. I didn't think she would but maybe she would have anyway. She couldn't afford to love me anymore. That's what she reckoned. Fuck, she was a bitch.' He gulps. 'She wasn't. She . . .'

'What did she say the day she left?'

'I've told you. Nothing. She was at the hospital to see you would be okay and then she had to do the interview with Community Services.'

'You thought she would come back.'

'I don't know.'

You wait for him to say that she left a message, she left a note, but he doesn't.

He nods, doesn't look at you for too long. 'Are you living here now?'

'I'm going to find her.' You watch for a jolt, a little gesture, but it doesn't arrive. He doesn't believe you.

'I remember when you and Jez did that circus performance with the cartwheels. God, that cracked me up.' He turns to you, waves his arms around. 'All bashing into each other and clashing accidentally. Slapstick. Laurel and Hardy, I thought.'

You say: 'He hated being called Jez.'

Your dad's face bleats for pity. 'Did he? I didn't know.'

'They used to copy you at school. Follow him round, calling Je-ez. Jez the spaz.'

He sinks his nails into his palm.

'You did a good show, all right.' He steps back and both of you look at the thin ridges of black in his nails, the bitten skin around the cuticles, the tiny red marks on his palm.

After you have left, you look back over your shoulder and see he has picked up a stick and is drawing shapes in the dirt with it, picking and digging into the hard earth as if there is some rich relief lying just beneath the surface.

And it's much later, on the long trip back to Alice's, at a small greasy coffee joint where you smoke butts out of the ashtray and drink coffee for two dollars, that you do it. Stand on your hands and try to walk on them the way you once could when you were Jeremy's twin sister and everybody knew he was brighter than you and maybe better. You smack a waitress's hands with your foot and tumble over.

She drops the tray. How the crockery comes down. You pull yourself up and fling yourself over into space and then it is cartwheels, glorious cartwheels with the chipped plates crunching underfoot and the agog floating faces upside down – even a woman clapping in the corner. The past is gone even while it bites at your skin and bleeds in your eyes. You can't return to how you used to be, not even for regret's sake, not even for comfort, if you want to keep alive.

Alice's place is not an apartment with many hidden places. The bottom drawer of her dressing table is filled with half-deflated bath baubles in Christmas colours, old letters and bills from years ago, a school photograph bent in two, some dank mothballs, a bottle of cheap perfume without a lid, an expired chequebook and a black lace bra that has removable straps. One of the letters is from Sarah, Alice's oldest friend. She's written: *There's someone now but I guess I don't know what I'm doing as usual.* A few pages later: *You should stop giving Louise money.*

On her bookshelf there are curriculum reforms, notes from her teaching degree, superannuation statements. Nothing. You find it behind a glossy art book about house designs – the solar system project Jeremy finished just before he died. Right in the middle of the scrapbook is the photograph of his model. Stones and rocks collected from the front driveway and the train tracks near where your family used to live, suspended on string to show the size and arrangement of the planets, each one labelled carefully. A replica of space.

You rush to get your plastic bag of papers. There's another photo. He's smiling and holding a stick for a wand. Nine years old and crouching next to a circle of stones. It was your birthday that day. Blowing out the candles, you made a wish you can't remember.

Maybe your mother fell on the step itself, or she hit the damp and dusty crates of junk that gathered in the corners of the front yard: a plastic scooter with punctured tyres; mouldy clothes washed months before that had not been hung on the line; spare mechanical equipment that your dad cleaned and forgot about. If your mother saw the circle of stones left behind wouldn't she have also known that Jeremy was nearby, his leavings like breadcrumbs pointing out the path he had taken?

What you carry inside you is the blackest deep, an oil slick sea. When will the black mass rotting inside your chest dissolve? The front door was locked when you and Alice came back from the park so you'd pushed open the back one, warm to the touch and heavy, sticking because the doorframe had swollen in the heat. Your father was yelling 'stop'. Already there were sirens; the Whittakers, your new neighbours, had rung the cops. You wanted the bracelet and your jewellery box. You didn't go back in for Jeremy and now you won't ever know if the squealing, the high thin shrieking you heard, was just a feeling. In the ambulance, you had tried to cover your dirty bare feet with the white sheet they'd tucked over you.

Now you put down newspaper on the ground and prime the canvas stretched across the floor. You draw first, sketching in the bracelet you'd owned as a kid. The background will become a wash of fairy floss colours, each bead containing a tiny black letter of the alphabet, miniature and typewriter-official. You work in the living room on your knees, bent over the painting until the blood rushes to your head and you get dizzy and then you lie on your stomach, propped up on your elbows.

The bracelet runs across the canvas over and over in looping lines like a barbed wire fence, lit up with the shades of gelati. You want it to feel like an assault, too, with the effort it demands of the viewer to put the letters back together into some intelligible order. But the painting does not work.

You find a new section of canvas and stretch it out, pinning it down with the sofa legs on one side and Alice's desk on the other. You recreate soaring trees, jungle plants, succulents with winding arms and thin ferocious tentacles, and ferns in golden hues with blue stems. You use Dr Seuss colours and thick oil paints. The garden's inside a Bio Dome, an isolated bubble you design to resemble the scientific experiment of the biosphere with all its self-supporting systems and artificially reproduced worlds. Other circles pattern the page like soap bubbles. Jeremy's a blot in the corner of the dome, looking out. Over the dome you layer the ghost of a clock face or a viewfinder of a rifle, with many hands pointing at precise angles fanning out like crosshairs. You sit back for a while, face on your knees, arms around you, before you can look at the painting again.

By the time you're halfway through, your shoulders are stiff and sore. Your fingers ache. The paint's not dry but you move the canvas anyway and manage to spill paint on the carpet. Dishwashing liquid and water won't move the stain so you shift the chair leg forward over it, brushing at the carpet with a nail brush as if you were shining the coat of a prize dog, to get rid of the old indentation.

You put on the television and smoke a cigarette, leaf through Alice's magazines. You roll up the painting, still damp, and hide it in your pile of clothes.

You let the afternoon fade away until you give in.

'Can you help me out with this, mate?'

The person who answered the door lets you in. He's only a boy really. Just a boy. He won't hurt you. His hand is on your arm and he is propelling you down the corridor as though you cannot go forward without being pushed.

'Trying to get some pills or whatever's going.' You are talking very quickly but the walls seem to soak up your voice.

North Melbourne greeted you with the smell of stale vegetables and the melancholy romance of the sky at dusk. When you arrived, a man was hosing down the entrance to the market, and the stench of slaughtered meat was enough to make you cover your mouth. Katrina's dealer used to live in one of those huge rambling houses so you had taken a chance and knocked on the door and asked the man who opened it if they'd got anything.

Another boy jitters in the corridor. 'Who's she?' In the dark of the hallway this kid's face is young and sweet. He doesn't seem dangerous at all. Heroin loves him now. He's dreaming your old dream, the one that got away. You ache for him because he'll never have this moment again, the one that comes free.

'Please.' You aren't sure how crazy to seem. 'Someone said there might be something going.'

You lurch into the teenager's room and he pulls out a bottle of gin and a packet of tinfoil. He says, 'Rick can get you some smack.' He reckons his name is Sam. He's a kid. He doesn't live there. The dealer's been and gone.

'I've got some ice,' he says. He tells you his mum is dying but no one knows. He's been taking her morphine and then getting the prescriptions filled again. That's how he started. Sounds like crap to you.

You wait and study the mucus or coffee stains on the faded purple velvet couch. In the room next door you hear scraps of conversations – 'and then *I* said, "I don't think so" and *she* says, "Well you wouldn't"' – and your head thuds: time to go, time to go.

You can't pay much. You take a slug from the bottle and he doesn't know what to do.

'Let me taste first,' you say.

He leans in, giggles. 'This isn't even mine. You seem really nice. No, I *mean* it, really nice. Just take some. But quick.' He sips at his own cup of gin. Everything is said as if it's a secret he's disclosing.

'Whose is this?' You ask, dipping your finger into the powder and sucking it, rubbing it across your gums.

'Ssh. You should go.'

Your palms are sweaty and the jitters travel through you like a pinball, rocketing from your ankles to the soft part of your arms and up the back of your neck.

An older guy flings the door open with a packet in his palm. 'How much are you after?'

You see stringy, pale yellow hair, high on top, with a mullet. All you can think about is how much he looks like Rod Stewart. You laugh and laugh. 'How much is it?' You can't stop. His face is sallow. It is not going to be okay. But the dread is lifting. You hear the wind outside and your heart is opening up.

'Look, you want it or not?'

Perhaps it's how it should be: the delay, the schoolkid, methamphetamines. Not today then. You shake your head.

'Fuck off you dumb bitch. Out. And don't be a fucking moron, letting strangers walk in, she could've been anyone.' This to Sam, sweating and scared in his school jumper. There's something about the colours of his uniform. You throw yourself into the freezing cold of the night. Oh fuck. Oh joy. It's the uniform for Alice's school.

Sick. Sway on the bar, put your hands up on the shiny wood, keep your money in your fist, sweating closely on the notes. Grind your teeth, think about lollipops, sugary foods, bones.

There are shamrocks on the coasters, green streamers bunched in the corners of the room. Waves of confusion ripple through the air. The cushions that coat the warm booths have Irish proverbs written across them. There's hardly anyone drinking in this part of the pub. And the ghosts in your head whisper words of comfort.

Nineties pop on the jukebox. Synthesized. Inoffensive. And still you're humming without even knowing it, tapping on the bar in time, and letting the notes slide from under your fingers.

A man sits next to you. 'This music is bloody awful.' His accent's English.

You ask him: 'What're you doing in here?'

He tips forward on his bar stool, takes another look. 'Do I know you?'

'You should be off oppressing the Irish in' – hiccup – 'Belfast or something.'

He shrugs cheerfully, gets back on his feet. 'Just asking if you want a game of pool. None of them bastards'll play with me.' He waves over his shoulder at a small group near the door, then stops. 'Oh wow.'

'What?'

'Your pupils are just . . . very impressive.'

You tell him, 'Thanks,' with glee.

You can barely hold the cue, let alone sink a ball, but he comes behind you, puts his arm over and helps you aim. His name is Jason, he's thirty, he emigrated four years ago after a backpacking trip through Bondi and Byron Bay; now he rents in Essendon and works in admin support. 'What about you?'

'Louise.'

He pots balls quickly and carefully, leaning forward over the table so that his T-shirt rises and a gap of pale flesh hangs out. 'You've taken the honour for the crappest game of pool I've ever played, Louise.' When you waver he holds you up straight.

You're laughing, then spinning, in a hurry, tomorrow, and the long night to come, flashing before you. 'Get me a beer then.'

He brings back drinks for all his friends, who are playing cards now, hands you a Carlton without really noticing, and shoots the black diagonally across the table so it rebounds neatly into the pocket. 'Cheers.'

He turns and gives a 'thumbs up' to the boys.

Bile in your mouth now, salt and sweat creeping over you. 'I have to get outside.'

'We're going to try and have a bit of a dance, if there's anywhere open. Come.'

'Nah, I'm . . .' Your stomach heaves. Look at the floor, the black, the creamy skirting boards, the floating ash; see tiny sparkles litter the ground, glittering the way diamonds do in kids' cartoons.

'You want a drink of water?'

The exit sign is fluorescent and you try not to look away from it as you walk.

You hear him announce to his friends. 'She. Is. *Fucked*.'

You push into the door and as you feel it resist then give way he calls after you, 'Good luck then.'

You vomit into the bushes outside, wipe your mouth with the back of your hand. You start running. See tiny alleyways break away from the street like secret tunnels. Hear the hidden scuttlings of the night. Old strains of music from above the shops, windows thrown open. Step, skip. Hop. Jump. Kerb. Horns blast. Back into the blackness. Jogging. Leap the puddles of water, outpace the boys hovering on the corner with a joint. The world's beginning and ending. Up the big hill where the streetlights fade into fairy lights in the distance, one blinking on/off like a lighthouse. Into the sea and the spray's on your skin now, salting away your shell. And you're almost out into the highway.

'Stop.' The men are outlines forming in the blackness. You're panting. 'Is someone following you?'

They peel away from the fence and stand in front of you on the footpath. Cops.

And it's good luck, Louise, good luck to you.

Stay away from the streetlight. Slide into the old years of camouflage. 'Nah. Just running late.'

'An appointment at this time of night? You nearly ran under the wheels of a truck.'

You've got to placate them, exhibit some fear. 'Sorry.' Now that you are closer you see one of them is a woman.

She takes out a notepad. 'What's your name?'

'Why?'

Her partner comes closer, too. 'We're trying to look after your safety.'

'I'm fine.'

The man shines the torch at you. 'Look at her, she's speeding. She's high as.'

'It's Louise.'

'What?'

You have your hand in your pocket and it brushes against the cards. You think of the summary offences, the unpaid Met fines, the cautions, and the possession charge, and try to calculate if the good behaviour bond's expired. 'Alice,' you say.

'And where are you headed now, Alice?'

To hell. Fuck off. 'Home.'

'You've had a few drinks.'

'Yes.' Keep your eyes down, your chin in your hand.

They step back and mutter together while you wait for a good time to run. The woman is saying, 'She looks out of it; probably got stuff on her.' The man's telling her he can't be bothered. 'Let her sleep it off.'

They move closer. 'We'll need to see some ID. And have a look through your bag.'

'I don't have one. Just these.' You take the cards out of your pocket, offer up the licence. The meth is crashing through you. It's hard to be still.

They take Alice's licence and her teacher's registration card, and copy down your details. The woman clucks. 'Are you going to be able to get home? We can see you're under the influence of some kind of party drug.'

'I'm okay.'

The man gives you a formal warning, says you need to think about your safety and the safety of others.

'Thanks.' Your legs are trembling. You grind your teeth rhythmically. 'Thanks, you pack of cunts,' you say, and you are racing away before they know if they've heard you properly.

On the walk back to Alice's you see a club where people in their thirties and late twenties are dancing. There are couples practising swing-dancing to the tunes of a live band. You sway and swoon too, on the footpath, counting the beat as you step. Alice used to do Irish dancing in primary school. The whole family went to her show. Onstage she'd gotten out of time and was smiling too hard. You never knew when you were bad at things as a kid, but Alice hated it.

You find a fluffy seed pod on the ground. You cradle it close, blow and make a silent wish. Forgiveness.

When you unlock the door, she's asleep on the couch, arms crossed over her chest as though she's in a coffin. The note on the table says: *Pasta salad in fridge. I'm an old woman and can't wait up. If you're drug-fucked, go elsewhere. If not, love to you Louise.*

You crinkle your forehead, uncertain about whether you've earned the love or not. No heroin. Whatever Sam gave you is wearing off. The note's cheerful but she's drawn anxious lines around the writing in thin pencil.

You tuck the cotton sheets under your makeshift mattress and get ready for bed but your heart thumps on. You turn on the lamp, pull out Jeremy's magnifying glass and look at your skin naked. He'd been so disappointed when he looked through the lens and realized the glass was ordinary, that what he held was a prop, not a scientific instrument. He'd said, 'They use forensic pathology to solve crimes in a laboratory, not a magnifying glass anyway.' He'd said, 'This is kid stuff.' But your dad had given it to him and so he'd clung to it.

Your scars are pale. Time bleaches them. You smack the magnifying glass against the ground and push out the lens, trace your scars with shards of sharp plastic, digging into your skin to see what you feel.

'Louise.'

You shriek, leap back. Alice is in the door. She's wearing bikini underpants and a loose top. She looks less angular now she's nearly thirty, and more undisciplined. Her hair curls around her shoulders.

'Where have you been?'

'I broke this by accident.' You hold out the shards in your palm.

'Oh no.'

You feel terrible for yourself as if it really was an accident. You say, 'My life and other disastrous experiments in humanity.'

'I'm sure it can be glued.' She takes the pieces. 'Do you want to eat?'

In the early hours of the morning a siren wails.

Jeremy sees lights on at his house when he comes over the hill. The sky is an old enemy, a thick black coat above his head. His legs are tired now. People are cooking onions next door and the TV is up loud when he goes past. Before he goes inside, he plans excuses for why he ran away. He imagines the house settling around his father's urgent stride and the fluttery twitches of his mother, following. When Jeremy walks into their garden he feels strange. There is an unusual lightness to his shoulders. He is not wearing his schoolbag. He can't remember if he left it in his locker or if he shrugged it off at the railway tracks and left it to get wet in the rain, or stolen. He will have to go and get it or else his mum will make him carry his pencil case and lunch in a plastic bag. But he can't remember where he took the bag off.

He veers into his overgrown front yard. He sits in the long grass and the weeds that cover the sodden pebbles, which used to be part of a driveway. Jeremy makes his fingers into a circle and spies through so that what he can't see, what isn't contained within his hands, ceases to exist. He limits his vision to the tunnel and imagines he has a telescope. The sky isn't flat. It's expansive. He feels a rush of excitement. He talks to himself about the Southern Cross and the Milky Way. There are other galaxies and solar systems. Astronomy explains that even the stars above him have burned to nothing by the time their light reaches earth's sight. It's the light of absence that he's seeing. The stars are already gone. The night clouds over and he is left staring at grey wisps and ghosts.

He places the rocks in patterns around him. There are pieces of gravel buried beneath the clumps of grass and he collects these in his palm.

He climbs into the lap of the big oak tree right out the front on the nature strip, where his sisters used to play dares from the danger game all those months ago. He wants to eat dinner. He will walk up the path, soon, and say sorry. He gets a fright and almost falls when Louise and Alice come out into the garden.

There's a rigidity to Alice's skinny limbs, as if she has metal inside her. Alice used to be a monkey who climbed trees and turned her elbows inside out for laughs. She's holding herself carefully as if any lapse in attention might have catastrophic results.

Louise is crying. 'I *did* take him there. I walked all the way.'

Alice stops and waits, very still. 'Did you see him go into the exam? Going inside?'

'They think a pervert got him, don't they? Or he's dead?'

'You're being stupid.'

'He's hiding, Alice. I betcha.' Louise opens the tiny door that leads under the house and calls out his name.

Jeremy jerks his head up. He has done something extraordinary. He is invisible at this moment. His father has no idea where he is.

Alice grabs Louise's jacket and pulls her along. 'He's not there. Where do you want to start looking? Park?'

Louise has her arms folded. Her face is screwed up, lonely.

When Jeremy's father comes out, he trips on Louise's jewellery box and almost falls. He throws the plastic toy, with its dreamy unicorns drawn on the side, and it bounces on the ground.

He sees Louise flinch. 'That's *mine*,' she says, but she doesn't move.

'Tell me the fucking truth. Did you walk him there or not?'

Then Alice yells too: 'You were meant to do it.' She picks at the skin on her face.

'He was never there. The school rang and told us. So you're a filthy thief and a liar, Louise.' His dad picks up the jewellery box and turns it over. Jeremy can see the fear in the touching, the need for a thing to belong in his father's grasping hands.

Louise says, 'And you take money out of Mum's purse to get drunk. People hate you.'

Jeremy knows that he has to call out, to let them know he is right there in the tree. But it must be very late, later than ever before. Missing is a good place to be. He can't go back yet.

Then his mother snaps open the flyscreen door, banging it hard so that it swings back and crashes against the house. 'Leave the girls alone.'

His father puts on his ugly laugh. 'Did you hear what Louise just said? Tell *them* to leave *me* alone.'

Jeremy watches as his mum stands in the war zone between his father and the others. 'Shaun, I'm not doing this out here on the footpath. Come back in. Come on.'

Jeremy sees his dad sag back. He recognizes with relief that his father's rage is flowing away to nothing, like water leaking into the earth.

'Do they hate me, Alice? Do people?'

Alice shrugs. 'Some people do.'

Jeremy feels faint when he glimpses the pinched clutch of Alice's fingers. She is afraid, too.

His mother has her hair down around her shoulders and no shoes on. 'Get out,' his mum says. Louise sniffs. 'Go to the corner. Walk down and wait. Stick together. I'll come and find you.'

He can see the tops of his sisters' heads, the parts in their hair, when they leave. They walk right below him and he wishes one of them would look up.

When his parents are walking back, Jeremy climbs down from the tree, his sneakers slipping on the bark in a rubbery scramble. If they just look, they'll see him. When they go to search, he will be right there and they will know it.

His mum looks up the street to see if Alice and Louise are gone. Jeremy barely hears her when she talks to his dad. 'Come and help me ring around.'

'Did you try his teacher?'

'I left a message.'

'Who else?' Jeremy's dad asks loudly. 'He doesn't have any friends.'

'Stop it. He could be dead.'

His parents are on the porch now but still they don't look out. His father sits on the doorstep, trembling. Jeremy's mother stands over him with her hand on his shoulder. His dad shrugs her off and eats the skin around his nails.

His dad drops his head on his knees. 'Are we going to ring the police now?' Jeremy doesn't know why they would call the police. His parents seem to shrink a little when they see the cops. The neighbours have rung them when his dad gets too loud, drinking at night. Jeremy has opened the door and seen their bright uniforms, their firm, prepared faces.

His mother doesn't answer. She rubs his father's back. She shifts her foot against the bottle near the step and it spins and rolls. His dad lunges for it and misses, scraping his palm against the concrete.

Then she lets her shoulders slump. 'They won't take us seriously. Look at you.'

'If he's just run off, why hasn't he come back yet?'

'He's afraid of you.'

Jeremy is shocked to see the red swelling of his mother's face. She does not cry, his mum, not for a long time. She won't; she says crying is a waste of energy. You can cry about it or you can fight it.

His father tilts forward on the step in a drunken defensive dodge.

Jeremy picks the stalks of weeds and crushes them in his hands and weeps in time with his dad's sobs.

His mother pulls back her pale hair. 'You were meant to take him.'

It's a long drone now, his father's story, words tumbling into one another in a vacant, musical drawl. 'You were the one who was so keen on the exam. Show off to the world how smart he was, not like his dad. Funny, because you didn't even know if you wanted him. Remember the ultrasound? "Twins," you said. "Just what I need."'

He hears his mother's voice, as flat and sure as he has ever heard it. 'If I didn't have him I would have left you years ago.'

'I thought you were happy before' – his dad gulps – 'this.'

She shakes her head. 'So did I.'

'You want to leave me?'

His mum sighs and Jeremy bites his lips. 'Maybe you only know somebody when you see what they do when things go wrong,' she says. The phone rings. His mother goes back into the house and Jeremy watches his dad walk in dizzying steps, as if he might fall at any moment, into the backyard.

Jeremy creates a circle around him with stones but he knows real magicians' circles are drawn with chalk. And anyway – he has a book on it – all the tricks have a scientific explanation: a false bottom, a trapdoor, a hidden chamber, a distraction, an optical illusion. The circle of stones can't make him safe.

Jeremy takes his stones one by one and spreads them across the front doorstep and wishes – though he knows already that wishes don't change things – that they will keep the house safe.

Then he pushes open the front door.

*H*ad my parents ever been joyous together? I could remember being lifted into the air by them both: my mother grabbing one hand, Dad taking the other, swinging me up between them when they walked down to the shops, before Jeremy and Louise were born. My father, sunburnt in the summer, reading his books about philosophy and geology in the wilderness of the backyard. He'd been another sort of man then, easily transported, easily ashamed. He'd fancied himself as an autodidact. Showed his friends at the factory how the boy from Galway, Ireland knew the meanings of words they'd never heard. Had it been different before the rolling logic of hunger and doubt? Or was it only nostalgia that made me think so? There were flashes of memory, of warmth, the sound of my mother's voice, lively and unconstrained, but they came to me without context, lit up and then dark again.

'You're crying, Lice.'

I flinched. That had been Dad's nickname for me when I was very young. We'd been Lice and Fleas instead of Alice and Louise.

Saturday morning. When had Louise woken up?

I said weakly, 'I'm crying tears, not lice.' I held my face in my hands, gingerly pressed my fingers into my skin. 'I wish you'd tell me what's going on.'

She shifted, put her cool hand on the back of my neck. The bracelets jangled. I looked at the hollow of her neck, her prominent collarbone.

My sister stroked my cheek. 'Is it work?'

I had forgotten how comforting she could be. 'I was thinking about when we were younger. Remember that cape Mum had?'

'And when she borrowed a bike it got caught in the spokes?'

'And she wore it in the rain with the hood up and then it never dried properly and smelled?'

'What I think of' – Louise sat up properly – 'is how when Dad went away for training, she went to that group in the scout hall on yoga and they were going on about the trees and lily pads and the great open paddocks and communing with nature and she tells us, "I've spent my whole life trying to get *away* from nature."' Louise picked at her toenails. 'Then she grew up.'

'You forget that, don't you – that she was ever like that?' The last memories I had of my mother saw her dressed for work in the morning, bright blonde hair greasy and tangled, the pockets on her blue dress sagging down and her body emitting defeat in a million ways. Grimness hovered around her mouth. But she had never even sent a postcard or rung us up since she left us so there must have been more to her, some hidden fury.

I had loved my father more, when I was a kid, before the rages and the despair. My mother was too practical, too earthbound: he was fierce and funny, would let me sneak a cigarette, sometimes smoke one with me, though he'd given up years before. He sometimes took Louise to work after school and showed off her storytelling, her exaggerated imitations of her teachers, to his mates.

Our mother must have been achingly lonely for a long time. She was twenty-four years old when I was born, and planning to be a receptionist. She listened to jazz and folk music. My father had photos of her before they moved to Melbourne. She was wearing pink lipstick and a short skirt, grasping me under one arm as if I were a bag of shopping, and grinning, a hand shading her eyes. By the time Jeremy died she was living in some flat grey suburb, knowing that all the people in her street pitied her.

'You're like her,' I told my sister, unkindly. 'You don't even realize that you're inventing things. You know why you think she threw stuff around at work and told them to fuck off the day she left? Because that's what *you* would have liked to do.'

'Fuck off.' Louise folded her arms. 'She didn't invent things, anyway.'

I scrambled onto my feet. 'Surprise! Guess what? She invented an entirely new life for herself.' Why was I so angry with Lou?

Louise crouched back on her heels, impervious. 'If she was going to leave us, why have us?'

'They were different at the beginning, better.'

'I think she was planning it, already.'

'What?'

'Leaving.'

That Louise suspected this too left me breathless. I got up and washed my face, scrubbing at the dark skin under my eyes, willing a cheerfulness that wouldn't come.

'Al, did he look okay in the morning? He wasn't planning anything . . .'

I felt bleakness descend. My dread grew. The past was a set of cruel claws that raked through me, slicing into blood and bone and tissue. 'I don't know. You saw him after I did.' *I* had told him not to come home.

'Did you know there were stones on the front step?'

'What are you talking about?'

'He left a circle of stones out the front.'

I had wanted to stay in the park the night my brother burned to death. I'd thought Dad might hit him hard, injure him, and so I sat on a park bench and read a magazine by the street light; and all the while he had been doing whatever it was he did before he died. 'I don't remember. It was too dark. Do you want breakfast?'

'Toast. Please. I went to see Dad yesterday.'

I got up from the couch, scrabbled in the black leather handbag for my cigarettes, and came across the battered report about downsizing the school.

After the fire our dad had said he didn't know anything about the kerosene. He'd said this for months. Such is the nature of our denials.

I sucked in the first cigarette of the day, coughed like a flu patient, until even my ribs and back ached. 'How was it?'

She tucked her knees under her. 'He thought I was living in Townsville.'

We both grinned. I told her: 'That's a holiday destination. Resort town. You could have been a waitress at Burger Grill and got a great tan.'

'He thought I was Jeremy.'

And there it was. All the things Louise and I had never spoken of pulled us together and held us apart like two beads on a tightly banded bracelet. I wished we could forget everything.

My throat stung. I swallowed. 'Was he upset?'

'He said she went to go back in the house and fell on the stones Jeremy left.'

The stones had littered our lives, small deposits, chipped and hard. They'd been irritating, a hasty arrangement to keep anxiety at bay. I remembered the patterns, the tight circles. 'He never told me that.'

She went into my bedroom and looked at herself in the mirror. Picked up my hairbrush and started brushing her hair. 'He wasn't pissed. He remembered.'

'So?'

'We were at the park. We didn't know he'd come home. I thought he was getting beaten up by the kids from school.'

'I know, Louise, I know.'

'They thought he'd been kidnapped or hit by a car.'

'Yeah.' I got up and took two eggs from the fridge. I took a couple of slices of bacon out of the packet and pushed the thin strips around in the frying pan. 'Please. You're upsetting me.'

'What if she knew he was inside? Saw the stones but didn't go in?'

'You don't know when he left them there.' I cracked one of the eggs on the side of the bench and dropped it, shell and all, across my floor. The yellow leaked out over the pale jelly of albumen, splinters of shell stuck to the tiles. 'Maybe she didn't realize they were his.'

Louise watched me sadly. 'Maybe.'

'There was junk out there. It was really black. Or, she saw them before . . . thought he'd left them ages ago.'

'Ages ago, when?'

'*I don't know, Louise*. I didn't see them.'

Louise stood in the middle of the room, hands loose and gentle, back taut. So regal. So unrelenting. 'She probably didn't even notice.'

'Anyway, she turned back. She didn't try and go into the house.'

Then my heart turned. It was as if an anaesthetic or sedative had worn off and I was disoriented, unknowing, entering a conversation or job interview midway through, and expected to provide answers. I was adrift.

I picked up the remaining egg and threw it hard at the wall. It splattered with a satisfactory smashing sound, crumpled, and flowed down the wall onto the carpet.

Louise fell back onto the sofa. 'That was a very me thing to do.'

Then we were both quiet, watching the egg drip thickly onto my floor, the pattern of impact spread like blood over the wall.

She was easier to love when she was silent. I went over and touched her hair. 'I'll help you,' I told her. 'I'll help you look.'

I hadn't told Louise about the staff meeting yet. She'd been so extreme when she arrived home in the early hours of the morning and I wanted to get Sarah's advice about what to do. Kirsty had been showing everyone her engagement ring before the staff meeting began. She taught Year 7 and was an irritatingly effective teacher. The kids adored her. She wore her hair in a golden ponytail and owned thin, silver jewellery, including a delicate pendant in the shape of a K. I thought there was something irredeemably fifties about her: she claimed to want hundreds of children and was organizing a wedding with the full trimmings, including earnest discussions about napkin colours and the embossment on invitation paper. I tried not to despise her.

I had watched the second hand on the clock tick around as Tom worked his way through the agenda. Kirsty had a special needs kid who needed an integration aide but was only on the cusp of meeting the new criteria for assistance. Tom said he wanted this year's reports to follow a different format. I'd been drifting, putting my hopes into the weekend. There was a tangle of tension because Year 9 permission forms had been wrongly drafted for an excursion to the Immigration Museum.

Then Tom had stood and rubbed his hands together in the pose of a man ready to give an unfunny speech at his best friend's wedding. He held the leaked document aloft. 'Most of you will have seen this. I'm not sure how it was circulated but *since it has been* I want to clarify that no decisions have been made.'

Anastassia was our union delegate. She asked why the union wasn't included in the discussions around the report.

I pulled out my copy of the paper and went over the finely pencilled initials, M.F., in pen.

Tom thought the report wouldn't be a surprise to anyone: there had been concerns about results and enrolments for some time, and the union representative had already been included in a committee to examine retention problems.

That's when Anastassia said, 'We are concerned that the school is going to be closed by stealth,' and I realized how far things had already gone.

'The report wasn't to be released. It was a preliminary draft.'

'But you knew about it.'

Tom rocked back on his heels and breathed deeply in an exaggerated way. 'It was meant to provide the boundaries for a consultative process. We didn't want parents yanking their kids out of here because of rumours.' He raised his voice. 'I'm on *your* side. I'm on the side of the staff and the school.'

He handed round a thickly stapled document. 'This policy document has the new funding profile in it. It hasn't been passed yet but it will be.'

'What about jobs?' Kirsty rifled through the pages.

'Permanent staff, including anyone on leave, will be transferred if we're in excess of requirements.'

Anastassia sat down quickly in the red plastic chair. 'When is the decision being made?'

'The union will be invited to make a submission. But given our enrolments, the education department of the state government has done some preliminary investigation into the possibility of us becoming a middle school only and re-streaming into the other secondary colleges.'

I had been foolish, slow. 'How long have you known about this?' I asked.

Tom put his glasses on. 'Let's not panic. It's just an exploration at this stage.'

Kirsty said, 'Where would the older ones go? The Catholic school's expensive and the girls' secondary is academically selective.'

He shrugged. 'That's what I said. It's all in my report to the department.'

'Why is this happening now?'

'Apparently our enrolments aren't meeting the new outcomes targets. The concentration of new migrant students means our results are down and our completions don't compare well.'

'Isn't this just procedure to make it look better when they close us down?' Anastassia put her thick arms on the table. I saw my own resentment and surprise in the sour set of her face. Kirsty sat with her mouth open, touching her engagement ring.

'*I* don't think so. It's not even a proposal. It's a study. There's a lot of good faith here. The department won't force us to do anything. It'll be our choice ultimately how we manage it.'

'Is this something you suggested?' asked Anastassia.

Tom's mouth was a straight line. 'Certainly not. I've been here for ten years, some of them as head teacher. Let's be honest. We get fairly crap academic results. We're in one of the poorest postcodes in the state and we don't have the numbers.' He spoke dryly but waved his hands out in a 'what can I do?' gesture full of good-humoured helplessness at the mess we were in. But where was his outrage? Tom was not known for indignation or fury. He liked calm. I could not see the subtext, if there was any. I could not tell if Tom was playing the game or being played by it.

I sipped my cold coffee. 'Then why would anyone suggest they go on to a selective academic college?'

'I agree, but we have to seem prepared to make changes.'

It was an old story. We didn't have the numbers. We didn't have enough completions. Maybe this was another exercise in paying attention, in the government pretending to worry about schools like ours, another fuss that would lead to nothing more than an enquiry that ticked boxes and hurried us back to the status quo. But I thought of all those kids: their impudent, shining faces, their insistence on teaching me lessons about the real world, their enviable, unremitting resilience and that long walk from their public house high-rises, their hungry homes, from their generous, hapless parents into our school. The kids whose parents ironed and patched school uniforms perfectly after completing eleven-hour days sewing some company's garments for piece rates. They would shatter at an academically selective school, be left behind to read grade five storybooks in a language that was not their own while their classmates talked about tragedy and Shakespeare – if they travelled the forty-minutes to the big public school in the next suburb, gentrified in the eighties. Somebody had to teach the children of new migrants, the children whose mothers and fathers worked night and day in taxicabs or kiosks, or who nursed three children under five and comforting addictions. Didn't they? Except I knew I was monstrously naïve. I could hear the government's arguments already. They were part of a social ghetto. It would be better for them to mix with other kids who were academically engaged. There is only so much that can be done. New migrants needed to learn how to adjust to Australia's school system. Schools aren't charities. They ought to be efficient. Every child deserves an education but we can't force it on them. I started to feel sick.

The phone rang loudly. Tom put his head down and ran a hand over the polished top of his scalp where the hair was sparse and wiry. 'Leave it.'

Kirsty had looked at her watch, a dainty silver affair with a diamond-patterned band. She told Tom, in a near whisper, that she had a dress fitting in the evening.

He looked up at us. 'Can we finish? Any other business?'

'What about teachers on temporary contracts?' I knew Anastassia was talking about me.

'I can promise you that if we lose the senior years, those staff will be reallocated. No one is going to be sacked.'

Tom painfully adlibbed for a few minutes more about responding to challenges and giving the kids the chance to mix in different environments and meeting the students' needs in flexible ways and not looking at the teaching process narrowly, not getting fixated or attached to any one solution. Because he seemed to know both too little and too much, I was already certain that they wanted to shut the school.

Anastassia asked me to stay for the union meeting and I did. But I just nodded limply and raised my hand at the motions about consultation and liaising with the branch president and condemning moves to close the school, in the strongest terms.

I saw Kirsty in the car park when I left.

'Those poor kids,' she told me.

'Poor us,' I answered.

I felt unprepared, ripped apart by my own assumptions. When I went to buy a ticket I found my teacher's registration card, licence and union card were missing from my purse.

I had travelled through university to get away from my father's heart-rending aloneness, and the noise of my mother's absence. I had learned to read clever books and wear smart clothes and argue about Freud with a man who already had a wife. Now I was hopeless at reaching the students I taught, distanced by my authority and their willingness to see through my forced optimism. And yet somehow, like my father – for whom history was a trick, for whom each month and year somehow led back to that moment when he was told he was surplus to requirements – I was now also well on the way to losing my job.

The whole trip home I had thought obsessively about what we could do. Tom might sell out and take a quiet retirement. It was a wrench when I recognized that despite all the humiliations and failures of my classes – the older kids who had graffitied crude pictures of fornication into my desk, the parents who wanted to know when I would teach their kids real history with exams about dates and names – I desperately wanted the school to stay open.

We'd had students arrive in Year 7 functionally illiterate, and leave the school reading. I'd taught the children of Iranian asylum seekers whose parents had resisted their own government and fled in the night, as well as teenage potheads and girls like Selena who loved school but pretended not to. I realized I had been smug, quietly self-satisfied.

I missed my stop and pulled the cord on the tram too late. I rushed down the stairs and into the 7-Eleven for cigarettes. If Louise got in debt again I wouldn't be able to help her. I was jumpy with impulsiveness and uncertainty, and the old fear that had once haunted me during the danger game as a child jolted in my veins.

As I approached the counter I bumped into another customer. I turned to apologize and, because I recognized the woman from somewhere, I opened my mouth to greet her, until I realized the woman was Jon's wife.

We had met only once before, at a party. She'd had shining hair that reached to her shoulders, and she touched her mouth a lot. She hadn't seemed suspicious. She had been smiley and polite when we'd been introduced.

She stood grasping a leather handbag in both hands tenderly, as if holding a gift. She was tall with broad hips and narrow shoulders. There were mild frown lines on her forehead. Her earrings were tiny silver birds and looked horribly expensive. I wondered if he had bought them for her. She smelled of Nivea skin cream. I did not know what to say and I felt caught out in the most enormous lie. My private life – the sex, the half-asleep, mundane conversations and the messy, sprawling rages – suddenly seemed childish, ridiculous, spiteful. I hovered at the counter, struck by the complete lack of social mores governing the situation. I couldn't remember her name. I tried to appear diffident, disconsolate, restrained.

She folded her arms quietly in a sure, fluid movement. 'Just so you know, I'm not the mad woman in the attic.'

Jon had never pretended she was awful or psychotic. I kept my head down and asked for cigarettes from the young Indian guy behind the counter. I tried to appear like an ordinary kind of person but embarrassment made my voice high and I said 'please' three times in the one request.

She waited, admirably unhurried. She watched me put the smokes in my pocket.

'Do you know how long I've been with Jon?'

I shook my head.

'Fifteen years. That doesn't seem so long to you because you're young.'

I rested the weight of my upper body on the counter and looked from her to the teenager who was watching me expectantly behind the counter. I hadn't been able to break the frozen tableau.

Then she had clicked open her handbag. 'I think he wants you to pay.'

I handed over the money and waited dumbly for my change. And then I was out into the night.

Louise and I sat at the big wooden table with cups of black coffee and a ratty exercise book she'd dug out of her bag. She had come out of the shower with her hair dripping, stepping gingerly across the lounge with wet brown feet. The impressions left on the carpet by her damp footprints were shallow and disappeared while I was watching. Her pupils were normal, her arms unmarked. When she'd been absolutely in thrall to heroin she would inject into her toes if she had to. This life had given her a secret knowledge, another language, of deceit.

Now, her hair smelled of apples. 'We could try her parents.'

'Are they still alive?'

'Or I can make a list of people she used to know.'

'I think we should start with Dad, ask him more about it. And Jean. She was her best friend.'

She scribbled into her book. 'What about friends? Births, deaths, marriages? What happens if you change your name by deed poll?'

I was remembering last night. 'Hang on, Lou. Did you take my teacher ID card?'

She didn't pause. Her eyelashes fluttered. 'Was it in your wallet?'

'Yep.'

'I might have borrowed it when I was doing the application. To get back the Community Services records.' She smoothed down a page of paper.

My voice was high. 'Well, don't. Don't just take things from me and don't bullshit me all the time.'

'I forgot about it. It wasn't a secret.'

I felt cool, removed. 'Did you even speak to Dad?'

She snatched a fag, got up. 'Yeah.'

'And he remembered?'

'I just said.'

I held the cup of coffee tightly with two hands. 'You say plenty of things, Louise; it's knowing which of them are true that's the difficulty.' Jeremy's death, the dreams, the detective kit, the wearing, wearying compulsion. I hadn't seen the fantasy in it, the distraction, the element of ruse.

She grabbed the telephone and dragged it over. 'Ring him. Ring him and ask him.'

'I won't do this again. Phone calls from debt collection agencies for things you've ordered in my name, waiting up all night in case you've passed out in the middle of the road smacked up to your eyeballs . . .'

'But I'm not, I'm not.' She was pacing.

Then the telephone rang. Louise shoved it at me.

'Where did you go last night then?'

She was ashen-faced, unreachable, picking up her things.

I took a breath, told myself *careful*. 'Hello, Alice speaking.' The receiver was cool to hold.

'Hi, Alice, it's Anastassia Theopolous. I hope I'm not calling too early.'

'Oh, hi Anastassia.'

Louise had her backpack on. She slung the plastic bag of papers she carried with her over a wrist. She wrenched open the front door, then waited. As she was leaving she told me: 'You lie to yourself all the time, Alice, *all* the time.'

'Sorry, Anastassia. Shitty line. Can you say that again?'

'Things have got a bit more complicated since the last meeting. I thought you'd like to know Tom's called a community consultation meeting about the future of the school for next week.'

'Well, good. The parents will be furious about it.'

'The unofficial word from the education department is they're submitting a preference to Tom for closing us down and they'd rather do it quietly with his acquiescence.'

'How do you know that?'

'There are rumours Tom's already agreed. I've got a source that works in policy and procedures and she thinks that this has been in the pipeline for months. She says there are plenty of stories flying about that Tom's happy to see the place shut. She's going to forward me some emails, but you don't know this, Alice; you haven't heard it from me. The state branch says this has been the strategy all over. Rather than have a huge battle all over the media that looks as if they're being nasty to poor kids, they starve the schools of funds, watch them collapse into total dumps, and then look like they're doing everyone a favour.'

'So you don't know anything for sure.'

She sighed. 'Tom hasn't objected to the new guidelines. This letter has invited a representative from the department to speak and the state Minister's going to have a statement. It would have been drafted before the staff meeting.'

'Because of this report?'

'I don't think the report matters. That's just a bit of cover. It's the declining enrolments, crap results.'

'He just told us he was submitting a proposal for a middle school. At the meeting.'

'I guess a day's a long time in the politics of sucking up. He's drafted an invitation to the union, and this letter to the parents for a forum would have been written days ago.'

'Honestly, Anastassia, I don't think he'd lie. I know he's hardly a unionist but he cares about the school. And himself.' Otherwise, I thought, why had he stayed there so long?

'I'm calling our members for an emergency meeting so the branch can do a press release and get in first. And we'll have to elect someone to speak at the forum. Tom may be on the side of the good and the great but he can retire in six months with a package.'

'Someone should talk to Tom before this all goes ahead and try to get the facts right. We can't assume he's going to be on the wrong side of this. Why would he want to close the place he's been in charge of for a decade?'

'No, Alice, I don't think that's smart. Whatever he has to say about the school he should be willing to say publicly.'

'But you don't have any reason to think he's abandoned pushing for a middle-school model.'

'Then why has he been so secretive about a whole raft of funding decisions and that the report was commissioned?'

'I could ask him quietly, unofficially, what he thinks should happen. I'll say I'm worried about my position.'

Anastassia sighed. 'Alice, I think it would be much wiser to wait until the public meeting and ambush him, demand that he speaks out on behalf of the school. He's not stupid. But we can discuss tactics at the branch meeting.'

'If you're right, then what do we do?'

'It depends on what support the national branch can offer, what the other teachers think, how much of a fuss the parents make. We'll have to fight this in a few strands, find out whether conditions and positions will be protected in a new environment if teachers are shifted, emphasize that we're servicing a marginalized group of kids.'

'Can we take industrial action?'

'What? At a school that no longer exists? Slow down, Alice, you're too impatient. We'll talk about it but half the teaching staff's not even *in* the union.'

'How long will it take? Not the forum – I mean for the final decision?'

'Depends on Tom. If he stands with us to keep the school open it'll be much more difficult for the bureaucrats. If he agrees, no time at all. They'll shut at the end of the year. If they're smart they'll let it drag on until parents rip out their kids, everyone's fatigued and teachers start leaving voluntarily.' She sighed. 'I don't know. This Foley report's a bit strange. Either he knew about it for ages or they've had their eye on us to close for quite a while.'

'What do the others think?' Anastassia had been at the school for years. One of her daughters went there.

'I'm ringing around now. We'll figure out a proper strategy at the meeting. But I'm asking you not to approach Tom personally.'

'They can just let my contract expire, can't they?'

She said gently, 'Alice, if you get involved in this campaign to keep the school open they might do that anyway.'

I lay down on the red rug in my bedroom and tried to stop shivering. I wanted to get drunk. I looked at an old photo of Jeremy and thought of the way he used to bury objects he loved in the garden, create treasure hunts for Louise with real clues and tests, his milky breath when he was a toddler, the soft pads of his hands in fists as a baby.

And perhaps our mother stepped back as the fire grew and spread and Jeremy burned and burned and burned.

Tom had hired me to fill a maternity leave position when I was just a Bachelor of Education graduate with patchy results but he'd never tried to sell the school as more than it was.

He'd been patient with my mistakes but largely disinterested. His wife, who was hopelessly ambitious, had carried on to me once or twice about how Tom could have been a research scientist but wasn't prepared to spend the years in postgraduate education and how she'd never thought he'd settle in teaching because he didn't have 'super people skills'. 'Not like me,' she'd said, and laughed without humour, leaning in so that I could demur, her perfume too strong, varicose veins spread like bright pathways across her hands.

I had to trust Anastassia's instincts. I had to shut my mouth. Instead, I called Sarah and got her voicemail. 'Hi Sar. Can you ring me? It's getting a bit chaotic here. I need your sensible thoughts. Thanks.'

Louise wasn't outside. I drank a glass of red wine. It tasted sugary. From the balcony I watched the street. *Ring back, Sarah. Ring me back.* A small balloon glided high in the sky, yellow with gold trim, trailing a wavy ribbon like a tail. There was a warm wind and the black roads looked like sticky liquorice.

*

But when the phone rang it was my old friend Timothy who'd flown into Melbourne first thing. I'd promised weeks ago I'd meet him for lunch.

'Hello honey. Much as I love the suspense, when exactly *are* you arriving?'

'Oh no.'

'Why, yes. I've entertained myself by devising song-lists of hate and fear that I can download onto a compilation CD for my ex-boyfriend.'

Timothy had been my saviour at university. He had known how to make awfulness funny. He was, very briefly, just a tall, pale boy from the country until he found a certain crisp pitch in his voice and a knack for cruel humour. He was irreverent. He fucked strange men in the park and he had trained himself to raise a single eyebrow.

'I'm awful; I can't come now.' He did not reply. My voice sounded wheedling. 'I'm sorry I forgot you. Too busy arguing with everyone.'

Always a muscular, solid person, Timothy was now bony. Each time I saw him, he was fading a little, losing his old shape like a receipt that had been through the wash. He was in Melbourne for a couple of weeks to visit his mother and to try to make amends with his ex-partner.

'Don't you want to know what's going on the CD? I'm in a sticky-carpet pub pretending not to be a hundred years older than everyone else here and washing down my bitterness with watery pots; what's not to love?'

I looked at my watch. I was hours late. Timothy sounded ebullient with desperation and fatigue. I thought of the washed-out grey of his eyes, almost the same shade as the pearly insides of shells on the shore, of his dyed, bright-red hair.

'I didn't know the breakup was that final. Aren't you seeing Jaryd?' They'd been together for two years, shared an apartment in Bondi and then a house in the suburbs of Sydney.

'I rang and left a message. He hasn't called back yet.'

I picked up a piece of paper and folded it into small squares.

'I'm lonely. Why aren't you lonely, Alice?'

'Louise is staying with me.' He did not say anything. 'I am. I'm sick of being trapped inside my own thoughts. At least I have Sarah here.'

'You know how young he was.'

'Mmm.' It had been a cause of some ill-tempered humour in our fraying circle of friends.

'I think he got bored.'

'Is that what he says?' I cast around to try and find my packet of cigarettes.

Timothy yawned into the phone. 'He never wanted to be home, picked and poked at me. Moved out into a studio apartment in a warehouse and drank ginger tea and went on the liver cleansing diet. You know these places – drawings right onto the walls, someone playing bass guitar in the room below. He liked watching the neighbour get undressed through the overlooking window.'

'He's restless. Sounds like he wants to be nineteen again.' I dug out the cigarettes from under the sofa then did a double take. 'He wasn't nineteen, was he?'

'Very funny.'

'I like to keep my public entertained.' How had we become reduced to these feeble one-liners?

'You're not coming, are you Alice?'

There was a fluid sadness in his voice, sharper than resignation, more subdued than grief.

I could have gone to meet him, caught the tram along Sydney Road, and the leafy back streets behind the university, into the city. 'This school thing's happened.' Filaments of dust swam and turned in the golden light. I rubbed my neck. I wanted coffee.

'Oh, yes.' He could not comprehend my job. It was anathema to him, a sign that I was a bit of a hypocrite, a bit of a fraud. 'I'm still glad I majored in boys, bongs and . . .'

'Bravado.' I finished the line for him. This was an old joke. He was repeating himself.

'And you like teaching?' he asked, the rising inflection tinged with carefulness or disbelief.

I swallowed. 'That's the million dollar question,' I told him, evasively.

'Still saving the world one child at a time?' Timothy worked in computer programming in intense spurts to earn the money to garden and read and go to protest rallies and take drugs for months at a time. I was the sell-out, the frightened one who'd finished my degree and taken the first job I was offered.

My skin prickled. 'You make it sound like sponsoring a child complete with morose photograph and fifty cents in the charity box at church.'

'How do the kids like you?'

I sniffed. 'About as much as the church charity box.' I laughed. 'A bit more. If I can get them interested they'll forget they hate school.'

'What excites them?'

'War. At least for the boys. And porn magazines.' I was not being accurate. I was using the kids I taught as fodder to impress Timothy with the banality of my life. 'They all hate Australian history; they think nothing's ever happened here.'

'Good for them.'

'The Australian history?'

'The pornography. Got to get a bit of pleasure somehow in this world.' Timothy had started, since the end of his relationship, to watch pornography the way other people watch television: constantly, in a numb, private trance.

'I'll make today up to you. I'll come and visit. Bring singles to add to your CD?'

'You might want to give your sister a ring.'

'Why?'

'When I saw her in Sydney last year, she was all thin and scraped together, with some creep of a man standing over her. She was a bag of bones, Alice. She's not imbibing anything that isn't injected or snorted.'

'You're charming, really.'

'Be kind to her, Alice. She was miserable.'

'Anyway, she's here now.'

Before we hung up I told him I was sorry about Jaryd.

'He loved to live a cliché. Wanted more "me time". It was *all* him time.' The last time I visited, I had been surprised to see sharp lines around Timothy's eyes, his trademark insouciance nearly lost to him.

I put out my cigarette. 'You don't get that with an affair – the us and the me time.'

'He's got a friend in Northcote that he's staying with. He says it's a friend.' A ragged breath. 'Why do you think you're so fucked up about men?'

I smiled. 'I blame men.'

'Honestly, why?'

A rush of despair juddered through me. I hadn't realized how obvious I was.

St Kilda was a palimpsest where old stories still lingered. On the steps of McDonald's a boy, perhaps seventeen, was cradling himself, touching his skin with his fingertips. He could barely raise his head. The smack was peaking. The skin on his face was clear, the crook of his arm unmarked and his cheeks were still fat with the sponginess of late adolescence. A tram cut off my view. The boy had looked like Sam from my school, Sam of the gentle hands and great responsibilities.

A fat guy wearing a singlet limped forward as the tram doors closed. The Vietnamese tram driver shook his head and rang the bell. The fat man flung back his head in a wild jerk and asked, 'Didja see that Ching Chong cunt?' to the open sky.

I glimpsed Sarah in the park. She was trying on mournfulness, staring at the alcoholics who were huddled together. Her thin lilac and white cotton shirt was stretched across her work uniform, half buttoned despite the heat. She tugged her hair out of a ponytail, shook her head emphatically.

'Don't you touch me,' a woman in the group wailed to the grass and the sky.

I waved to Sarah. 'Hey.'

'Delirium tremens.'

I steered her away from the park. 'You're off-duty now.'

'I started at five today, so if a single human being asks for my assistance in any way there will be blood.'

I laughed. 'So you didn't get my message?'

She frowned. 'I haven't been home.'

It had been late in the day when she rang, asking me to meet her after a shift in the south-eastern suburbs. We pushed through the press of people, the surfeit that was Acland Street. Cakes with high towers of whipped cream, lemon tarts piled with glazed fruit and custard, were lined up in shop windows. Pink and silver tops clashed with pale yellow fisherman's pants in the discount stores. We negotiated our way past struggling children and tourists, and let the drunks fade back into the short shadows of the trees in the park.

A middle-aged woman wearing a pencil skirt and very high heels almost collided with the empty hat of a homeless man. She leapt back and dropped her bag. I picked it up.

'I've heard they send their kids to ask you, to make you feel sorry for them,' she hissed as I passed it to her. 'But then they just take the money off them and use it to buy drugs.'

'They have plenty of money,' Sarah told her, and the woman began to nod. 'I think begging is like a sport for them, a sort of game.' The woman drew back, still smiling uncertainly. 'You can make thousands of dollars doing this – more than CEOs do. They go back to their mansions on the cliffs and change out of their homeless uniforms.'

We cackled – we were twenty again, we ran the world – and the woman stepped jerkily away.

The footpath pulsed out heat as we walked towards the beach, tipping our heads back into the tangy breeze. Sarah tugged at her skirt where her uniform was creased. 'I need to get changed back into my own skin.'

'You know, on the way here I thought I saw one of my students – well, old students – smacked out of his brain on the tram before.'

'You always think you recognize people,' Sarah told me. 'It's like some kind of syndrome.'

'I couldn't get close enough to see.'

'Tch tch. What *are* you teaching them?' There was a dimple in her left cheek that only appeared when she smiled.

'History, this term.' She wasn't really listening.

'What do you tell them about that?' Sarah was taller than me and had to stoop to hear. When she leaned down, I smelled the hospital on her: anti-bacterial hand-soap, disinfectant.

'Whatever's on the curriculum. Who discovered Australia. Federation. The Anzac tradition. Civil rights. Ancient civilisations. Revolutions. Wars. Twentieth century mostly.' I shaded my eyes with a hand, squinted into the sun. 'Teaching the syllabus.' I drew out the words so the sentence was almost one undulating, extended sound. After I spent time with Tim, I often found myself speaking like him. Drolly, with an undirected sarcasm.

'Are you meant to make them see it as the world improving?' She spoke coolly but kept her hands clasped tightly together in front of her.

'I'm not sure what I'm meant to do.'

'You didn't even like History at school. Remember Mrs Fisher in Year 8?'

'We had to fight the English Civil War and you got to be the king and I was stuck in the new model army. Thank God I changed schools.'

'What was it with all those weird re-enactments? She'd say: "if you're on the left-hand side of the classroom you're a squatter, on the right a landowner." Or she'd divide us down the centre into workers and peasants or old regime and revolutionaries. *You* don't do that.'

'Nope.' I did not mention my failed exercise on stereotyping. 'The Year 7s get to do genealogy, or "my personal history". They draw and collect things and paste them into their books.'

'How I became the person I am today by Alice Reilly.' She clapped her hands together without enthusiasm.

'That sort of thing.'

'What about the older kids? Do they see history as progress? As things getting better?'

'Only in the sense that it's one thing and then the next. They don't think of it like that. They like student protest stuff, of course.'

'We were like that.' She was walking quickly. She bent her head. 'I just want to get these ingredients for tonight and go.'

'Do you have time to get a drink?'

She grabbed my arm. 'Hang on a sec.' She edged towards the gated mouth of deserted Luna Park, and started to unbutton her top. She handed me her bag. 'Can you hold this?'

'What are you doing?' I took her heavy sports bag. She handed me her damp blouse. Her bra had lace straps. 'Don't get changed here.'

She peeled off her navy skirt, which had her hospital ID card clipped to its belt. 'I need to get out of these clothes,' she told me, speaking steadily through clenched teeth and giving the finger to a bemused cyclist who'd paused to see the show. She pulled on a vintage cotton dress over her head, and turned so I could do up the zip. The fabric was a wash of peachy-watermelon.

We walked on slowly. A light rain fell, although the air was humid. We watched drizzle fall on damp sand, boats skip and toss in the shucking, billowing waves of the sea.

'Did something happen today?'

She took off her huge sunglasses and tucked them into her bag. 'I had an Alzheimer's patient again. It's not even my regular hospital and I've seen her twice.' She paused and then spoke softly. 'In my worst moments I think: take a bottle of pills, shoot up some morphine, marry someone who can afford to fund your comfortable deterioration, just don't get old and lose your mind if you're alone.'

Since her return from her years in the country, Sarah had given in to these jolting, short-lived streaks of bitterness.

'You're very morbid today.'

'I'm just being practical.' Her voice was still light and gentle.

I snuck a glance at her but she was not smiling. I linked my arm through hers. 'I thought *I* was meant to be the cynical one.'

Her eyes could look dark – inky and full of grief – but not today.

'We're all cynical ones. How could we not be? It's only you,

Alice, that thinks of me as Saint Sarah, patron of the left-behind, the not-quite-right, the lost.'

'I don't think that.' I did. I'd known her the whole of my adult life. This belief was an old habit. But things were shifting and settling into new shapes. They were becoming, transforming, like images in a kaleidoscope.

We reached the bridge across Fitzroy Street. I stared out at the aqua sea and waves crashing near the pier.

'Come on, dopey. Where are we going?'

I wheeled around. I propped my hands on her shoulders. 'Shall we go and sit down somewhere?'

Sarah took my hand and swung her arm back and forth. 'Yes. I want an omelette full of cheese, and Borscht and a decent coffee, and then I'll be human again.'

But we couldn't get a table. Instead we ducked into a minuscule café, which was decked out in bile-coloured citrus colours, and were directed back outside. We chose a pair of tiny red seats positioned under striped sun umbrellas and sat crunched too close together, jammed next to a thickset man on a guitar who was singing a Cold Chisel song out of tune with terrifying gusto. It was a perfect day. The north wind was driving away the drizzle.

The waitress thumped two glasses of water onto the table. Her hair, tucked firmly behind her ears, was the colour of muddy honey. I ordered green tea and Sarah asked for espresso.

'We've got this woman in her early sixties who gets brought in. It's probably happened four times. Today she was burning up her paperwork in an incinerator so that no one can get her money. Forgets to put the fire out, falls asleep on her own front step, can't remember where she lives. The neighbours drove her in. Early-onset Alzheimer's.'

'Aren't you in casualty?'

'They can't keep her in the psych ward. Don't want her in a bed. She's too far gone to live at home. The state'll sell her house to pay for a bargain basement gasoline-baths nursing home. By the time she dies her brain will be a moth-eaten mess.' Sarah stirred sugar into her coffee, tapped the spoon on the saucer.

I burned my mouth on my green tea. 'No family?'

'Some daughter she didn't recognize first off. When she figured it out she was really upset. Moaning: "This is not the sort of daughter I thought I'd have. Why did she turn out this way?" Etcetera.'

I caught site of my worried face in the mirrored glass that edged the door. 'What does the daughter say?'

'She didn't believe me until she heard the diagnosis from the doctors. Her mum's fine, just has moods.' Sarah swallowed some coffee.

'I'm sorry your work's so crappy at the moment.' I stood up and put my arms over her shoulders. I rested my forehead on her head.

She blew her nose into a napkin. 'I love my job. I'm lucky.'

Once this would have impressed me: Sarah's resilience, the quiet pleasure. 'So, the plan's to marry a rich man or live in a country where it's legal to die an assisted death. I'll try to organize it for us.'

She smacked her palms on the table. 'Thanks.'

'My mum would be in her late fifties now,' I calculated. 'If she's alive.'

'You think about her a lot, don't you?'

After the fire, when we moved away, Sarah had phoned and written me letters in green strawberry-smelling pen in her looping handwriting, but we weren't friends again for two years.

'I think about if she ever thinks of us. Idle, morbid, curiosity. Come on, you grumpy tart, let's get your ingredients.'

Sarah went to an Asian grocery, sifting through packets of wonton skins and piling up sticks of fresh lemongrass and damp bundles of coriander.

I waited outside for her, and sauntered into one of the upmarket hippie stores. I drifted past bottles of lavender oil and books with high production values and arty pictures of rainforests. I hadn't expected Sarah to be so unreachable. I had wanted the sunny, uncomplicated version of my friend, the advice-giver.

At the counter lay a straw basket with slips of glossy paper, a collection of fortune teller flashcards. I ruffled my hands through, closed my eyes and clutched a card in my palm. It told me: *Open your heart*. There was an indistinguishable fuzzy animal drawn at the bottom of the instruction, perhaps a rabbit or a toy bear, that was smiling a lopsided, half-encouraging, half-admonishing smile.

'Oh Christ.' I held it up so Sarah, who was at the other side of the store window, could read it. Her arms were full of packages. She seemed puzzled.

I walked back out.

'There are worse sentiments.' She put her bags of shopping down on the street and leant forward and kissed me, her mouth warm and soft on my cheek, as people streamed around us.

By the time I finally got ready to leave her house, Sarah was chopping wombok at the bench. I sat on the floor in front of the tall, clear windows that overlooked her garden and warmed myself in a patch of sunlight. Eggplant pieces lay on a cutting board, sprinkled with salt. Stock was simmering on the stove, parsley lay limp and green in the sink.

'What's in the pot?' I lifted the beaten lid of the huge saucepan and breathed in the steam.

'Old bones and ends of vegetables.'

'Yuck.'

'Don't worry Alice, it's not for you.'

'What are you making?'

'There are three courses. Soup first.' She brought the knife down with neat quick strokes, and she was not really looking as she sliced on the diagonal.

'Who's coming over?'

'Just this woman at my work.' She put the eggplant in a colander and rinsed it. 'But I'll make a meal for you and Lou if you're good.' She began peeling galangal. 'How are things with Jon?'

'I think it's ending. I don't think he's interested in me anymore.'

'Don't you want something more from a relationship than what you get with him?'

I lay on my back with my feet against the wall, my shoes splayed out on the floor next to me. 'Like what?'

'Plans? Kids?'

'No. Are you a closet moralist? You don't have those things.'

She poured herself a glass of red wine and took a slug, running her tongue over her lips. 'We'll see.'

And it wasn't until we were at the gate, Sarah snipping at her plants with a pair of secateurs while we spoke, that she asked me: 'How's school?'

'It'll probably be closed this time next year.'

'What?'

'Our school.'

She cut the head off a drooping rose. 'Why? What's going on?'

'We don't have enough students. Apparently. According to the new funding guidelines. And we're now classified as an "under-performing" school. That school's been there for thirty years. One in three kids comes from a non-English speaking background.'

'New funding guidelines. *Blech*.' And the subject was closed.

What had I forgotten? There was something I hadn't remembered. Back at home I shunted back and forth, reading over my employment contract, my scribbled comments from the conversation with Anastassia and the state-wide funding submission the union had put together last year on disadvantaged schools in low-income areas; and hunting in the scraps of paperwork Louise had left behind, writing lists of people who once knew my mother. I kept walking between my bedroom and the lounge, treading a repetitive route in the same obsessive way I had once seen an armadillo at the zoo trot a figure eight so incessantly that the earth had deep grooves worn into it. The afternoon was nearly over when I realized.

Anastassia had called it the Foley report. Foley was a common enough name – English, I assumed, perhaps Irish or Welsh. Still it had been *M.F.* and she worked in the public service. I couldn't remember which department. I should have listened when Jon spoke of her.

His mobile rang out. I dialled over and over but he didn't pick up the phone. Tucked into the back of my wallet was his home phone number. 'For emergencies,' he'd said, as he scrawled it down six months ago. We had both known I wasn't to ring.

We'd only fucked at his home once, when his wife was away on a girls' trip to the Yarra Valley, and I'd had to lie naked on their expensive cotton sheets and listen to her leave a drunken message on their machine. She used a pet name for him and asked about his mate's wedding that she didn't want to go to. She'd sounded gregarious, mild, kind.

Usually we met at my place or his studio, which was uncomfortably small, and so cold in the winter we'd have to warm ourselves at the electric bar heater, turning one way and then the next to get an even temperature, our naked limbs like meat on a spit, before we lay down. Our breath puffed out visibly as though we were perpetually exhaling cigarette smoke.

We'd tried a weekend away ourselves, right back when it began, when the future wasn't known, when even a casual touch would make me shiver and just the thought of him thrilled me. I would smile quietly, privately, trying all the while not to assume anything.

I had gone down on him in the hotel lift, his hand on my neck, while my eyes kept straying to the mirrored wall and the uncomfortable reflection of myself on my knees. A woman with a cleaning trolley, who quickly turned away, had interrupted us. He'd told me, 'You can keep going. It's just the maid. I'm sure this happens all the time,' and we had laughed together uneasily: how abject were we prepared to be?

Later, under the table at dinner, when we were sitting outside on the deck in front of a crowd of strangers, he'd lifted up my dress and manoeuvred his fingers beneath my underwear and touched me to orgasm. It had still felt like a love affair.

Even so, we had packed up early with relief, his guilt and my diffidence circumvented. There were times in the day when we'd had nothing to say to one another.

It had been easier to admit things then. 'You only like me 'cos I'm great in bed,' he would sigh, and I'd nod gravely.

I fished out the crumpled number, which was inked heavily and followed by a couple of jaunty Xs. I dialled it with trembling hands.

Hi, they chorused, in stagey unison. She continued, *Obviously we're not here at the moment –*

Then Jon's voice. 'Uh, hello.' The machine cut out.

'It's Alice.'

A beat. 'Right. Hang on a sec.' I heard the sweep of a door closing.

'Sorry. I really need to see you.'

'Yup, I don't think that's going to work.'

It was too humiliating to reply.

'I can give you a ring from the studio next week to set up a time?'

'Please,' I said. 'Come over.'

He cleared his throat loudly and raised his voice. 'Okay, if you'll fit me in that's fantastic but I've only got half an hour.'

By the time he arrived I was drunk. I watched from the balcony as he parked his car deftly and jogged up to my apartment building. He had on dirty Levis and black Dunlops. His tight T-shirt was expensive. It was patterned with blocks of colour and flecks of white. The bottlebrush tree swayed drunkenly. I saw a parrot flash past – a flurry of blue and red unfolding. Jon handed me a bunch of damp oak leaves. 'Beautiful, hey?'

I let them fall to the carpet. I put my hands in my pockets. 'Let's go somewhere; let's walk.'

He put his hand on my arm. 'Alice, I can't stay.'

He looked like he had been crying. His face was red. I felt terrible. He never let me see him hurt. 'Are you okay?'

He frowned, then grinned. 'No, no, it's hay fever. What's happened with you?'

'Can we go out? I don't want Louise interrupting us.'

'You're not taking me out of your flat so you can break up with me are you?' He took my hand and turned it palm up.

'I don't know. No.' I felt limp, uncouraging.

He let go of my hand swiftly, shifted his own into his pockets. 'You just asked me to come *here*. Alice, I love you, you're gorgeous, but I am going home in half an hour.'

'Right.' I shut the door behind him and we went into the lounge. I poured us drinks.

'There's stuff all over your wall.' He dabbed a finger on the rough white paint.

I had not cleaned up after I smashed the egg. 'Never mind.' I didn't know how to begin. 'Where are you?'

'I said I was getting a suit fitted for the design prize and they snuck me in.'

'What design prize?'

He shifted from one foot to the other. 'Just this industry award.'

'I thought I'd know when important things happen for you but why would I? I suppose that's a silly thing to expect.' I picked up my glass and took a sip.

Jon looked at his hands. 'Is it your sister?'

It was the combination of generosity and ignorance that was painful.

'Remember that whole, *let's be loyal and good to one another even if we can't make*' – I swallowed – '*certain promises, or not try to give promises we can't keep?*'

If I drew a cartoon of how he looked in that moment, I would exaggerate the slump in his shoulders, the charcoal smudges under his eyes. He'd be despair, disenchantment.

He nodded, meshed his fingers together, and cracked his knuckles. I noticed his new watch. Its face was a pop art image of a woman from a fifties comic book, mouth open, brows raised, terrified and titillated by an invisible threat. 'I thought that's how you wanted it, too,' he told me.

'I need to know what's going on at my school. Everything that you know.'

He grinned, relieved. He clasped my hands. 'Okay, but I know what you told me. That's it.' He attempted a bizarre French-German accent: 'I know nothing.'

'I won't get anybody in trouble. I can even keep it quiet. I just want a heads up.'

He settled deeper into the couch now, reassured. 'I've been worrying that you wouldn't see me anymore – I was expecting you to say, "that's it."'

'Your wife's in the public service, right?'

'Mmmm she is.' His voice had an upward lilt, a warning.

'Which department?'

'They sort of ship her around; why?'

'Jill of all trades,' I said unkindly.

'I guess.' He didn't get it. 'There's no point obsessing about it.'

'Do you listen to what I tell you?'

'Alice, what are you so angry about?'

I was calm. 'Do you remember the name of the school I teach at?'

He fiddled with the braiding that hemmed the arm of the sofa. He suddenly remembered his drink and picked it up. 'Let's talk about where we're going here. Just kindly and truthfully. What do we want to do with this mess?' He raised his head to look at me.

'Does your wife know that it's me?'

'She told me she saw you. I'm sorry. She guessed, said she'd suspected for ages. It's pretty awful and I haven't . . . been able to promise her what will happen with us.'

The pronoun seemed ambiguous. It was better not to know which 'us' he meant. 'She's in the education department at the moment, though?'

He looked annoyed.

'You always want to talk about her; let's talk about her,' I said.

'I don't understand what you're asking me to say.'

'Where do I teach?'

'I'm choosing to be here. I came here and now you're acting like a dissociative.'

'Do you want a minor reward? Is there some kind of sliding scale of remuneration for people who lie and cheat but come when called?'

Jon stayed unruffled. His palms were huge and square, fingers narrow and elegant. He grinned, swept out his arms. 'I'd say something in the minor to median range would be fine.'

'Did Mary write a report on low enrolment state schools?'

The recognition was slow in coming. 'That report was written months ago.'

'And it didn't occur to you that my fucking job might go down the drain because your punitive little wife –'

'Don't speak like that about her.'

'Speak like that about her? *You're* the one fucking around on her with other women.'

'Not *other* women, just you.' He clung to the point doggedly, a pinpoint of clarity. He was breathing fast.

'Did you see other women before me?'

He flung out his arms, furiously. 'What? I don't understand this paranoia. I mean, you never wanted any strings, you didn't want a man in your life *full-time* you said. You were happy to have company but really you wanted the life of an ageing spinster in an Agatha Christie movie: privacy and freedom and no one to be responsible for.'

The longing for our old relationship, for the unknowing hope I'd had when it first began, rushed forward without my even knowing where it had come from, leaving me bereft in its wake. 'It's not as if I was hanging about but privately hoping that if I was undemanding enough, and shaved my legs regularly, and wore expensive clothes, and never told you what I wanted that one day you'd realize how fantastic I was and leave Mary.'

'Good.' He ran his hands through his hair. 'I knew you weren't doing that. You're not that kind of person. You look after yourself, you're strong, you like being alone.'

'How long has she known?'

He pushed his hands through his hair again. 'I'm sure she has no idea where you work. She takes her job a bit more seriously than to make recommendations she wouldn't stand by professionally.'

'You're saying you never even knew?'

'I didn't read the report and, no, my life is not so small that I memorized the name of your school. I try to keep things – my thoughts – separate.'

'I won't have a *job*.'

'You'll get a transfer. You don't even have to stay in teaching, if you don't want to. You'll have great references, plenty of experience. Don't be so dramatic; you thought it was crappy pay and bad hours. Here's your chance.'

This from the man who'd read me *Gulliver's Travels* in bed, the man who'd cooked a terrible cake for me when I was sick, the man who'd worked through the night painting pictures of mountain bears and ghostly horrors for a young adult novel cover.

I said, 'Lemons from lemonade?'

He shook his head. 'If you like. I was thinking spilt milk.'

The words rushed out. 'You really are an idiot, aren't you? No one can be that naïve. This is an attack on everybody who lives in that neighbourhood and wants a basic education. It's not just where I happen to work. We've got parents with incomes lower than what you spent upgrading your car this year. They're closing the school because the kids are struggling, they don't speak perfect English and if they miss out, drop out, fuck up – well, who gives a fuck about them? Not people like you.'

'Stuff like this happens all the time and people learn to deal with it. However much you'd like to make this the full dog-and-pony show, it's actually pretty simple so far as I can see: the school's draining money and losing enrolments.'

'You arsehole.'

He held a smile on his face, bitterly, quietly. 'You have plenty of resilience. I've never met anyone as tough as you. Alice will look after Alice.'

'Are you talking about our relationship now?'

'You like control.' He shrugged. 'You maintain an unnatural amount of distance.'

I was flummoxed, winded by how unfair he was being. 'You're married. You've never had any intention of leaving the marriage. What am I meant to be doing? Wailing like a banshee and threatening to hire a hit man to take out your wife?' I kept hold of my voice, kept it light.

He didn't laugh or fall back. 'But I have thought of leaving. There have been nights when I wanted to try and make it work with you: when we'd been trundling around here in the warmth, just putting things together, and making dinner, and I've dreaded all the dishonesty and the evasions and the silences I have with her, and years on years of recrimination and regret. *Hated* going back to it. But I can't speak to you then; you won't allow me to even contemplate it. And I do have years with her, good years with her too.'

'That's so *great*, Jon, that's really wonderful. Gosh I admire that sometimes you even think...just let your mind wander where it will... that you might one day, not yet, reflect on your screwed up marriage.'

'Why are you being so *vicious*? You never wanted this to be more than it is. You *love* the fact I'm married.'

'Oh yeah. It's a real riot for me. A source of constant comfort and reassurance.'

'Because it means you don't have to make any decisions, or take any risks or make any commitments at all to anything or anyone other than yourself.'

I stood. 'You're screaming at me because you won't admit your honourable, faithful, nineteenth century character of a wife actually fucked over my job exclusively because you were fucking me. Go home.'

'You talk about the kids you teach as if they're projects, not people. Look at your sister, walking round like a fucking ghost, or the way you feel about your father. You want to treat fully grown human beings like sparrows with broken wings, propping them all up, extorting gratitude.'

He clasped his hands together. They were trembling. He turned the gold circle of his ring on his left hand, slowly, and with painful care. 'How did we get here?' He got to his feet, looking far older than before. 'I'm sorry. I'm so ashamed.'

I tugged open the lock, which slid back easily. Jon walked stiffly to the door.

He hovered. 'Wait. Just wait.'

'Wait for what?' I left a silence. 'What's the difference.' I said it to myself as much as him, swinging closed the door, shutting out the draught and the night and remorse.

Later, I looked at the landing but he had gone without leaving a note or a drawing. Although I felt bereft, hesitating near the telephone, I knew this was a reprieve, a free chance.

That was how things ended, not so differently from how we'd gone on when we were together: half-heartedly, not knowing whether to be relieved or disappointed.

As I was walking up the steps to my father's flat, the rage nearly unbalanced me. My breath was coming so fast I was almost panting. I held my fists tight so that the blood pounded in my wrists like the stamp of distant feet. And then I saw the warm haze of sky behind the balcony, so full of longing, so full of hunger. I climbed the stairs and noticed the twitch of dirty curtains behind a window, the rustle of men left behind, the lumbering shape of Diane approaching the laundry room, and I felt overwhelmed by sudden recognition. My father lived here. My father was one of these men. He couldn't hold a job. He was terrified of history. He didn't have close friends, or 'interests', as the dating agencies and aged-care facilities called it. He got up each day alone and clung with the same amnesiac determination as a sufferer of hypothermia stuck on a mountain, lost in a blizzard, to the present moment, to surviving. For this very moment, with the warm sun falling on me, and the smell of stale smoke and takeaway in the air, the fury subsided and I admired him, almost loved him again.

Like the others who lived here he would have become used to all the tiny calculations that made life possible: using teabags twice; checking your change; doing the divisions for the meal, the day, the week. Black and Gold butter, reading the newspaper at the local library, the bargain trolleys at the supermarket. Potatoes in their jackets, bread, noodles, carbohydrates to fill you, pre-made meals frozen or in cans. Fishing through the bins at railway stations for a discarded ticket. Filling up his days with checking the mailbox, eavesdropping on conversations in nearby flats, a list of favoured TV programs (sports, cop shows) taped beside the bed, walks along the overpass to the shopping centre and the park, the preparation of small meals; and projects like painting a piece of furniture or cleaning the shower, spread over hours.

Jon had said: 'You make it sound like old-fashioned class war, Alice.'

I thought of Dad explaining how you learn the age of a tree, and where the oldest-known living tree in the world grew. Or the time we made a snail farm under the house when Louise and Jeremy were babies, one held in the crook of his arm, the other in a sling.

I could see him in my mind's eye: peeling the newspaper wrappers off steaming hot fish and chips, smiling and helping Louise make up a story while Mum poured tea and wiped the table.

I paused at the landing, giddy with grief and joy. Once, in an old argument about whether I should leave my job, Jon had told me: 'It's as if you imagine your life to be some kind of grim black and white Depression-era documentary, with barefooted mothers forced out of their homes and eviction notices nailed to the front door. Things aren't like that anymore. Everything's more flexible now. You just have to learn how to make the change.'

A Vespa gleamed on the floor below me. A bright bumper sticker was splashed across it. 'Ex-wives are like old horses. You can't ride 'em but you still have to feed 'em.'

My father came to the front door flushed but sober. Down the hall I saw Diane seated at the green card table, sipping a drink. They were playing cards. My father pulled out a chair for me. 'Just let us finish this game, love.' His eyes were glowing. He looked happy.

'Whose is that motorbike parked downstairs?'

'That'd be Jake's, wouldn't it?' He nodded at Diane, who was pushing potato chips into her mouth furiously and didn't answer. 'Won it in a raffle, how about that?'

Diane swallowed. 'My mother used to serve good drinking sherry every Sunday afternoon with the main meal.'

'Okay,' I said.

'Thought it was all class, all lady.'

My father was frozen midway through dealing the next round of cards.

'She had photographs of the Queen up. Used to hide food from us, scared we'd get too big.'

'Have a drink.' He pushed the bottle towards me.

'Since when do you drink sherry?' The sweet smell was overwhelming.

'It was a present. I'm saving mine for later.' I saw Diane's lip tremble. She was wearing an oversized pinafore dress over grubby jeans and a charm necklace.

'How are you, Diane?'

She blinked slowly, put her cards face down in a fan on the table. Hissed: 'I'm undercover.'

I kept my expression blank.

She got up and spoke in an exaggerated voice, taking a polite interest. 'And how's your affair?'

I put my head down on the table and didn't raise it until she'd left.

My father turned on the electric burner and poured a can of beans into a saucepan, flopped some bread onto two plates. The teabags looked ancient, pale and ghostly, so I pinched them in the hot water to extract some colour.

We sat at the card table.

'What day is it? Wednesday?'

'Saturday.' I put crisps in my mouth. 'Why does Diane come here?'

'She likes cards.' His voice picked up. 'I was thinking about putting in for this job. I want to stay off the booze for a while.'

'Sounds like you're off to a good start.' The cynicism was automatic. Jon had said: 'Alice will look after Alice.' I looked at my father's face carefully. He was banal, friendly, gentle, this man I had loathed an hour earlier. 'Sorry.' He shook his head.

Then, as if for the first time, I noticed the careful arrangements of decorations in the flat: the cut out magazine images of Ireland, the op shop postcards, the dusty red and white curtains.

I had meant to see if he could remember the night Jeremy died but something closed in my throat. 'They're shutting down my school.'

He put his hand out as if to touch my shoulder and left it waiting in the air, holding back an invisible intruder. 'I'd say you could put up a good fight.'

I picked at the dull mustard-coloured fabric of the chair. 'We'll try.'

'Be glad you come from a long line of people used to making a fuss.'

My laugh was a scoff.

'Don't let events overtake you.'

And now I couldn't speak of the fire. Instead I asked about his factory job. 'Do you think if you'd done things differently you would've kept that job?'

'Which one?'

'The first one.'

'You're kidding.'

I took my crockery to the tiny sink. There was grease shining on the door to the grill. The ends of soft white bread had been saved under plastic wrap on the counter and the crusts were dry and tough when I touched them. My elbow bumped an out-of-date jar of jam.

It had been a long time since I had been ashamed in front of my father. I sent a cheque to his real estate agents when I remembered.

He called out, 'There's Coke in the fridge. For me too.'

I pulled out the bottle. There was a carton of milk, a huge block of cheese, wilting lettuce. 'Are you *going* to apply for this job?'

'Jake knows they're looking. It's just test driving cars at night. You just take them up and down the freeways, follow the same route. See if they break down. I didn't keep up my licence . . . and you can't . . . well, you're out all night.'

You can't drink is what he didn't say – not unless you want to kill someone.

I brought him the glass of Coke. 'What about your sherry?'

'Cough syrup.'

'Why don't you just tell Diane you can't drink?'

He winced.

'Louise came over?'

'Used to be a real live wire that kid, always schemes going. She's still pretty.'

'Pretty pretty for a junkie,' but I said it more to myself than to him.

'When it's your kids . . . Like your mum used to say, "I'd love you if you had four noses and seventeen eyes and a mouth full of teeth."'

'That's how much,' she used to tell us. 'That's how much I love you.' I thought of her whispering this to me before she went out, when she was working night shift, sliding a paper bag of lollies under my pillow when I was almost asleep.

'Did you tell Lou that Mum tried to get Jeremy out of the house?'

'He couldn't have been in there, Alice. When I put down the kero I was bluffing. Then all I see is Louise crying, burned up. That smell. The ambulance was coming.'

It had been a terrible day. I let myself free-fall. 'Do you remember him dying?'

Nothing. I brought him a glass of water.

'Thanks.' His long body was cramped into his chair.

I tried to smile at him. 'Anyway, the union's involved now, with my teaching job.'

'Yeah.'

He swallowed and wiped his mouth with the back of his hand. 'I was in cars to start, you know? Ford.'

'Why wasn't it illegal when they sacked you?'

'They did it right smart. We were a closed shop or as close as you can get. Some of those guys were amazing. You wouldn't believe how they could get up in a crowd and say the right stuff. Zero accidents in two years, not even a fucking paper cut.'

'How did they do it?'

He got up and offered me a snack, then put the leftover bread in a bowl and sprinkled sugar over it. He added a tablespoon of milk and ate standing up at the sink, his back to me.

'It was a huge company. We'd gone on pattern bargaining. Then they sold it off to a new owner. Took them a year. Offered contracts with sky-high penalty rates to the bastards who didn't give a fuck. Fought it out, took their time, voluntary redundancies, said the industry was going broke. We hung on.'

I drank my tea.

'Seven months till they registered the agreement. We went out, came back, they locked us out. Got a few onto the contracts, it's all rosy. New machinery, now the older blokes are redundant whether they like it or not.'

'What did you think was going to happen?'

'I was a patsy. I was a bloody moron. The boss's son takes me aside, says they're going to lay me off, they'll pay what I'm owed, it's all fine, they're sorry. That's how they did it, quiet and smart. If you had done a chart . . . every diehard union member was gone by the time they finished. Individual contracts stayed. Hired again six months later.'

'What about unfair dismissal?'

'They got benefits back for most of them. I fucked myself, Alice.'

'Yeah.'

'Summary dismissal. I belted him in the mouth. He's holding his chin, dripping blood and grinning.'

'I thought there was a whole bunch of you.'

'By the time it was over, the managers outsourced, drove the company broke, made sure there's nothing there to pay out the blokes who stayed. Got themselves pay rises then bankruptcy.'

Even in the dark I saw the tears.

'But, like I say to you three kids, "You play the cards you're given."'

And the gnomic wisdom felt too bleak even for me.

Through the gap in the cupboard door – a sharp slice of lemon light – Jeremy watches his father. The picture is cluttered by details. There's the loose leg of the chair tilting his dad slightly towards the plastic cover on the kitchen table. There's the great stack of old papers and the mug with Santa Claus, broad-faced with blushing circles for cheeks, half-beaming, half-scowling, on the side. There are his dad's trembling fingers. From this angle, and in this moment only, his father is a small man. In the bright fluorescent light of the kitchen, in the dirty smells of the pipe running down from the sink, Jeremy's father is not someone to be afraid of. If Jeremy stares long enough, things will slide back into their usual places again and there will be a pulsing in his chest and he will come out and talk to his parents.

His mum didn't notice when he walked into the house. She was calling out to his dad that somebody had found Jeremy's bag. When his dad didn't answer, she started putting some money in a pile with her keys and some clothes. She rang and left a message, asking someone not to come over; while she was speaking, she tucked the telephone into the crook of her neck and counted out notes. He waited and watched when she pulled out bills wrapped in an elastic band from the top of Alice's wardrobe. Then she took out a knife, too, but shoved it back in the drawer and put on her coat. That was when he hid.

He tells himself this is what a detective would do, but really he is just tired, and afraid of being caught, and wondering if his mother is going away for good.

There is a long-lost box of Velvet soap in the cupboard, so old that the cardboard has stuck damply to the blocks of soap and there is a sticky yellow residue that has leaked out. Louise used to eat soap for the danger game. His sister's old treasures are kept here. There is the sewing box where Louise used to hide the jelly beans she nicked from the chemist's. He loves the smell of black jelly beans; stale aniseed lingers in the container.

Jeremy leans into the water pipe, which is still warm against his back, and his foot nudges the deflated rubber of the soccer ball. Before his dad got wrecked, he used to take Jeremy to the park down the road where they'd kick the ball and pretend to find secret gardens behind the swings. They would keep secrets together, and sometimes when they all went out to dinner at the place where you could get a token for a kid's drink and take it up to the bar, his dad would wink and make jokes that only he and Jeremy could understand. The secret garden was at the bottom of the little hill, behind the swings, at the back of a thick hedge, and his father saw it too.

Through the gap, Jeremy sees the pale legs of his mother and the dirt smudged across her feet. He stays undiscovered.

His mother says, 'What do you want to do?'

'What have I done to my kids?' His father pushes the Santa mug away. 'Come here.'

His mother sits down suddenly and the angle of her elbow in her arm is precise, like the side of a triangle. His father is saying words over and over in a gentle rhythm. A whispering chatter. His mum takes his father's shoulders and strokes his head. Jeremy can hear his father saying 'forgive me, forgive me, forgive me.' He says it so many times that the words begin to sound like something else or it seems as though his father has always been saying these words and just these words.

His mum separates and stands up and still his dad murmurs. His mother says, 'I can't.'

'Just tell me. Just say it.' Jeremy watches the Santa mug as his dad hits it and it rolls off the table.

But his mother puts her hands on the back of her chair and does not look up. She says, 'If he comes back you'll hug him and say you love him. And then next week you'll want a little drink and you'll become jealous of him, and talk about how you were never encouraged at school and he has all the chances and I shouldn't favour him. Then you'll say sorry but you *won't change*. You can't help yourself. In a minute, even though you don't want to, even though you love me, you'll start screaming at me. And I'll give in, like I always do, or I'll go.'

Jeremy closes his eyes but he can hear the shudder of the back door frame and his dad asking his mother to come back, quietly at first and then yelling, 'You come back here now.' Jeremy hears his father walk towards the cupboards and he pulls the door closed so that he is sealed in tight. His dad opens the cupboard next to him and slams the door shut. 'Do you want me to do it? I'll do it.' There is a tinny echo and then a trickle and the sound of water sloshing. Perhaps his dad is tipping out all his drink onto the ground. 'I'll burn this fucking place down.'

'Why don't you . . .' his father is bellowing. 'Why don't you help me?' His mother doesn't answer. 'Get back here.' Jeremy presses the sewing box to his face and sniffs in deep from the pale crumbs of black jelly beans.

On the day of the public meeting everything seemed sharper and more chaotic. School was scattered with streamers and balloons for the Year 7 sports carnival. Children in sneakers and maroon and white windcheaters poured out of buses. It was a silvery morning.

Louise had woken me up at dawn, listening to the Clash and getting dressed for a trial shift at the sandwich shop around the corner from my apartment.

I avoided the staffroom, the thin lines of tension that would be curving through the air. But I glimpsed Anastassia inside, slumped forward over the Greek newspaper. The State branch had sent a press release condemning any closure or downsizing and was liaising with the admin and cleaning unions. Anastassia's carefully worded summary had been added to an email bulletin to members, but she was enraged about a few teachers who were already murmuring about taking packages and travelling, or finding work in the private sector. At the branch meeting she had chaired to help plan the union's intervention into the public meeting, she was unable to concentrate, fiddling with her packet of unfiltered cigarettes and making a list of the teachers who weren't there. 'They've *no* principles.'

My first class of the day meant preparing for the end of term test. I unlocked the door. Without students, the room felt bare, oddly austere and preserved, as if the school had already closed. I drafted revision questions on the 'Australians at War' photo exhibition my Year 10s had seen, alternating between trying to be inventive and feeling irate about the curriculum.

Sam knocked on the door. He'd hardly been in school since he told me that he might be leaving. He was out of breath.

'Hi. Still here?'

'It's my last week.'

'You're early; the bell hasn't gone. Are you going to sit for the exams?'

'I have to ask you stuff, Miss.'

'Come on in.' I pulled two seats over to the near corner of the room and left the door open, remembering Tom's warning. Sam kept standing.

'How's your mum?'

'Okay. They say she's "comfortable". She doesn't reckon. My brother's back.' He jittered his feet on the wooden floor.

It was then that I realized. 'She's dying?'

'She's got the cancer in her bones now.' He picked at the sleeves of his school jumper, which must have shrunk in the wash. It reached only to a few inches before his wrists. 'How do I get more painkillers? It's not enough.'

'You know I can't tell you that. Get your brother to speak to the hospital.'

'She doesn't wanna go back. She wants to die at home.' His heavy school shoes jittered on the floor, kicking rapidly, a demented tap routine in fast-forward.

'Are you on something, Sam? You know the policy on drugs.'

He swung his head back and forth slowly. This brought to mind an elephant sadly rocking its trunk in time to music at the circus. 'Nah, Miss. I'm not.'

I let it go.

'This is my last instalment.' He pressed some folded up sheets of paper into my hand. 'The story.' He'd wanted to write a three-part tale about interspace and mind-reading. His writing never had apostrophes or capital letters at the beginning of sentences, though he would occasionally capitalize a letter in the middle of a word to wake me up. The stories were beautiful and curious. He hadn't given me a history assignment most of the term.

'Thanks, Sam.' If it hadn't been for the rules, the non-negotiable borderlines, I might have hugged him.

'Hamish and Chris are twins so maybe they could learn to read each other's minds, d'you reckon?'

I had to grapple with a smile. 'No.'

'With ESP – they could have ESP.' He spoke far too quickly.

'I don't think so, Sam. They've done studies of twins and how their lives develop, though; you should look in the library.'

He scowled. 'It's *possible* they have ESP. That's what my story's about.'

I gave up, put on my SBS world-news commentator voice. 'They say there's a lot we still don't know about the mind.'

The bell went. Bodies bustled in the aisles. 'My sister was a twin, fraternal. And I wouldn't taste-test your mum's drugs, you'll fuck yourself up.'

His head snapped up. He was probably thinking, *Miss said fuck.*

I got out worksheets for the students who were streaming into class. 'Okay. Morning. Last class before the dreaded test.'

The boys shoved and pushed so as not to take the seat next to Sam. I put my hands on my hips. 'What's the problem?'

Nicholas whined. 'He's got a cold, he's all germy; I don't wanna sit there.' Even Chris was playing along, whacking the history textbook onto the wooden seat next to him as Sam moved towards it. Sam waited, uncertain, his skin burning up, his fingers jostling the air.

'This seat's taken, someone's sitting here.' Hamish, who was listening to an iPod he hadn't owned last week, put his feet up on a chair. Rage Against the Machine pounded out through the earpieces.

I stood in the front of the room. 'If you think you've got a good reason not to sit next to Sam, stand up.' His eyes fastened on the floor. A few of the boys sitting at the back jeered one another and started pushing back their chairs. 'And get out. *Out.* And don't come back in. You can all go straight to the principal's office. Each and every one of you.' The two boys stood with bent backs and tried to get back into their chairs without making any noise.

Hamish moved his feet. 'There's a seat here.'

Sam lumbered into the seat.

I yanked Hamish's earphones out. 'Stop showing off.'

'Sorry, Miss.'

'Who's going to tell me what's going on?' I tried to get control of myself but I could hear that my voice was too shrill, too high. 'Fine. Try to answer questions one through five individually then we'll discuss them in groups.'

I walked around in the silence, watched them scribble down definitions of conscription and alliance. Then I found a scrap of paper with a scrawled stick figure of a man with an arrow pointing to him and *Poofter. He sucks dicks* written in a neat speech balloon. Then there was the line: *Your hole family is gay as Sam's brother*. Of course. The handwriting was Chris's. I didn't have the energy for a patient, token discussion of discrimination and sexuality and inclusion. I scrunched up the paper, breathed carefully, and went to the board. 'Swap your sheet with the person next to you and we'll go through your answers.' As they were called out, I began writing up the major military altercations Australia had been involved in throughout the twentieth century. 'So, what is the US alliance?'

Nicholas waved his hand in the air. 'Like ANZUS.'

'Okay, good. And what was that?'

A silence.

Hamish put his hand up. 'Miss, if we have go to another school, will you still be our teacher?'

'I don't know. But this is your school for now.'

There was a burst of enthusiasm in the room. 'But Mum got a letter and there's no funding.'

'That's what the meeting tomorrow's meant to talk about. If you want to keep going to school here you should come.'

Nicholas muttered, 'What if you don't want to go to school at all?' but it was mostly bravado and he said it quietly.

'If you think you deserve a publicly funded education, come to the meeting.'

'My dad says you'll strike – that means *no classes*.'

I coughed. 'Anyway, for your short essays you might be asked to explain why Australia sent troops to Vietnam, or World War One and Two, or to provide an analysis of the explanations for these wars.'

I scribbled the revision sections up on the whiteboard. 'Let's keep going. What are some of the other features of the alliance?'

Chris read from the textbook. 'Shared intelligence. Joint facilities. US bases.'

'So, what's the point of an alliance? What's meant by it?'

'America is a superpower and Australia's not even a middle power so it helps protect us and they get stuff back.'

'Mmm . . .'

Selena put up her hand, shuffling through her old notes. 'Australia needs a shield, so it used to be Britain, but now it's America and they have a special relationship.'

I ticked off questions on my list. 'And looking at the person's paper in front of you and correcting as we go, what was significant about Australia and the Vietnam War? Sam?'

'TV.'

'What about TV?'

He shrugged. 'Happened on TV.'

'No, it didn't happen on TV, some of it was broadcast on TV. What else?'

I looked at the clock. Class was finishing late and I hadn't got through the revision.

'For homework, have a look at the copies I made of the photos of World War Two soldiers and then I want you to write down how you think it might feel to be in the army. If you haven't yet, do the short answer in your book on why you think Australia went to war – it's in one of the case studies, one of the situations, on page fourteen.'

Chris curled his lip. 'What if you don't get why?'

'Then you can write about that – whether you think it was the right thing.'

'Course it is.'

Selena was waving her hand again. 'Can we do this war now?'

'Not the war in Iraq.' I told Selena, 'It won't be on the exam.'

They streamed out of the classroom. 'Can I see you for a moment, Chris?'

Selena slouched next to her desk, one hand on her hip, her books held tight against her chest. 'Even if it's not on the exam, what if I want to do it?'

Chris made a noise that was meant to sound like a missile falling to the ground. I studied Selena's face. 'You're that excited about the war on Iraq?'

She chewed gum rhythmically. 'Not *excited.*'

I straightened up, nodded my head. 'Okay. Off you go.'

I held the paper out to Chris so that he could see it. 'How did you feel when the others used to call you a fag or a poofter?'

'Don't care.'

'You didn't mind? You thought it was fine?'

'But Miss, he *is* one. Sam's brother is. I saw them and he was there with some guy and they were kissing.'

I thought of the danger game. I was almost thirty. 'He's gay. But when you say he's a poofter, you don't mean it as a compliment, do you?' I wanted to say, stop fucking me around; you're thirteen, not three.

Chris shook his head.

'You need to leave Sam alone. His brother has a boyfriend and that's perfectly fine and natural. He loves men.' Sam's parents were probably not going to love me. 'There's nothing wrong with that so stop treating it as a disease you can catch or pass on.'

'Yeah, whatever dot com.'

'Do you want to sit in here at lunch like a child?' I couldn't keep hold of my rage, which was mostly disappointment – not even at Chris, but at my own naïvety, my lack of realism. Hadn't 'poofter' been Louise's favourite term when we were kids? Perhaps Jon was right: my empathy was conditional, my commitment to the school drummed up.

'Chris, there are things that happen in your family, your life, that you wouldn't want broadcast everywhere.'

I was confusing him. Now I was talking about horrible, shameful things that should stay hidden. Before I had been telling him that it was okay to love whoever you want. My analogy translated as a threat.

He got up. 'Yeah. Sorry.' I heard my own mood in his voice: impatient, without conviction.

I drank instant coffee with Anastassia in the classroom overlooking the basketball court. Kirsty was unhooking the rope lanes she'd pegged up for sprint races, tugging down her skirt as it ballooned in the breeze.

The lines across Anastassia's forehead were deep grooves that dashed across her skin. Her daughter had the flu but Anastassia hadn't stayed home to look after her because she was afraid of how it would look if she wasn't in class. She'd been elected delegate during a statewide pay campaign but she had just recovered from an ulcer and had told me her husband thought she was insane for putting herself at the forefront of the struggle to keep the school open.

She was drinking a Big M from the canteen. She was a short woman who carried extra weight around her hips and belly. Her build was motherly but her voice was gravelly and I often heard her telling off students in her mathematics class, even through the closed door. Her sense of humour was deadpan and occasionally dirty, and I guessed I giggled at the wrong moments when she told jokes to us at lunch.

We sat on a bench under the canopy of a huge tree. 'I nearly exploded this morning,' I told her. 'They were being toxic little bullies. I almost swore at them, told them to give up, get out, go home.'

She clucked. 'Wish they'd bring back corporal punishment.'

When I started I had heard rumours that Anastassia had smacked a child.

'Joke. Everybody has those days.' She was unperturbed, scowling into the middle distance.

'Not Kirsty,' I said.

'She's joined up.'

We watched Kirsty talk to a boy who'd lost his sneakers; he was standing in bare feet, crying. 'She's incredibly pissed off with Tom,' Anastassia told me.

'But unions are so *out of date*.' I recalled her objections.

She nudged me, grinning, holding out a piece of a paper. 'Have a look at this. From the staff noticeboard.'

I took the document.

'Read Tom's unilateral policy. We're not allowed to talk about it in class.'

'What?'

'The school closing, the public meeting, any of it. He'll address assembly but we're not to discuss it with the kids.' She made a sour face, copied Tom. 'It sows confusion if staff speculate about facts they can't possibly prove.'

'Oops. I think I've already done that today.'

'Delightful, isn't it? No discussion, no attempts to include the staff. But now Kirsty's enraged. That's Tom's problem. She swallowed all the honour and trust and teamwork he peddled, hated the idea of industrial action, and now she feels betrayed.'

'I went and spoke to him yesterday.'

'What for? Anything he promises you privately he should be willing to say in public.'

'He asked me to. But you were right; he's not going to speak out about the funding or us closing. He thinks we're ruining our chances of negotiating.'

She snorted. 'Actually, that's probably what the local organizer thinks. I know that a bunch of people on the State Branch do.'

'Because they think we can't win?'

Anastassia blew on her coffee cup. 'Pick your battles.' Her singsong imitation made me think of Louise and the way she was able to copy the intonations of politicians and TV characters.

'They haven't even offered us anything.'

Anastassia stood up. 'They will.'

'What about the argument that by lumping in low-income kids, migrants, and teenagers with behavioural problems, we're creating a ghetto?'

'Did we create the demographic makeup of this suburb?' She turned back, accidentally sloshing coffee onto the ground.

'But if it comes up in the meeting?'

Anastassia laughed. 'Tom's not going to tell the parents he thinks their poverty and country of origin is giving the school a bad name, is he?'

I felt sick. 'Sorry. I just . . . things keep changing, shifting.' I didn't trust myself, and I was meant to be speaking at the meeting about my experiences and concerns as a teacher on contract.

'It's not as if they're trying to replace it with something better.' She paused. 'You should write out what you want to say tonight.'

'In case I get mixed up and forget which side I'm on?'

'By the way, your sister called this morning. She said ring back, it's about your brother.'

So much of the urgency about finding our mother had begun to slip away. At the beginning of the week, Louise had tried to access any legal change of name our mother had registered but the Office of Births, Deaths and Marriages wouldn't release any information. I'd located a single person out of the list of my mother's long-ago friends that Louise and I had drawn up, and then realized, when she answered the phone, that I didn't know what I expected from her, and so I'd hung up.

The hours when Jeremy was lost, after he'd skipped out on the exam, were a kind of vanished time. Maybe he'd hidden. Louise thought he had been beaten up by boys from school.

He used to line Louise's dolls up for her when her friends came over to play, set up the toys for tea parties, hoping to be part of the game. The year I'd given him Lego for Christmas, funded by my mother, he'd hugged me so much I'd toppled over.

I hadn't told Sarah we were looking for our mother. Yet I'd found a new kindness with Louise. When I told her about Jon, her voice had soared. She had reassured me: 'You have to admit he looked a bit like a ferret.' If she came home late I tried not to ask her where she'd been, or to worry when phone messages from people I'd never met collected on the machine. I let the evenings

I used to spend with Jon pass drinking too much and playing backgammon with my sister.

Louise had taken some objects we'd kept of Jeremy's – the space project, the player's tokens of the detective kit – and was gluing them into a giant collage. She pasted these directly onto canvas tacked on the wall. My flat was littered with her things: apple cores lolled next to pillows on the floor, sneakers with worn soles went forgotten on the balcony.

I returned her call in the staffroom where Kirsty and Deirdre were sharing lunch.

'Hello?'

'It's Alice.'

'Can you come home?'

'No.'

'Yes you can.'

'I've got a staff meeting after school and a bunch of stuff to do. Aren't you meant to be at that job trial?'

'I'll come into your school. These documents came back. The ones about us. I'm not feeling good.'

'Louise, *I can't*; I've got to work.' I kept my voice down, spoke into the wall. 'It will look really bad if I leave now when I'm speaking tonight. I'm meant to be representing the position for contract teachers. Did you try for the job or not?'

'It disturbs them to discover I don't know the difference between pumpkin bread and pumpernickel bread or silverbeet and silverside, or salami and mild salami.'

'Silverbeet is a vegetable,' I volunteered.

'Piss off Alice.'

But as I put down the phone I thought of Louise pacing the flat, compulsively rifling through the paperwork gathering in her plastic bag of misery, inciting herself to some new incarnation of the danger game.

'Kirsty, can I borrow you?'

'Now?'

'Two secs, I promise.'

On the brick path next to the art room I asked her to cover my afternoon classes. The Year 7s were having a half-day because of school sports.

'When will you be back? Anastassia thinks you're helping to plan. And Tom's called a staff meeting beforehand.'

I fixed my eyes on the pretty vintage broach pinned to her lapel and tried not to show how embarrassed I was. Instead, I gushed. 'Kirsty, you'd be a total lifesaver. I'll be on time for the evening meeting.'

She hesitated. 'It might look a bit unreliable.'

I didn't say anything.

'Can do, but you'll need to tell him yourself.'

Tom opened the door to his office abruptly, talking on his mobile, and holding a mug of tea in his hand. He waved me in. There was a bright green school calendar up on the wall. A big ornate jug he'd been given as a gift from a parent was displayed on the shelf. Various out-of-date certificates and nominations for awards were pinned on the noticeboard. I sat on the cold vinyl couch. Tom's work was spread across the desk in mounds. The grey carpet was lifting away from the floor in the corners of the room. Sometimes this room reminded me of a dishevelled private investigator's office.

'Gotta go, Therese, I've got someone with me. Okay. I will. Bye now.' He put the phone down on the desk, sat opposite me.

'Sorry, Tom, I need to go home. Kirsty said she could take this afternoon's classes.'

'Kirsty was here at the crack of dawn to set up.'

I nodded, clasped my hands together. 'It's a family thing.'

'I've been very distressed, very tense, about these recent events.' He turned pages in the diary on his desk. There was low-level panic in his voice. 'The way I see it, this school's at the end of the road.' He struggled to find the appropriate clichés. 'We've done good things, useful things, but the momentum is gone.' He nodded to himself. 'Whatever the outcome, Alice, you'll still be expected to fulfil your responsibilities to the school.'

Tom took off his reading glasses. 'How have you found your time here?'

'In what way?'

'Do you feel I've been fair to you, you've been supported enough?'

'I do.' This was half true.

Tom rifled in his drawer and drew out a packet of biscuits and pushed them towards me. 'I hope you've considered the realities of what's happening carefully.'

I crunched on a ginger nut. 'Tom, I have accumulated sick leave. I can go home.'

'Of course, of course. Kirsty can do it. *I* can even step in.' He was puzzled, benign. 'I just want to be completely transparent about this. You are in a difficult position but if there's an easy transition, *if*, then I hope you'll be transferred, or at least recommended with good references and given priority for upcoming vacancies. My concern is that there's a lack of reality in the union's response. Dig your heels in and hope for the best.'

I ate another biscuit.

His hands were shaking. 'It is so demoralizing to see people you've taught with for years, staff you've hired, assume you're malevolent, to be treated as the enemy.'

'What are your own plans?' I asked at the door.

'I haven't decided yet. Not thinking that far ahead.'

Back at the flat, Louise had papers spread across the table. She was wearing an old striped singlet she'd found in the back of my wardrobe, grubby yellow Converse sneakers, and a short black and green kilt. The bones of her spine protruded as she leant forward. A trail of scrunched-up tissues was scattered around her. Cigarette butts had amassed in a rose-coloured saucer on the bench.

'Shit. I'm afraid. I'm afraid.' Her eyes were shining darkly. She started pacing.

I dragged a chair over to the table. 'Lou.' Her lips were trembling amphetamine-fast. On the top of the mass of paper I saw a letter. Louise's freedom of information application had come back. Then I saw the social worker's report from after the fire.

And where had she gone, the sister I knew, so shiny and pointy-edged and brimming with stories?

I lit a cigarette myself. 'Will you make me a coffee?'

She went into the kitchen, turned on the tap, and opened and closed cupboard doors. She dropped the coffeepot on the tiles, where it bounced and spun.

'Forget it. Where's the bottle of gin?' I put my arms around her and breathed in the smell of her hair.

'He nearly went to jail.'

'Dad?'

'Yeah. Criminal negligence. The police report's all blacked out but that's what it looks like.'

I unscrewed the gin bottle and found some ancient orange juice in the bottom of the cupboard. Bits of pulp floated on the surface like debris in a river. I got a glass for Louise. 'Here; have.'

She raised her glass, toasted the air. 'A pardon, Pandora.' She reached across for my packet. 'I think this occasion calls for yet another cigarette.' The jauntiness was familiar. It was my own. Our camouflages, our hidden selves, were becoming visible to each other.

I sorted through the pages. The coroner's report said 'accidental death by asphyxiation'. There were notes from Community Services interviews with my father but the detail of these had been blacked out. Reports from inspections of the public housing unit we'd moved into were as revealing as shopping lists. There was even a psychiatric report on Louise from when she commenced the methadone program, and a note that some of her Centrelink file was exempt from freedom of information claims.

The past seemed simply a litter of documents on the public record, reports and debts stretching back in a line of fluttering flags that led nowhere.

'What's that smell?'

'It's fine, it's fine.' Toast was burning under the grill. 'I'm making you lunch, Al.' She tossed the burnt bread into the bin. 'When you die of asphyxiation I think your lungs collapse. Do you think you would feel your skin burning or would you be unconscious?'

'Unconscious.'

She hugged herself. 'I felt it. Like my skin was melting. It hurt more later.'

I unfolded the social worker's report.

Counselling report DHS & CS. CASE # 3353, Meeting 2

Summary:
Louise appears to be sheltering herself from the reality of her brother's recent death by assuming roles and playing out desires and fancies. Her playfulness belies a deep injury. She refuses to discuss her brother's death except by inventing quite convincing and detailed stories, which she then almost immediately undermines. She does appear to be getting some solace from the fantasies she is creating, though when this collapses she may well struggle. Although Louise is impulsive, at this stage she is controlling her negative instincts, albeit by strategies of projection and denial. She exhibits attention-seeking behaviour but is noticeably uncomfortable when pressed deeper about her feelings and reactions to trauma, including her own physical injuries. Louise appears to envy her older sister's equilibrium. Alice describes her sister as highly imaginative, demanding and extremely social. When complex questions are asked of Louise she tends to slip into the voice and mannerisms of a much younger child. Throughout our interview she consistently changed the subject and 'phased out'. When encouraged to use other engagement devices – drawing, role-playing – she becomes hostile ('you are annoying me' and 'don't be dumb').

During the first session, I interviewed both girls together and then separately after speaking with their mother, who was sedated. Louise has already been kept down a grade, and may have been deliberately under-performing as a defensive strategy. Louise was extremely imaginative and able to master quite sophisticated abstract concepts well beyond her age-level.

The most significant element of Louise's self-description is the dissonance between her own self-image (her idea of her own qualities and faults) and the reality. She claims, for example, to be an outstanding student and a mime artist.

As the interview is concluding, Louise says she loves her brother but also that she thinks he is coming back. She does not explain further but it appears she assumes his death will be found to be a misunderstanding or a trick and that he will return. She tells me, when I speak with her alone, without her older sister, that she is waiting for him. Grief reactions of this kind are common in the early stages of bereavement.

Alice presents as an extremely sober teenager, who is nervous about the perils of adult existence even as she tries to shield her father and sister from criticism. She is extremely hostile to authority figures. She declares, upon entering the interview room, that she doesn't want to be taken away and that she wants to keep living with her parents. She expresses a fear that the entire family is now dependent on her and cites Louise as a source of her anxiety. Alice seems naturally a quieter and more solitary character who has developed an assertive and forceful side as a survival strategy. Alice feared questions about money, repairs to the home, living arrangements, and so on. While both children had normal physical and social development, Alice shows certain signs of immaturity for her age; for example, she finds it difficult to articulate the fact that she had met a boy at the park when her brother was missing, although this may be connected with her sense of hyper-responsibility. (She blurts out 'I don't have to tell you' when I ask her why she finds this hard to talk about.)

Although more cooperative than Louise, Alice becomes silent when I ask about her neighbours' claim that her father drinks often. Alice agrees her parents often argue about money but doesn't expand on this. She seems to be replicating some of her mother's coping strategies, such as stoicism and defensiveness. Louise identified more with her father; Alice, increasingly with her mother's position. When asked if she is generally happy at home Alice told me: 'My brother's dead.'

While I do not detect any immediate risk of self-harm with either child, Alice may be prone to depression. Her strategies of detachment are quite disturbing. In my professional opinion Louise is a likely candidate for truancy, and potentially liable to engage in risk-taking behaviours. The suspicion towards institutional involvement from welfare agencies appears to have been passed down from the girls' parents. Also, there is much shame and fear involved in talking about the family dynamic, which makes it hard to assess or support these children.

Both felt in some way responsible for their brother's death. Alice had encouraged her brother not to return home the night he died, and Louise expressed a belief that she had induced him to engage in risky behaviour through a particular game. When asked whether their brother was usually supervised and if he was ever allowed to use chemicals when on his own, Alice has said yes and Louise said she didn't understand the question.

While neither child expressed this overtly, there were some indications of a history of family violence. In any case, the home life has been highly dysfunctional and socio-economically deprived. Regular counselling support is recommended, as their circumstances are crisis ones. Subsequent casework should include further interviews with teachers, parents, and a visit to the family's new home, once it is established.

Recommendations: Regular monitoring of home environment and school attendance; approach mother/father (guardians) regarding continued counselling and bereavement support.

Removal/state care: Not at present, subject to outcome of police investigations. Guardianship claim may be made by grandparents.
Legal caveats: No, subject to interrogatory requests if police investigation results in prosecution.

Casework status: Open/ongoing.

Louise read over my shoulder. 'Highly imaginative. That's me. Why do you get called sober?'

'Hang on.' At the bottom of the page were some handwritten notes. *Suicidal thoughts. Preventable accidental death. Fear of injuring children. Missed work days. (Husband unemployed.) Disturbed sleep.*

There our mother was in the traces, in the tacked-on lines at the end of someone else's story, thinking about dying.

She had left behind so little in the new unit we'd been allocated after the fire: her work uniform hanging on a hook behind the door, her last pay stuffed into the pocket of my father's pants, a worn-down lipstick lolling in a handbag.

I remembered Louise being dragged to the social worker's office, done up in a scratchy cardigan and too-big boots that had been donated from a local charity, crying and pretending she didn't know us. Dad had thought it would make a good impression but Louise wanted to wear what she called her own clothes, systematically nicked from major department stores.

Now Louise puffed out her chest. 'God, that social worker. Tell me how you're feeling, *in here*,' she echoed and patted her chest with a fist. 'We were under investigation to see if someone was going to be charged with a crime and she's prattling with do-gooder determination, promising that if we let out our feelings like slugs into the garden we'll be better.'

'She was a monster.' I had a vague impression of a young woman with sharp eyes and a glossy bob, carrying a clipboard. 'What was she called?' The name had been removed from the document.

'Janice.'

I drank more gin and juice. I felt dizzy as the memories fell like ash from the fire. 'That night, I had fucked some boy from school in the park. That's why I didn't want to answer her.'

'Fuck.' She grinned uneasily. 'Did you really do that?'

I put out my cigarette. 'Why didn't they tease you the way they teased him?'

'He was weird. He was embarrassing. They thought he was a snob, that he looked down on them. I didn't care what they said about me and I wasn't afraid.'

There was my brother: drawing maps of Africa, tracing the continents of the world on butcher's paper at the kitchen table. I saw his awkward left-hand grip on the pen, his legs not reaching the ground and dangling strangely beneath the chair, the humming song he'd made up for himself, sleepy and tuneless.

'Do you dream about Mum?' Louise asked me, standing at the window, watching cars flash past.

'No.'

Louise used to sit on the warm footpath outside the new flat waiting for Mum to arrive at our new home, chalking hopscotch patterns onto the road.

'Do you?' I asked.

'Nah, I dream about him.'

'Dying?'

'Just, him. I thought he'd been murdered that night. I thought he'd been thrown in a ditch somewhere because Dad forgot to pick him up.'

I could see the shape of her collarbones under her singlet. Her arms were sinewy and frail.

'Although . . . I dreamed she visited me when I went back to hospital for the skin graft on my arm. After she'd left. But I don't reckon she would have, do you? To go away and to stay away you'd have to draw some kind of line. There'd be things you couldn't ever think about.'

'I think we have to stop this.'

Louise sat stiffly. 'This conversation or the search?'

'It's not a search; it's not anything. We know he's dead. She's fucked up, she fucked off, it's gone.'

'I tried to make him play the danger game, Alice. You remember, I never even waited to see him go into the test.'

I felt desolate but also strangely sullen and light-headed. 'I'm sorry.'

'Did you see the report from after she left? The notes about Dad?'

I looked at the pages but there were too many black lines across names and other privileged material.

At first he'd rung the police, wanting her on the Missing Persons list, before he saw that some photographs salvaged from the fire had been taken. Then she'd rung a few weeks later and told him she wouldn't return, that he should stop looking for her. Louise had written our mother a letter and posted it to our grandparents' farm more than a decade ago. It hadn't been returned or replied to. We hadn't known she had called. Dad had never told us.

They'd asked him to promise we'd get to school and that he'd do anger management programs and report to them regularly; otherwise we'd be taken away, put in foster care. He must have threatened them with disputes in the courts, though, because the handwritten comments were full of anxiety and suggestions for tying his Centrelink payments to our school attendance.

When I lit the stove for coffee I thought of Jeremy, alone in the cold, damp house and full of dread, lighting the stove to make tea for Mum and Dad, or poking a bit of burning newspaper through to light the faulty pilot light for the heater in the living room.

Our house had burned so quickly, collapsing like a plastic bag under a flame, melting in on itself.

That night, after the fire, Mum had been feverish, brutal, washing our clothes in the tiny bathroom sink of the motel room we'd been given, unable to really look at me, pulling open the curtains and then yanking them shut. After he came back from visiting Louise in hospital, Dad slept in the bed, moaning in his sleep. Mum and I slept on the floor, her body curled away from me, her fingers clasped together, rigid, like a snap-frozen prayer, through the night.

'Alice?' Louise had stopped shaking. She was reading a document, grasping it firmly. 'Did we see our grandparents?'

'Her parents?'

'Yeah.'

'Sort of. We visited once. Mum took us to their farm. It took hours.' The flat paddocks had stretched out in all directions as far as I could see. Everywhere there was dry dust, cows. I had not liked the country. I took the coffee to the table and handed a cup to my sister. 'You were too young.'

'From what's written here, I bet they tried to make a deal with Dad for them to look after us. So we wouldn't be wards of the state if the police laid charges or they took us off him. They wrote a letter.'

I drank the hot black liquid, inhaling the bitter steam rising from my cup. I had a vague memory of a tin shed that smelled of fertilizer, adjacent to the dirt road that ran beside their house, and a hallway with worn pale green carpet – but they were the sorts of scenes that might not even be real memories, but dreams, or other people's descriptions. I couldn't recall my grandparents.

I rifled through the documents. There were notes on how clean our house was, what was in the fridge, our health. Interviews we'd assumed were counselling sessions that had actually been assessments. The grandparents our mother had cut contact with for years were put forward as temporary custodial guardians but then backed out. Our father had fought to keep us out of foster care for almost a year after the police investigation had finished. Judging from the letters back and forth, not losing us had been a kind of full-time job for him. He had never told us.

Louise snatched a cigarette from my packet. 'So.'

'So?' I felt my fingers slip on my cup.

The breeze brought the smell of warm croissants from the bakery as I rushed to meet Sarah. I was late. I wanted her advice on what to say at the meeting that evening. My bag was stuffed full of pamphlets, union minutes, and the mail, which I hadn't had time to open.

I saw Sarah while I was crossing the road. She was near the counter of the café, her hands in her pockets, back slumped a little, her face soft. I pushed open the door, which was decorated with red ribbons and tiny silver bells that clinked together when it swung closed behind me.

Sarah hugged me and we sat on the fat pink couch near the window, beside a plastic orange lamp. In the warm circle of light her hair was feathery and her skin glowed pale brown. 'Oomph.' I sighed and made a face. 'Sorry I'm so late.'

'You look weary.'

Sarah and I had still not had the chance to talk properly. She'd promised to help me prepare, and now I had missed the union strategy meeting. I thought of the spreading staining mess of my family, of my own harsh dismissals, the careful signature of my dad on legal papers, and I nearly wept. 'How many things have you done in your life that you completely regret? That you think made you a blacker, crueller person?'

'Including saying you look weary?'

I didn't smile.

She shifted her bag down onto the ground. 'A few.' There was an anxious silence. 'What's wrong, darling?'

Sarah ordered fruit and vegetables every week from a farmer's market. They were delivered to her door in a cardboard box. She went for walks along the Maribyrnong River. She wanted me to take care of myself. I wanted her to comfort me but I felt my eyes sting, my face grow hot. She'd worry and pick at my decision to help look for my mother so I didn't mention it. 'I just need to get ready for this thing.'

She shrugged a shoulder. Her red lipstick was bright against her teeth. 'Give us a look at your speech then.'

Before I handed the draft to her, I charged into the next topic. 'Are you going well?'

'I am not. They shifted me into intensive care for two weeks because we're understaffed. I drove piece-of-shit from the other side of the city.' Sarah had taken to thinking up new names for her car.

'You're lovely to do this for me.'

She lifted her chin. 'I had a date this week.'

'You don't go on dates.' My voice was too loud. 'Who with?'

'This guy, Andy, in his forties. I'm doing Spanish classes with him.'

'Any good?'

'Lovely. But Star Trek geek.'

'Oh.' Sarah was trying to be pleasant, but I knew she was angry with me because I'd been so late, and now I was angry too, but I didn't know why.

Sarah said, 'I hope I can help you. I'm probably not the best person to ask: I'm hopeless at public speaking.'

I handed her my speech. 'You've got more experience at it than I do.'

'The union stuff is exhausting, isn't it? Trying to keep your balance while the politics shift this way and then that. There were days when we were campaigning for a pay rise, when I first started nursing – there'd be mass meetings; I'd have to nick into the toilets for a cry before I'd go back to it.' She laughed. 'Mostly frustration. You need a thick skin.'

I pinched myself gleefully. 'Fortunately I have one of those.' When I'd told Sarah about the report and the public meeting she'd been so quiet on the phone I'd wondered if it was all decided already and I was the only one who didn't realize. 'But I missed the preparation meeting in the afternoon.'

She straightened out the pages, licked her finger, and sifted through them. Her face was clear but I saw a line of tension in her neck.

Soup arrived for Sarah. I ordered a cup of tea and a sandwich. 'You know, I leave the staffroom and then I eat the same food when I go out. Chronic failure of imagination.'

'Practise saying your speech to me,' Sarah said, as she kept reading my paper.

'Why did you get married?'

'I don't think that's a very good opening. Too personal.' Our laughter was weak.

Sarah had met her husband when he tried to sell her a stereo at

JB Hi-Fi. She became alien to me, as if in her old life she had been a piece of playdough, waiting for a man to come along and leave his impression, to make her into something new. We had not liked each other in those days.

'I was eighteen. I was full of shit. And deeply suburban. I wanted to be safe.' She exhaled heavily. 'So I tried to be a good wife down to the last pavlova recipe and free set of steak knives.' She smiled. 'Then I missed playing music and being a teenager. Except by then I was twenty-three.'

'I'm terrified Jon's wife will be at the meeting.' I didn't know whether Jon had told her he'd stopped seeing me.

She put her hand on mine. 'You're jittery. Breathe.'

I sucked in my breath and exhaled, exasperatedly, then lit a cigarette. Sarah thought I was paranoid.

'She can't be that high up in the bureaucracy; she sounds like a public servant dogsbody. And you told me that report covered eight schools.'

I took a drag. 'Mmm.'

She looked pleased with herself. 'Where does that leave Jon?'

'We split up.'

She put her hand on my arm. 'Good for you. I thought he was a wanker but I'm sure he didn't know about your school.'

'How could he not know?'

Sarah shrugged. 'If they didn't talk. Or didn't talk about *you*.' She slurped her soup. 'Not talking keeps many marriages alive.'

'Now I'm dreaming about him. He's about to declare his love for me and then some *stunning* woman appears and she's all of twenty-two and just before they walk off together he says mournfully, "Sorry, Alice, I thought you knew. I thought you realized."'

Sarah was unsettled. 'You should have told me. I would have come around and looked after you, fed you Barbecue Shapes and Ribena.'

'Why did you leave Greg?'

'Alice, I married someone who used to make me scrapbooks of cooking recipes as *presents*.'

'But what made you finally decide?'

'I don't know.' She was smiling faintly, as though remembering a pleasant occasion in the long-distant past she had forgotten until now, like a birthday celebration with paper hats and bowls of punch. 'It feels so long ago.'

'It is.'

'Anyway, Jon's married. Why do you care how many other women there are?'

'In my dream, as soon as I see him, there's this incredible sense of rightness. I see I've had this longing for him to appear.'

'I guess the dream's not really about Jon.'

I chewed on the sandwich, which oozed butter and cheese and was garnished with some limp parsley. 'You should have done psych. Yeah, dream's about alligators. And World War Two fighter pilots.' The bitterness in my voice was rancid. She was my oldest friend. I thought of acid peeling paint off a cabinet, eating away at skin.

Sarah's hands were pressed firmly together in her lap and the knuckles were white.

She went back to my draft. 'You're very thorough.'

I gulped some tea. 'There's a lot of data on schools and disadvantage in low-income areas.'

'It reads more like a briefing paper.'

My hands were shaking. 'Too much material?'

Sarah twisted her hair around her finger. 'If your school rep is speaking she'll probably cover some of this. Certainly the state organizer would.'

'I thought it would seem more authoritative.'

She looked at me carefully. 'It's good, Alice. But who are you trying to convince?'

I wriggled in my seat.

'If the new funding profile's been passed, the department's decided and nothing you say will make any difference. It's not a lack of information, or the right information, that's behind their decision.'

'Who do you think I should be focusing on?'

'Really, you're talking to the parents and the other teachers, trying to get them passionate about fighting for the school. So you don't have to be so impersonal and measured. Speak about what the school's meant to you, how vulnerable you feel as a teacher on contract, that sort of jazz.'

I swished the tea leaves at the bottom of my cup around glumly. 'Seems a bit fake.'

'Does it?'

'Often I hate teaching.'

'So why do you care?'

I didn't answer. It was almost time to set up for the meeting. 'What's it about then? My dream?'

She packed her things into her leather handbag. Sarah had long been a hoarder and her bags usually bulged with an assortment of random objects: tissues, scraps of paper and old tickets, books. 'I don't know.' She smiled but did not look at me directly. 'With Lou here I suppose you might have been thinking about your mother.'

I couldn't think of any answer.

'How's Lou-Loubelle?'

I'd forgotten that our mother used to call her that. 'What made you think of that?'

'Louie? I've hardly heard from you since she arrived. She's not still using?'

'Don't think so. She's working in a café. Not that the two are mutually exclusive.' Sarah gave me another half-smile. 'I meant what made you think of the nickname. Mum used to call her that. Do you remember my mother?'

'Not that well. I only met her a few times. She had really tiny wrists and she made crap kid jokes. She kept telling Lou to calm down. I'd like to see old Lou. You should invite me over.'

'I'll make dinner.' Fear fluttered like a heartbeat. 'Actually, I'm looking for Mum too.'

Sarah buried her surprise in pushing her keys back into her bag. 'And if you find her, what happens then?'

'Louise' – my cough was hacking – 'Louise says Mum must know more about the day Jeremy died.'

'What sort of thing?'

'I don't know.'

'Why does she think that?'

I waved the speech at her. 'I'll go and redo this.'

The last fifteen minutes before the public meeting were tinged with a dispiriting irony. Putting out jugs of water and paper cups with Kirsty, arranging Monte Carlo biscuits on trays and unstacking chairs, it almost felt as if we were preparing for a school fundraiser or parent-teacher night.

Anastassia was back in the staffroom talking to the state organizer about tactics. While I'd rewritten my speech, I'd missed the union planning meeting and Anastassia had clucked at me to 'stop being so *flittery*,' in a scolding, bemused voice that reminded me of my Catholic grandmother correcting me when I'd forgotten the words to hymns.

The Minister's contact had arrived in a wide, gleaming car and was dressed for a photo opportunity in blue jeans and a 'support PUBLIC education' T-shirt.

Tom was writing out name tags for the speakers and scrambling to greet people as they arrived. There was a sallow greyness to his skin and he wrung his hands slowly, turning them in the careful, repetitive fashion of someone kneading dough to make bread. His wife clung to his side. She tried to smile and nod at parents as if Tom were a presidential candidate and she the first lady in waiting. I felt a pang of sympathy for her. She had put on mascara, and her silk blouse looked new.

People crowded in, scraping chairs on the wooden floor of the assembly room and fanning away the smells of kids' feet with the union statement we'd placed on the chairs. The sounds of chatting gave way to the anxious silence that institutional buildings invite.

Anastassia introduced me to the union organizer who was a chunky man in his early thirties. 'Ned knows the department guy, says he's pretty low down in the scheme of things. Won't make any promises or statements beyond what they've already given.'

Ned shook my hand. 'Mmm. They're cagey. It's not a closure; it's a reprioritization. No firm decisions have been made yet.'

Anastassia grinned. 'It's not an arsehole, it's just a . . .' We took our seats on the stage. She squeezed my hand. 'Good luck, Alice.'

I looked at my watch, my heart beating fiercely. It was starting. Tom got up on the stage and welcomed everyone. There were more than a hundred people in the room. I saw Sarah find a seat up the back and wave at Louise who was sitting behind her. Sweat gathered under my arms, trickling down my back. Tom spoke first.

'I can't tell you how difficult it is to see you all here under these circumstances. I began working here, as some of you will know, as the head of science twelve years ago, before I took on the role of principal, which I'm still in. That's long enough for me to have seen two entire generations travel through our school from Year 7 to Year 12. I've seen students arrive as new migrants with barely two words of English and leave with places at university. Throughout my guardianship at this school I've been indebted to, in a hundred different ways, the support and skill of the teaching staff, who I'd like to thank.

'I've seen your sons and daughters learn and triumph, go on to apprenticeships, to trades, to professions, to tertiary study, and to excel not only as students or workers but also as *people,* young adults who've learnt how to be generous, how to contribute, how to participate, how to be kind to each other.' He sounded like a Democratic presidential candidate.

'But in recent years the school has faced hardship. We've seen enrolments fall; we've seen increased problems with drugs, petty theft, truancy. So, of late, the road has been difficult and it hasn't always been clearly marked. Some of you have spoken to me personally about these challenges. As you know, the school's results and new enrolments aren't sufficient to meet the current funding profile, the minimum standards for increased and ongoing support.

'My own opinion is that it's time for a fresh approach, to consider moving *this* community back into the broader education community. There's a larger public secondary school with greater resources than we have here that could accommodate our students. And I know the department's set aside a grant for relocation to make that possible for those of you who don't have the finances to pay for new books and uniforms, if that's what eventuates.'

Next to me Anastassia hissed, 'nice bribe,' and was shushed by the union organizer.

'It's tempting to see the learning process as belonging to, or limited to, a particular school or set of teachers or learning environment. And we should value each of these things. But I believe it's the *whole* community of learning, of committed staff and engaged students – not one particular school – where teaching and student welfare and growth can be protected and promoted.

'I know there has been too much confusion circulating. Today, more than anything, I'm here as a facilitator so that you as parents and members of this community feel consulted, involved and considered. If you have questions, they'll be answered. If you have objections, they'll be recorded and, more than that, heard. So I appreciate your patience and your time tonight.'

There was a long pause. Parents nodded, one or two even clapped. The question had begun forming, though, in their crinkled foreheads and half-raised hands: what did he mean? I'd underestimated Tom as a simple man searching for a quiet retreat, the simplest exit strategy out of a conflict. He'd managed to reassure the audience without clarifying anything for them and I couldn't reconcile this person with the man who'd chatted to me about football all through lunch on my first day at work, the man who'd given me time off to visit Louise the last time she was a chronic user and who'd spoken of his nephew who was in Barwon prison for drug dealing. Even as I waited to speak I almost expected him to change his mind, to speak passionately about saving the school.

Anastassia seemed small on the gaping stage. She held the microphone too close with broad, blunt hands and spoke too close to it, so that her voice was both amplified and distorted. She spoke about a lack of transparency and consultation. She talked too quickly, in a throaty, slightly accented tone. As she got more incensed her words grew longer and louder until they approached a wail. I saw Ned, the union organizer, cross his legs, look at the floor, flip open his mobile phone.

Anastassia talked about the importance of job security for

effective teaching, and how you could not put a price on the value of education. She said that she'd always been proud of how the school had taken up the particular needs of migrant students and those from low socio-economic backgrounds. The audience shuffled. Anastassia talked about how our class sizes were still large, the huge proportion of students with literacy and learning difficulties we encountered, how more prestigious schools with lower enrolments in wealthier areas remained open, and why she considered the new funding profile unjust, targeting schools in poorer areas while exempting those that were already well-resourced. Sarah had been right about information: it cluttered the assembly hall like old furniture. The room was too hot and the tight black cotton dress I was wearing rubbed against the back of my neck, the tag irritating my skin. I felt light-headed already and wondered what Jon was doing this Wednesday evening – if he was with his wife, if they knew the meeting was happening.

Anastassia cleared her throat and took a piece of paper from her pocket. 'What we at the Education Union would like to know *today* is whether the school is being closed down or not, and will you make a commitment to keeping it open at least until the end of the year?' She stepped away from the microphone to a scattering of applause like light rain on the roof. Her question sounded defeatist, but then I'd missed the meeting to discuss what points we wanted the union to raise on our behalf.

Tom invited the departmental representative to answer the question. The man stood up. 'I don't think we're in a position to make any guarantees. My recommendation would be for the school to close voluntarily in a timely way so that we can resettle students. But I'll get to that in a moment.'

It had taken me an hour to get dressed. The decision about what to wear was inflected, strangely, by a sense of special occasion, as though I was preparing for a court appearance or a wedding. I'd chosen a black A-line dress, and polished my shoes. I felt unrehearsed. I had let my caution and control slip. I guessed I'd been rubbing at my eyes and that my mascara and liner were smudged onto my cheeks. Had I worn too much makeup?

My hands were shaking. Even my knees were trembling. Tom introduced me, ushered me towards the front of the stage with an arm hovering near the small of my back. For a moment, looking at the neat patterns of the chairs, the puzzled faces of parents and staff, I felt nothing other than the magnificent sweep of embarrassment. My speech was probably elevated and pretentious.

The Minister's representative was signalling to someone at the back of the hall: *five minutes*. The meeting felt like a set piece.

But I spoke. I read out the amount of money given to the private system and then the names of public schools that received the most funding in the state and the annual average income of families in the surrounding areas and then listed the locations of the poorest schools in the state. I gave examples of schools in wealthy areas with low enrolments that weren't under threat of closure. I said the suggestion of closure was irrational and ideological, that it was writing off students who came from less advantaged backgrounds, that the school had an irreplaceable culture and ability to assist students from non-English-speaking backgrounds.

I paused. When I looked up, the Minister's representative was making notes. People were listening. 'We keep hearing that our results aren't competitive, that we don't retain enough students in the final years of school. Some people think you have to run public services the way you marshal an army: send reinforcements to the side that's winning and if there are soldiers struggling on another front, well, you have to go where the results are and they'll learn to fend for themselves.' My militaristic comparison felt off-key, absurd, but I took a deep breath.

'Privately our principal has told me that he worries we're a self-fulfilling prophecy: seen as a school with a bad name, the place drop-outs go, and that we can end up replicating that culture. But *I* think pouring millions of dollars into schools in the wealthiest areas of the entire state ensures a self-fulfilling prophecy of another kind and starving schools in low-income areas of the funds to help them make the changes to *increase* their enrolments is self-fulfilling.' In my peripheral vision, Tom sat straight and did not look at me.

'Between last year and this year, how much did our enrolments fall by? Does anybody want to guess?' I saw Sarah smiling. 'Four students. There were four students less. The year before we had exactly the same number of students. And that's the so-called crisis in enrolments.'

I'd drafted a new section about my brother and poverty and my childhood but I didn't want to read it aloud. I bumped the microphone. I could see Tom preparing to come forward and introduce the next speaker. I took a step forward so I was directly under the fluorescent lights.

'I do feel vulnerable as a teacher on contract who doesn't have any job security.' I tried to explain how much living in poverty taught you that you had almost no control over what happened in the world, that you shouldn't expect too much, that you had to learn to be 'realistic', to settle for what you had, to do without – that I wanted what happened to our school to help break these ideas, not reinforce them. I didn't read the section that mentioned Jeremy. 'I said that closing the school would be making our students' and their families' lives invisible. Ignore it and it will go away. I didn't read the section that mentioned how the shame of poverty could be unbearable, the way it was for Jeremy.' I finished all of a sudden in the middle of a thought, like a cassette tape ejected from a car stereo.

I sat down, giddy with relief. Anastassia patted me softly on the thigh.

'And I'm sure Alice is aware that I will personally ensure no one is penalized in any way whatsoever for expressing their point of view on this, which is the properly legal position,' Tom spoke quickly.

The Department of Education speaker was introduced as Graeme Michaelson. I barely listened until he began correcting me, talking about how the new funding arrangements weren't calculated purely on the basis of enrolments but a combination of enrolments, results, program delivery and retention rates. He threw around figures of millions of dollars of government funding to the state sector and talked about 'self-starting' schools versus 'unviable' schools, about the solutions that already existed if the school closed at the end of term. Tom stood to the side, flustered, while Graeme called me disingenuous since 'enrolments over a five-year period have collapsed drastically and were already well below the state average.' When he summed up, much of his aggression had dissipated. He repeated: 'No one's being forced to do anything here, folks, this is a consultation. But next year these guidelines will come into effect. Regardless of what happens now, reduction in funding is what happens next. That's the decision of this government and it flows through to the school.'

Hands were raised and waved like stalks of wheat in a breeze.

'This sounds like doubletalk. If you're so good at teaching English, speak it.'

'Why don'tcha have a parent up there?' This was followed by Selena's mother giving a short and very loud speech in Greek and English – and then a thin Vietnamese parent, who I'd never met, wearing a pale anorak and synthetic jogging shoes, started reading painfully from a slip of paper and asking if the kids had done something to cause the closure, if they had done something wrong.

After more questions, at the end of the meeting, I saw several parents I knew talking near the door.

I climbed down from the stage slowly and made my way up the back to Sarah and Louise. My cheeks were warm and adrenaline rushed through me. Parents I'd never met before came over and shook my hand, introducing themselves, or patting my arm quietly and nodding. 'You a good girl,' Selena's mother told me in a thick accent. 'Very strong.' I was flushed. Exuberant.

A journalist from the local newspaper took a quote from Tom and then spoke to Anastassia. It was impossible not to feel lifted up by the crowd of people, the conversational harmony of voices falling over one another, the clatter and shuffle of chairs on the plastic matting of the floor.

I dropped my bag. Two of the parents reached forward together to pick it up. We all laughed. The gentleness, the quiet elation, was catching. We had surprised ourselves. The press of bodies didn't feel suffocating, the way it often had on the tram, pressing in with the grim determination of people who wanted to be somewhere else. It was reassuring. We were all holding on together.

A couple of my students were mooching outside in the cold, looking caught out as if they'd walked into the over-thirties night at a local club but thought the only way to keep their dignity was to pretend they'd intended it all along.

Louise had donned cut-off shorts over orange tights the shade of a fluorescent highlighter. She rolled up her sleeves. Sarah hugged me.

Louise rolled her eyes. 'What a sleaze.'

'Tom? Unlikely.'

'Hasn't been fucked in a long time, I'd say.'

'Stop it.' But I was smiling.

'The bureaucrat was so macho he practically had his dick out.'

Sarah grabbed my wrist. 'It went really well. You managed to put our friend Graeme on the defensive.'

'Not too bad at all.'

'They'll call it "successful community consultation",' Lou announced. 'And vacuum up the good press. You gotta fuck them up, Alice, force their hand.' She was wound up.

I saw Sam near the entrance, trailing his older brother, who was pushing their mother in a wheelchair. She seemed sunken. Her skin emanated an odd, stained pallor, greyish yellow, almost jaundiced.

'What do you want to do now?'

Louise flicked her head. 'Gotta take a slash.'

I called after her, 'The toilets are round the front,' but she was already marching away.

'How're you going, Sam?'

'This is my mum, Miss, and Toby.'

Her hand was dry and cool when I took it. 'Thanks for coming. This is my friend Sarah.'

Toby had neatly cut nails and wore a thick silver ring on his middle finger. He was lightly tanned, relaxed. 'How do you think it went?'

'I was pleased so many parents spoke. It's hard to tell, really.'

'What happens now?'

'Scuse me, can you hold still for a sec?' The local journalist snapped a photograph of us and copied down our names.

Kirsty walked over and hugged me. When she said I was brave I tried not to flee.

'I took some photos of you speaking' – she held out her digital camera. 'I'd like to talk to you about all this' – she leaned in and flashed her eyes towards the ceiling – 'now that we're comrades.' She said the word with curious emphasis, drolly, and I wondered if she had a hidden gift for irony. I didn't speak to Tom.

We saw Lou sitting out the front after we'd struggled past all the parents. She grabbed a hip flask of brandy out of her pocket. 'Ta da!' I gulped some down. It wasn't the time to be cautious. I wanted to shake off all the bandages that held me: the stiffness and the unkindness. Tonight I wouldn't think about Jon or his wife's document or our dead brother. I took Louise and Sarah each by the hand. Louise was skipping and singing a song softly to herself.

I found myself at Sarah's place, drunk, and it was only eight-thirty in the evening. Louise had peeled off after we'd left the first pub, bored. I had sensed the nervous energy humming beneath her skin. I knew I should have gone home with her. She was still reading and re-reading the documents she'd been sent from Community Services. She wanted to talk about Jeremy and I did not. When she left she'd said, 'I wish you wouldn't *do* that, milk your little sob story in public. *You're* not being paid eight bucks an hour.'

Sarah made me tea and took warm scones from the oven. 'You did a good job, Alice.'

'Do I have your ex-husband's scrapbook to thank for these?'

'Everybody knows how to make scones.'

I made a face. 'Do they?'

'Want brandy in it?'

'Err . . . absolutely.' We drank our spiked tea. Birds fought in the fruit trees in Sarah's backyard. We stayed outside in the dusk, until the sun began to set.

We collapsed onto her bed. I felt the warm beat of her heart through her wrist, which was lying next to my side. I stretched and put my hands above my head. The ceiling was creamy like a suburban dessert: meringue, or cheesecake. I was drowsy from the setting sun and the scent of fresh washing. I leant over and accidentally jammed my face into her neck. We laughed and I kept my face buried in her skin, in the warm humanness of it. She started tickling me but I edged away. I touched her back, slowly, and traced her skin beneath the blouse, the dip near the spine, the broad arch of her lower back. The desire felt like falling, like fainting, but the vertigo was glorious. I had a flash of déjà vu: I was climbing the stairs behind Jon the first time we'd fucked, watching his hips and back, the heels of his sneakers. It meant the rush of lust was also painful, strung into the past and to loss. If I kissed her, there was no disguising what was happening.

Her mouth was warm and sweet. She tasted of cinnamon mints. I touched the skin on her face with the very tips of my fingers, and her neck. She ran the back of her hand along my side from my armpit to my hip. I wanted her to touch me, to fuck me. We kissed more deeply and I sucked her fingers. It was dazzling and terrifying to be in bed with her. Sarah took off my dress. The sensation of her hands on my breasts made yearning and delight sing in me. We lay side by side, Sarah licking and cupping my breasts while I put my fingers inside her, a thumb sliding against her clitoris, feeling her open and wet, juice flowing thick and warm. She breathed shallowly. 'Mmmm . . . Oh . . . Put your fingers all the way in . . . That's . . .' and then I felt the pulsing of her muscles as she came. I kissed her belly. Her skin tasted of salt.

The flesh on her hip was dimpled and tanned. I ran my hand over the pale stretch marks that gathered like broken lines on a map. Sarah flipped over and kissed my thighs. The anticipation was also trepidation. My heart thudded gigantically.

I couldn't remember what underwear I had on. I'd showered in a rush this morning. Flickers of self-consciousness broke through desire. When Sarah finally put her mouth on me I felt as if I were underwater, pushed forward by ripples and waves. Where had this sexual chemistry come from? I came, all of a sudden. I lay with my whole body tingling. But then I thought of Jon again.

I realized the CD we'd been playing was skipping and that the Smiths' woeful bleakness was looping in permanent longing and despair. *There is another world. There is a better world. There must be.* I reached to pull myself up. I rolled over and fell off the bed.

Sarah pulled on tracksuit pants and a thin cotton shirt, turned off the CD player and rolled a joint. We sat outside in the warm breeze, sharing it. I asked her, 'Have you done that before?'

'Sex? Never. Don't believe in it.'

'With a woman.'

'Why?' She looked at her feet. 'I don't like my toes. Because the second toe is longer than the big toe. It's mutant.'

'I don't like my toes because they're hairy. Look.' I waved my toes out.

'*You've* been having lots of sex. Who did you lose your virginity to?'

'I've told you.'

'No you didn't.' Sarah waited, took a drag on the joint.

'His name was Robert. I think he was some kind of juvenile delinquent. He used to do really cool graffiti on the community centre wall. It was on a park bench near the Scout Hall. I got a cigarette butt caught in my hair.'

'Did you have any fun?'

'It was freezing. Actually, it was like those dreams where you want to move but you're paralysed. I liked the idea of it. When he was trying to get it in I thought: after this I'll know stuff, I'll be an adult.'

'Why didn't you tell me when it happened?'

I clasped my knees to my chest. Sarah's garden was so different at night. I saw ghostly waving flower heads whose stalks vanished in the dark, so they bobbed like balloons or small eyes in the air. 'Jeremy died the same night.'

She put her hand on the back of my neck. 'Did you see the guy again?'

I wanted a cigarette. 'He ejaculates in no time. Says, "thanks". Pulls out, zips up, walks off saying, "Alice is a slut." Wasn't it his good luck that I was a slut? I don't get it.'

'Weird.'

Sarah cut up oranges and brought them out to me on a silver tray.

'Fuck, I'm starving. Did we eat dinner?'

She shrugged. 'We drank dinner.'

'God, I don't want fruit. I want chips and biscuits and lollies. It's the dope.' I looked at my watch. 'I should get back to Louise.'

Sarah looked at me. 'Why don't you stay the night?'

I tapped ash onto the ground.

'I have had sex with women before,' she said firmly. A neighbour's window snapped shut with a bang. 'Oops.'

I gathered up the orange skins.

'They go in the compost bin. Garden loves it. But because they're so acidic you have to chuck a bit of shredded newspaper in there as well.'

I wanted to joke that I wasn't moving in with her but our old comfort hadn't yet returned. I tore up the pile of old papers Sarah had stacked next to the open fire in her house, sneezing at the dust. Sarah told me, 'I'm really glad that happened. Are you?'

I kissed her on the mouth and touched her cheek with the back of my hand. She picked up the paper and added it to the compost bin. 'We need a bit more. I'm too good at recycling.' She dug around in her magazine rack.

I pulled some papers out of my purse. 'How about my speech? Perfect compost fodder.' An envelope fell out of the stack of mail that I hadn't had time to read. 'And this, too?'

I tore open the letter. *We are writing to acknowledge your freedom of information request #665340. Further to our previous correspondence, please note that some documents fall under exemption clause 25 (3) and thus cannot be made available to you under the conditions of the act. If you believe such material ought not be exempt you may appeal this finding . . .*

I handed the pile to Sarah. 'It's about Louise's FOI thing. She doesn't need it. We got the papers already.'

'It's addressed to you.'

'It can't be – I didn't do one.' I was still holding the envelope with my name on it. Louise must have done one on my behalf.

Her talent for manufacturing people and stories that others would believe in was limitless. As far as I knew she had already taken out a credit card in my name, or a car loan, and she may never have even thought she glimpsed my mother on the streets of Sydney.

Sarah insisted I take her car. On the way home I pulled into a McDonald's parking lot, dropped my head onto the steering wheel and tried to calm down. Sarah's sensuality and her generosity, the language of her body, was exhilarating. I was already imagining a future for us but I had no idea what she wanted, whether she wished she could curl back into the certainty of the old friendship. My heart beat fast. A teenage raver swished and cut her way along the footpath on rollerskates. A cat clung to the fence, black fur prickling up, hackles rising, claws sinking into the damp wood as it pulled itself up.

Louise wasn't there when I got back just before midnight. She'd copied down Sarah's number on a pad next to the telephone. Her Jeremy collage had been taken down. The clock ticked persistently as I went from room to room, shaking out my pillows, wiping hair and toothpaste off the bathroom sink. Small delays.

She had not brought many clothes from Sydney. I rifled through a few pairs of stained underwear, some sleeveless sequinned top perhaps thieved from a costume store, two pairs of blue jeans, worn in the knees. The packet of foil stuffed into a sock smelled like weed, not amphetamines; I didn't open it. Her blue spiral-bound notebook was almost empty, except for a list of names and diary entries describing her dreams, none of which I could bear to know about.

If she had assumed my identity in other ways, there was no record of it.

All her hidden pockets of shame were here: detailed, voyeuristic lists of horrific ways to die, including research into war crimes, exotic diseases and car accidents. There was a recovery warrant for unpaid fare evasion fines, the notice she'd first been given in Sydney of her cancelled Centrelink support, an unfilled prescription for anti-depressants and a university offer for art school. Beneath these, dubious internet research on death by asphyxiation. A long account of many of the lies Louise had told recently with instructions to herself about how to avoid lying: *options: come clean, try to tell all others what actually happened, do not assume names, think first. You are not forgiven.*

And then I found the portraits: Jeremy (rendered pink and green with thick brushstrokes) held up a mask, which was Louise's face. In another drawing, only a sketch, Siamese twins in the womb with two sets of arms, one hand reaching out to saw off the other's head. In the next painting, there was a woman in a white apron holding out an enormous dinner on a silver platter. It was a too-shiny cheesy advertisement for an entire roast lunch, lush and vivid. The food was so realistic it could have been taken from a photograph, except the colours were crazed, glossy, and the lunch was a suckling pig that had a shockingly naturalistic child's face, drawn in pencil. It was Jeremy from a photograph the year he turned seven.

I put the portfolio back where it had come from and closed the front door tightly behind me. I summoned my courage and went back to spend the night at Sarah's and then went to work in stale clothes, smelling of cigarettes.

Even at recess, Tom's office door was closed. The blinds were down. In the staffroom I saw Kirsty reading aloud from the local paper. Deirdre, who wanted to take a package and teach in the private sector, left the room. But the other teachers crowded over the article and congratulated me on my fifteen seconds of fame, and made jokes about how photogenic I was.

'Wouldn't be hard to look good standing next to a woman with cancer,' I declared.

'Don't,' said Kirsty. 'That's awful.'

I bit down on my shame and my exhaustion, and sat quietly.

There was an interview with Sam's mother, describing her as a cancer patient and parent, and a sympathetic article about the threat to close the school.

'Did you hear Anastassia on talkback?' Kirsty asked me eagerly.

'I slept in.'

Vanessa, the part-time art teacher, said, 'There were *heaps* of calls, plenty of nasty ones. She said it's only happening because the school's got a high proportion of migrants. And that they know they won't lose votes in poor areas. One of the safest seats, practically heartland.'

'And we're having another staff meeting today and a union planning meeting for the branch on Friday.'

My head hurt. I made a cup of coffee. 'Okay.'

Kirsty followed me to the kettle and nudged me. 'You should be happy.'

'What's Tom's latest line?'

'No one knows. He's been holed up dealing with pissed off parents since I got here. They're talking about holding a demonstration.'

When Anastassia came into the room, we gave her a round of applause. She was wearing a blowsy floral dress and carrying bags of clothes for her daughter's birthday present. She bowed. 'Been shopping for Cassandra. And I got a call. I've a boy in VCE maths whose mum's African. Says she'll organize a community picket. She's calling Tom a turncoat, reckons they only want to support white kids with good grades.'

I sat next to her.

'Come out to lunch with me.'

'I can't; I have to do something with my sister.'

'Alice. Chin up.'

I tucked my chin in. 'I'm happy. I just drank too much. I'll be at the next meeting.'

'We've got the advantage; now we just have to press it home. The state branch advisor thinks we could go legal. The funding profile looks like it's designed to close us quietly and I'd bet Kirsty's bloody wedding ring they'll find an excuse to discard it once we're gone.'

Kirsty made a face. 'You can't bet my ring!'

'Why take this to the courts? Doesn't seem a great tactic. Won't there be endless delays?'

There was an education department bulletin on the table. I glanced over an article on support staff for students with disabilities or illnesses. There was a boxed ad for a fundraiser for Multiple Sclerosis.

Then I stopped at the photograph, chilled. My mother's eyes looked back at me. Her name was not in the image caption. The woman in the picture was the right age.

Yet hadn't Louise seen our mother everywhere in the years after she left? Louise had followed a woman off the train once, all the way to her door, until she'd understood that this person was far too young to be our mother. She'd been hoping for someone who didn't exist anymore: her 36-year-old parent of years before.

Heroin must have closed some kind of portal in Louise, blocked one madness in her with another. When she first stopped taking smack, in rushed all the ghosts, the armies of the dead and the gone. She'd been a kind of magnet for false hopes and misunderstanding. And now it was happening to me.

Tom plodded into the room. His shirt was crumpled and he kept his arms crossed. He saw the paper on the table and the cluster of teachers. 'As I'll say when I talk to Graeme today, it's clear to me that I've underestimated the level of staff and parent sentiment about this. So perhaps I've been hasty.' Deirdre pushed open the door and stood beside him. 'But I assume, unlike Alice, most of you don't believe I'm concealing and plotting.' He gave a dry, gentle laugh, to show me he could be joking.

Annie, the school receptionist, gave me a telephone message after my final class. 'It's a policeman,' she said, with a rising inflection. 'Here's the number. You're to ring back after five; he said he's on night shift. I hope everything's all right.'

Even at four in the afternoon, the day was bright and blustery; it was the proper weather for walks along the beach and sticky trips in cars, for lying on towels in the backyard and buying icypoles at the local service station. Louise was inside at work, sweltering over a coffee machine, mopping up milk and drying dishes. And I was in my dirty flat, stuffing pretzels into my mouth and licking salt off my fingers, looking at the half-painted banner she was making, with the slogans stencilled in, and the placards she'd glued together with balsa wood. They said: *School closures: just say no*; and *Education for all, not just the rich*. Louise was paying attention. Her instincts told her to.

You'd forgotten how much you remembered. There are two of you. The you now, with a shot of whiskey in your belly and all that useless energy motoring your flight, while fear pounds behind you. And there's the old you: the younger, better one, who stole chewing gum from this milk bar, hid it in your knickers and blamed Jeremy when you got caught; who swung on the swings in the park and watched your father use a stick to draw pictures of the galaxy in the dirt for Jeremy.

And you're eight years old and riding your pink Malvern Star bike all the way up the hill towards home, though you're puffing and your bare feet are sore on the pedals because you refused to wear shoes, the day your dad knew he'd lost his job for certain.

There's the tangle and the dread.

Station Street's bustling now, waking up. You walk the footpath you used to avoid the cracks on, count the same squares you used to count. Even though so much has changed, the old bones show through. As with X-rays, you are able to see what's not always visible on the outside. You hear the plaintive hoots of the trains but the sounds of the factories have gone: the thump of goods on and off forklifts, the packaged goods being stamped and labelled. New young families have moved here and work in call centres or in takeaway shops. Manufacturing hasn't gone entirely, but it's been edged out.

A florist has opened on the corner. 'Say it with flowers,' the sign advises. A few orchids are beginning to bloom. They lie wrapped in clear cellophane on display. You've been inside the shop when it was still a Chinese takeaway, and you'd eaten sloppy potatoes and carrots in a hot sauce. You went with Alice and her boyfriend the same week you dropped out of high school. He was Chinese and made small talk with the restaurant owners and clucked at the food when it arrived, sucked in his breath. They'd given him another bag of food to take home without charge. Alice's fortune cookie said: 'Like the eagle you will soar and swoop.' The boyfriend had laughed.

You were fifteen, then, still living with your dad, and Alice was out, home free, gone for good.

This used to be a tiny shopping strip: supermarket, fruit store, milk bar, newsagent.

The sky is getting lighter and people rush from the train station out onto the street. Cars pull up and beep. Kids slide out of them. A woman pushes a pram and the wheels squeak on the damp road. She tugs her older child by the wrist, sets her gaze on elsewhere.

You walk past where the community centre used to be. You and Alice once made clay mice there and baked them in a kiln. The tail fell off Alice's when it was cooking and so her mouse was just a rounded clump with ears of different sizes.

The building looks empty. Brown brick, peeling window frames, grass bunching over the borders of empty flowerbeds.

You think of Alice, perched on this fence, schoolbag at her feet, a book in her hand. The cover's bright, with a love heart on it. 'True love. I wouldn't bother with all that,' your mum had told her, and so Alice tried to read with the cover folded back. Alice sits on the fence and lights a smoke. She's probably waiting for a boy. She puffs hard into the air and your dad winks at her but says that smoking is stupid and she is killing herself. The wink is a painful thing. It's too large – it echoes the nervous twitch he gets in one eye, and flutters like blinds being dragged down and suddenly released.

It's been almost a decade since you walked along this street.

They've levelled out the ground where the old tip used to be. A new apartment building looms, balcony protruding like a stuck-out lower lip. The primary school's lasted. It's been renovated and it's a pleasant, light place to visit. There's a proper oval and a new library with huge glass windows tilted towards the sun, and a purple entrance way. Jeremy waits at the door to the science room, clutching a leaf to analyse under the microscope.

There are colourful paintings about the different seasons stuck up in the window of the Prep classroom. You bend over the water fountain to get a drink, kick your feet into the tanbark under the swings, practise walking the rope bridge; but all the old power of the school, its whiff of death and dying, has gone.

You're twenty-four and without really knowing it you've left heroin behind. But you remember its old call, the way it was devouring you, chewing off crumbs of flesh, dissolving your limbs with warm tongue and acid breath. Heroin was homecoming; heroin was ruin.

Jeremy's grave is thirty minutes away. The danger game says you should hitchhike and so you do. Traffic travels up to a hundred ks round here and it's a truck route. The drivers look through you when you stick out your thumb. You start walking.

The woman who pulls over looks a bit like Sarah, only younger and posher. 'Umm, where to?'

'The cemetery.'

'What?' She looks as if she wants you to get out again. 'I mean where are you going?'

'West.'

On the radio, the Pet Shop Boys sing, '*We were never being boring. We were never being bored.*'

When she drops you off she says, 'Are you from Melbourne? You could have just caught a bus, you know.'

'It was sort of a bet. Thanks.'

The gates are pinned open with blocks of bluestone. It's a huge cemetery, with a brown-brick crematorium and chapel in the centre, and paths fanning out like spokes in all directions. Even dying seems economical, pre-packaged, here: a one-size-fits-all experience. It's a late-twentieth century cemetery, so no sculptures of famous men, no beautiful old headstones, no one who died before the seventies, no history. The graves are close together, evenly placed. You stand under the shade of a poplar tree to catch your breath.

When you find his grave you dig in the dirt, which is harder than you imagined – baked with clay beneath the topsoil – and bury the magnifying glass.

Alice didn't come home last night. You haven't seen her so relieved, so abandoned, for a long time. You cooked dinner for her because you'd seen her face in the afternoon. When she didn't come, you started to make a banner, stealing a white cotton bedsheet for material. There'll be a rally. Some woman at the meeting said she'd heard that a developer's interested in the school's land.

In the middle of the night, after you'd tried to ring Alice's mobile and you'd read, and re-read, the documents you got under freedom of information, you got out of the flat.

You went to the backstreets alongside the Victoria Market, where pigs' blood and fish scales are hosed down the drain daily, cheap shoes are sold to tourists, and stalls offer homemade lavender soap, rinds of pricey imported cheese, and knock-off jackets in zany designs.

The door of the North Melbourne terrace flapped open, listlessly, in the still air. UDL cans marked the entrance, one either side of the hallway, like miniature pillars.

The boy, Sam, was in the backyard, pale and lolling. You guessed he might be at this old drug house again. He didn't look up when you walked down the side of the house.

'Who else is around?'

'Nuh, only me.' He hauled himself up onto his elbows. 'Why are you here?' He tried to inject some abruptness into his voice. 'I've got nothing.' Then you knew that it's him you wanted the comfort of – and to give comfort to – not the drugs.

He was blinking off the shreds of dreams and memories.

'Want to know something funny?'

He shook his head.

'My sister's your teacher.'

'Bull she is.' He leaned over a rumpled exercise book that he had been writing in.

'Miss Reilly, History.'

'You're identical.' He is drowsy, talking rubbish.

'What?'

'Can you think what the other one is doing?'

'Who? Alice? Now, you mean?'

He swayed and grabbed hold of his book. 'She reads my stories, Miss does.'

'Sorry about your mum.'

He drifted back into his blanket on the porch and closed his eyes. 'I meant your twin; can you know what they are thinking?'

You realized he was asking about Jeremy. 'No,' you said, but he was asleep.

You read some of the stories, his hunger for the future, the world of robots and galactic wars. Then you hugged him. He smelled like a man: pungent sweat, dirty skin. If he was on smack, you couldn't see it. The earth held together, didn't split in two along a fault line. Spit was gathered in the corners of his mouth. He felt warm and soft, like a little kid. You had to dodge when he woke up because he tried to kiss you. You told him to go home, to go back to his own house. He had been crying in his sleep.

At Jeremy's grave you take out the document that shows your mother's application, which you found last night in the pile of paperwork you'd been sent. Last year, under a new name, she filled out a foster parent application for temporary guardianship over a six-year-old girl with a severe disability who had become a ward of the state. She'd had to list the name change. She had written down your name and Alice's and Jeremy's under the section asking for information about children, and she wrote her occupation down as an aged-care worker. Her marital status is ticked as 'separated'. She withdrew the application a week after it was submitted and there's a red stamp across it. There's an address for her, a telephone number.

If you found her she was meant to be unbelievable or hopeless or both. She should be sexy, sassy, a TV-movie actress with a fag hanging out of her mouth and a satin slip. Not the way your grandparents were: deflated, evasive. Retorts crack out of her mouth, whip and sting. A woman working the prawn ships off the coast, with blistered hands and a peeling, ravaged face. Small-time con woman signing up people awash in spare time, drowning in it, to sell pyramid schemes, where she snaffles the cash. In jail for holding up a 7-Eleven, or welfare theft. A blubbery monster, yawning, unloveable, getting larger every day. Otherwise, why hasn't she ever contacted you? Otherwise, why didn't she come back?

Why are you so fucking stupid, Louise?

Alice says again, with her mouth full and sour: *it's TV, it's fantasy.*

Probably, you should never have been sent this document. Probably, it's a mistake. You fold up the paper, fold away the masochism and the lunacy and put it in the ground.

You cover up the game, the file, the broken magnifying glass, and whisper 'enough' to the bruised storm clouds in the sky, the gathering wind.

On your way back, a woman pushes a leaflet into your hand. She's scrubbed up, middle class. 'Jesus *saves* but those who set themselves beyond his forgiveness will *burn* in the inferno.' You tear the pieces up in front of her and sprinkle them like confetti over her head. She trembles. 'Repent,' she says, but it's delivered like so much wishful thinking, a kid's whisper over a magic wand, and just as powerless.

There are people queuing for takeaway coffee when you arrive for the second day of your job trial. They haven't taken down the ad in the window, which should bother you but it doesn't. You slice prosciutto paper-thin for a man in a rich silk suit and wrap it up.

The manager asks you to make coffee and writes a list of orders in inscrutable shorthand.

The customer is wearing a tight red-and-white spotted jacket, with tiny dots like exclamation points. Her eyes are bright, ringed with black eyeliner. Her nails are painted tomato. She taps softly on the counter. 'I don't know if you realize this but a macchiato only has a *tiny* amount of milk. Sorry to be fussy,' the woman tells you unapologetically. She turns to the other person on trial, assuming he's the manager. 'Is she new?'

'She's black/white colour-blind.'

'I see,' the woman says neutrally, and she frowns. 'What?'

'I'll get you another free of charge,' he tells the customer.

'Lovely.'

He takes you through the steps; he's proud of how he makes coffee.

Your manager comes up. 'Louise? You need to clear the till.' You slide the fifty-dollar notes out from the bottom drawer of the register and wrap an elastic band around them, push them into a plastic snap-lock bag and tuck the package beneath the bench. She stands behind you and checks as you count the money and scribble it down on a notepad.

At the end of your shift she peels off a couple of notes. 'Do you want this job or not?'

You let yourself into Alice's flat. She's working at the desk, grading papers with her shoes kicked off beside her.

'Where were *you* last night? Not the usual shape of things, for me to be asking . . .'

She doesn't turn around. 'Yeah.' The room is filled with the sounds of a whining saw from the renovations across the road.

'Did you stay at Sarah's?'

She keeps writing. 'Mmm hmm. I was drunk.'

'And how was your esteemed principal today?'

'He announced to the staffroom he's been "hasty".'

'I made signs for if there's a rally.'

She smiled thinly. 'Yeah. I'm not sure if that'll happen.'

'You should embarrass the fuck out of them. You could all chain yourself to the school like they do at forest protests.'

'Being *chained to the school* any more than I am already is not my idea of a good time.' But she grins a little.

'Those parents were pretty pissed off,' you tell her. She doesn't answer. The lightness you saw in her at the meeting, the elation, has faded. You go into the kitchen, rummage in the fridge and the cupboards. You find the peanut butter jar and scoop some out with a finger. She grabs the jar from you, snaps it away with too much force. 'That's disgusting.'

All the rage is held in her body. Kept precious, hugged near the bone, like blood or tissue.

'I went to Jeremy's grave.'

'That's not like you.'

'Sentimental?'

'Thinking of others.'

'Actually, I was thinking of myself.'

She does not smile.

You lean on the wooden island bench. 'Sister, resist.'

'You are *ridiculous*; did you know that? Rearranging words. It's compulsive. Not clever . . . just this babyish distraction. You're like a child. On and on and on and on.'

'And on.'

You see now that she's been cleaning the flat, rearranging objects, dusting down the blinds. It's not a good sign with Alice – all that compressed fury.

She laughs, and waits.

'What's up?'

Her face is blotchy. 'I'll tell you what I *do* know. I get sucked back into believing you, into hoping, thinking about Jeremy, and I know it's toxic and pointless but I keep –'

Alice's doorbell rings. 'Oh, not now. You get that.'

'Why?'

'I'm not home.'

'What am I going to say?'

Sarah's outside, holding a bunch of roses and fruit: a mango, pineapple, some berries. 'Hello, Lou.' She shifts the fruit in her cradled arms. 'Relax, I'm not going to bite you.' You give her a hug. 'Where's your gorgeous sister?'

You think quickly. 'She went out with Jon.'

The smile wobbles. Sarah's dressed up, wearing a black dress with capped sleeves, and dark lipstick. 'I told her I'd come round.'

'I've been annoying her. She's gone out.'

Sarah digs her keys out of her pocket. 'You take care, Louise. Say hi from me to Alice, pain in the arse that she is.'

Alice is calmer when you go back inside. She looks at you fondly, head tilted to the side. 'How do you have such a sophisticated ability to say precisely the wrong thing?'

'She knows you're home.'

'I heard.' She pulls out a glossy, stapled union newsletter. 'Can you look at this?'

You nick one of her smokes. There's an article about curriculum reform and another about students' attitudes to social studies – mostly hostile or indifferent, although the researcher notes that some of this is the product of a generalized hostility to school itself. A glossy photograph of a small girl with her mother next to an information campaign about disability support.

You are so tired you want to crawl under the covers and never get out of bed. The shame is burying you alive. The shape of the woman's neck and the narrowness of her back, this you know. The effect is like a child's colouring book where only a few sections have been filled in so the rest of the outline fades back into the paper. The child's propped against her.

Inhale the cigarette. Dream of yesterday or tomorrow, slide past time.

The woman isn't wearing a wedding ring. She isn't smiling. Her face is in shadow and slightly out of focus. The caption below says: 'Meredith is in Grade Two at Astonbury Primary.'

'Is it her?'

Keep hold of yourself. 'Dunno.'

'She'd be too old to have a kid. That girl's about seven.' Alice chews her hair. 'I tried to get her name from the editor, said I think I used to know Meredith, love to be in touch, blah.'

'Before we started looking properly,' you look just over her head, 'I kind of borrowed your ID for something.'

'I know,' she says. She lights a cigarette too. 'They sent a letter. I went through your things.'

'I was confused.' You bite down hard on your own hand. 'No I wasn't. I really wanted to find her. See her.'

You both sit on the couch. 'I'm surprised you didn't seriously take up crime as a career,' Alice tells you in a flat voice. 'Your talents are wasted on petty shoplifting.'

'If she knew what Jeremy was thinking about that night. Where he went to hide.' They hadn't told you he was dead until you'd been released from hospital and led into the new unit, the navy carpet smelling of steam cleaning fluid, the walls painted light grey. 'Did you look at all my stuff?'

Alice nods. 'I have thought she just left him to die.'

'Did you look at my paintings too? They're from the night-mares.'

She's pale. 'They're good. You've always had an eye for the ghoulish.' She takes your arm and strokes it.

'When my arms got infected, I dreamt she came and put her hand on my forehead.'

'I did dream about him,' Alice admits, her face to the wall. 'But not for a long time.'

'It is her. The photo.'

'*Louise.*'

'She tried to foster the kid in the photo.'

'What do you mean?'

'I got the paperwork by mistake with the other freedom of information stuff. She was going to apply to be a foster parent.'

'You didn't even tell me about it.'

'I didn't read it properly.'

'Why would they send you that stuff? Show me the application.'

'I chucked it out.'

'Please, Louise, just stop it.'

She thinks you are lying, now that you are telling her the truth. 'We don't need to see her.'

Alice stamps into the bedroom and tears open the window. 'Why did you come here? *You* said she knew Jeremy was back at home. That's what *you said*.'

'She couldn't foster. Cos of us. One dead, two dumped, not a great parenting record.'

'She wouldn't have adopted *another* kid.'

'It said fostered. She was applying to foster. I don't want to see her now.'

'They would never have let her.'

You run your fingers over the scars on your arms. 'That's why she pulled out the application.'

'And now you don't want to see her?'

'I'm finished with the danger game.'

She lights two cigarettes and passes one to you. 'All right, Lou.' She flicks back into efficiency: empties the ashtray, checks her mobile phone. 'I might go and see a movie with Sarah. You can finish your banner or come with us.'

'What would you ask her, if you could ask her something?'

Alice is tugging on her sneakers, pulling her hair back into a ponytail. 'Why she didn't take us with her. Anyway' – she stubs out her cigarette – 'this is masochistic.'

So all through the evening while Alice is out, you walk and walk, try to get lost in the night. Catch trains to stations you choose by closing your eyes and stabbing a finger at the rail map. You walk along the scratchy sand near the sea, the luxurious silence in tree-lined streets that whisper words of money and comfort, then the rubbish-trailed streets where men shuffle into boarding houses and women's legs are puckered with goose pimples beneath short dresses, their hips swinging as they pace up and down the block. You see a fat woman in a pale blue coat poised outside what looks like army barracks, below a sign that advertises the CROOKED PLACES MADE STRAIGHT CHRISTIAN ACADEMY. You pick up some rubbish from the bin and take pot shots at the windows. A milk carton bounces off the entrance. A dog barks cruelly. You can watch the industrial belt melt into outlying suburbs, scrubby farms, new estates; see the cramped inner-city terraces become roomy renovated two-storeys with glossy cars in the driveways, let the world fade and re-form through the limits of the train window.

They wake you up when Sarah leaves, feet thumping to the front door and their stage whispers full of suppressed excitement. You have a headache and your skin's dry and papery. You pull on the ratty manga-print T-shirt. It's morning. Sarah's bunch of roses is on the table in a vase now and Alice is making cornflakes and toast. You chew your fingernails, bite down hard on them, rip the skin around your cuticles off with your teeth. You walk over to Alice and put your arms around her, lean your forehead against her back.

'Her name,' you say into Alice's back. 'I know the new name.'

She turns. 'I can't hear you.'

'Mum.'

Alice slices tomato onto her toast. 'From this document?'

'She had to put it in. They run background checks.'

'Was there an address?'

'I buried the file. She changed her name to Lucinda Grey. Lucy. Last year she was on the outskirts of Albury, some shit-hole town.'

'Lucinda Grey.' Alice holds onto the rim of the sink. 'Maybe she'll be in the *White Pages* online. At least if we do this, it's done.'

'I'll go with you,' you say, 'but I won't go in.'

After reams of flat country, blond crops and grimy sheep lining the Hume, you stop near the border for a break. Alice brings two milky coffees to the table, froth slopping over the lip of the cup.

You are in a tea room next to a wide, open river that the sun bounces off in flashes of generous light. You want to be out there: barefoot on the shingled shore, up to your knees in shady water. You squelch the mud in your toes, knock against tree roots and slippery rocks.

The menu advertises 'Cuppachino'. Truckers order plates filled with hot chips and crabsticks and potato cakes. The soft drink fridge is almost empty. There are pastel prints of innocuous country villages on the wall.

'Why does she want this girl and not us?' you ask.

Your mother has found a child who is loveable, whose limitations, if they live anywhere, live in her body; this girl does not bring the dread smell of the past with her.

'Don't be a drama queen.' Alice stirs sugar into her coffee. She looks younger. Her hair is wild and gleaming. She says, 'Remember the stories you used to make up for Jeremy about the trains.'

'They went underground.' He used to ask if they travelled faster than the speed of light or if they were propelled by anti-gravity. But you both believed in the trains, at least for as long as it took to tell the story.

Your sister stretches, then lays her head in her forearms on the table. 'Did you check her date of birth?'

'I didn't think of that.'

'What if the names are just a coincidence?'

'Alice, Louise, Jeremy, Chelsea.' Want catches in your throat and sticks like an object that will choke you. 'It should be her.' You want to see your mother but you don't want her to see you. You are so tired. Only sudden circuits of anxiety – your trembling hands, your bolts of panic – keep you from drowsing.

You fill in the crossword in the local paper, which advertises feeding lots for sale.

'Thanks for giving my ID when you got caught.' Her face is calm, crafty. You spoon froth off your coffee and wait. 'The cops rang me to ask me to come in for an interview. I was on speed or ecstasy in Fitzroy weaving in and out of traffic,' she says.

'Sorry.'

'Now the guy's coming to see me so I can prove he's never met Alice Reilly.'

'You should've told them your wallet got stolen.'

She blows on her drink. 'It did.'

'I thought they'd forget about it.'

'Doesn't matter.'

'That boy in your class with the sick mother?'

'Sam?'

'Yeah. He's using lots of drugs.'

She puts her head down on the table. 'Are you, Louise?'

Tears drip off your checks, salty as the sea. 'I got some ice off him one time.'

'Is he on smack?'

'Maybe.'

'And you?' Her voice is thin and hard.

'Just methadone.'

'Why did we hate her and not Dad? He put down the kero.'

'*I* shared the hate around, thank-you-very-much.' You do a twirl and a curtsey but it doesn't dislodge the anchor of regret. 'Because she left and he stayed?'

'I went to his place the other week. He was so pleased to see me. Says he will never drink again. *Yeah right*. Why is he shadowed by that stupid woman from next door?'

'I would guess he is fucking her. Maybe they're a couple, Alice.'

Alice taps her spoon on the table edge. 'Sure they are. She keeps claiming she's getting marriage proposals from that young guy with the porn.'

But after you both giggle and drink the lukewarm coffee, you drive to the address written on the piece of paper in Alice's pocket.

It takes forty minutes to get there. The place is on the outskirts, near where a housing estate is being built, bisected by a shallow creek with honey-coloured water, the artificial lake still only a hollow in the earth dotted with bulldozers. The area is full of roads that go nowhere, looping back on themselves.

'48b,' Alice tells you.

You find it: half a house, just a bungalow really, brick veneer, with its own side entrance.

You are caught at the door again, your arms reaching for the handle, your lungs bursting, the skin on your arms blistering, a wailing in your ears. 'I'll wait out here.'

Alice takes your hand. 'Please.'

'I don't want to go in.'

'Just for twenty minutes.'

'I didn't know Jeremy was inside. I was getting my toys.'

'You're okay, Louloubelle.' Alice presses the buzzer.

There is the sound of several locks being drawn back.

This woman is not your mother. Her blonde hair is greying, her nose looks as if it has once been broken, and her shoulders are broad, like a Phys Ed teacher's. Where are the old smells of Velvet soap, or those rubber gloves she wore to wash walls; where is the heart's cut of recognition?

You used to know your mother's face. You knew every wrinkle and spot.

Now she's here you can hardly look at her.

You hyperventilate. The breaths come quickly. Your dad pushes you onto the ground, shoves you onto the grass and beats the fire off you with his hands.

She stares at Alice and then she looks at you and her face does not change. 'I was going out,' she says, but still she waits in the open door, clutching her cheap black handbag in her hands. She is pale and washed out, her placating stare almost abject. 'Just on my way to the shops.'

'Do you know who we are?' Alice asks so gently that it's hard to hear her.

'Yes.' Then she tries to slam the door. Alice shoves her foot in the way.

Both of your legs are trembling.

'Get out,' she says, as if she's shooing away a cat or a fly, but she's barely raised her voice and her eyes are on the floor.

She turns away and goes back inside the house.

You and Alice wait on the step, hovering until Alice flings the door open wide and follows her. During the walk down the hall Alice takes your arm. It's a narrow corridor, painted a lively yellow.

When your mother sits down she doesn't know how to greet you and keeps her arms pinned close to her sides as if to ward you off, as if you are small children still, who might cling to her and wrap yourselves around her like limpets. She puts out her hand to shake and then takes it away. Her hands are bony, knuckles large. They're man's hands, broad and thick. And all the while, during the placing of her bag back on the hall table, the scraping out of the chair, she's crying.

Your mother says in a soft voice – even her accent's changed, she speaks more slowly and her vowels are flatter – 'You look really happy, nice.'

She has cut her hair. It hangs to just under her chin. There are silver studs in her ears, although she never used to wear earrings.

There's no mess in her lounge room. It's bare but hopeful: some books about tapestry and wildlife on the makeshift shelf; a built-in wardrobe; a few spice jars on the kitchen bench; a half-sized fridge. You glimpse a pot of anti-ageing skincare lotion on the bedside table near the double bed. Her louvre windows are half-open, like many slitted eyes.

She's thin, with sad elbows and child's wrists. 'I like that dress. It suits you.' You touch the fabric of your blue-and-pink floral polyester tunic. She cries.

'Do you have *anything at all* to say to us?' Alice has never sounded so much like the mother you remember: so curt and flat.

She doesn't say, 'I wanted to see you,' or, 'I wrote.' She *introduces* herself to you, says her name's Lucinda. She tells you that she works as an aged-care assistant and lives alone and that you both look beautiful.

'Louise found you,' Alice announces.

She finds a tissue in her bag and blows her nose. 'You're both very big,' she announces as if you are still teenagers and likely to grow.

'We're not *too big*,' you say, although the entire conversation is permeated by a curious ache, not for anything that belongs to the three of you but for the world your mother excluded herself from, the time when you and Alice knew nothing at all. For here she is: harmless, almost powerless.

'Sorry.' She giggles and then puts her hand over her mouth. Your mother pats down her pleated skirt over and over.

'So, how have the last fourteen years been?' You raise your voice, weight your words with the cheery emphasis of a soap opera character's speech.

She cries some more. 'Louise.' All over the walls are photographs of Meredith, the girl she wanted to foster.

Then she looks at Alice and back at you. 'Why have you come here?'

Alice sits down and folds her arms. She speaks at a fair volume: 'Did you know Jeremy was trapped in the house with the fire? Is that why you left?'

'You girls . . .' She waits, as if there is a punchline you have not understood, as if there is a joke to be enjoyed. 'No.' She doesn't know where to look. 'I have a glass of water in the afternoon, I have a drink of water, just to, I'll come back . . .' She turns on the tap, fills herself a cup and returns.

'It's okay.' Alice rolls her eyes at you.

Your mother says, 'I feed the birds, outside; I put out a bath on the windowsill. Parakeets. Even a kookaburra.'

Alice nods but you stand up. 'Why are you acting as if we're going to beat you? Are you psychotic?'

She collects a pretty eggshell-coloured teapot from the small cupboard in her kitchen area, carries it to the table without hot water or tea. She smiles at you. 'You used to be so tiny I could almost hold you here,' she cups her hands together. 'Like that. Course you don't remember.' A husk of a laugh.

'No,' you tell her.

'Is your dad alive?'

Alice answers, looking at her feet. 'Yeah. He shifted into a new place when Louise moved out.'

You want to break all the furniture in the room, shower it down on her, smash the windows, ruin the birdbath. But here she is, a middle-aged woman afraid of her own kids.

It's Alice who eventually asks her. 'Who lit the fire?'

She puts some tea in the pot and boils water in the kettle, like she used to do every morning when you were young. 'I think Jeremy did.' She says the words quietly and evenly. An incantation. 'I nearly went back into the house. Thought we might save the place. It was the last thing we owned and the insurance would never pay it out. If I'd gone in, he might not have died alone.'

For a second, just as you breathe in, you are a circle, the three of you, bound by your own ancient regrets and the implacable, unyielding events of that night. For none of you will ever know what he thought as he crept into his home, ten years old and about to vanish.

Alice gets herself a drink of water and now you ask, 'Why did you leave?'

'I had a boyfriend then.'

You break in. '*Who cares?*'

But she keeps talking, patting the belly of the teapot. 'Wayne Colvert. I missed adult company. Being touched. Sometimes I met him in the offices. Mondays. Or he'd get me. Used to park his car across the road. He'd stay in the car until I came out, so your dad wouldn't see him hanging around. Then off I'd go. I was meant to meet him when the house caught fire. I was too busy worrying that Jeremy was missing, and that Wayne was waiting, to notice the house was burning.' She's stopped crying and now she rakes her hands over her cheeks, again and again, as if her skin is just a mask that will fall if she tugs hard enough. 'So . . . the things you think you'll never do, I did. I had an affair. I let my son die. I left my kids.'

'You left *us,*' you tell her.

'In the house that night, I knew, that was that, I was going. I would've taken you, all of you. I say to myself, if Jeremy comes home safe, I'll leave. I couldn't face the debt collectors and the phone calls.'

This time, you ask. 'But did you know Jeremy was home when the fire happened? Did you let Jeremy die on purpose?'

She pats the teapot. 'No. I have. A thing.' She breathes brokenly. 'It's. I get. I had a nervous breakdown. Actually, I was in the bin. But that was – not, not recently.' She pours tea for herself.

Alice straightens her back. 'The heart bleeds.'

Your mother jumps. 'What? It . . . I see.'

'Where did it all go, your strength? You used to be the most resilient person and now you're . . .' You break off. 'What happened to you?'

The question remains in the silence, like a musical note held too long.

She clears her throat. 'We never saw him. Jeremy. I thought your dad had lit it. That's what he had always threatened to do. I went to go in the house but I heard Shaun shouting for you, Louise, at the back.'

'What about the stones Jeremy left?'

She shrugs. 'I don't know about that.'

'Dad said you fell on stones.'

The smile was terrible. 'No. There were old toys on the porch, and I tripped. But I wasn't really going in. I did think I saw one of Jeremy's magic circles. But I'm sure he left them there weeks ago.'

She pats her hands together softly. 'You see, Shaun was right there outside with me, so I didn't think it could be our house on fire. And when I was about to go inside and check things, I knew Wayne was waiting. I thought it would destroy him, your dad, if he found out. So I went over to Wayne's car and told him to go, it's not a good day.'

The room is hot. You can't stop staring at all her things. You are trying to learn her life again. 'You didn't want to get caught?'

She cradles the teacup in her hands, looks at the tea leaves for signs. 'It wouldn't have made any difference what I did.'

Alice is watching her with tired eyes. 'Why didn't you take us when you went?'

She switches on a lamp. 'Shaun thought they would take you away, put you somewhere else. I thought it was just temporary when I left. So I was, "oh well," for a bit. I could get some sleep. Change my life. Shaun wanted to fight for you. After Jeremy died, I had nothing kind, no pity. I thought I'd come back for you. It took a year until I stopped wanting to cut myself, stopped imagining there were spiders living in my skin. I didn't love you anymore.'

'What do you tell people?'

You hear a trace of a tone you recognize: sly, light. 'Divorced. No kids.' She nods. 'You really have to believe it to keep it going.'

You rush to the bathroom and vomit on the floor, your stomach twisting. You wash your face and listen at the door while Alice stays and talks to her.

She spent months in and out of psychiatric hospitals, and now she works for a pittance in aged-care, volunteers her time for 'causes', visits Meredith, who is being shipped from one foster family to the other, and takes her out to the museum and the adventure playground. She's saving to help fund an operation for Meredith that will make it easier for her to walk.

'Good deeds,' Alice says tonelessly, and when your mother replies, 'something like that', she sounds so much like Alice herself, with the self-deprecation, the dismissal, that it almost breaks you.

He dreams. There are shadows with sharpened claws but slippery, kind smiles that lure him into a boat made of fish scales that can fly across the sea. The waves are tremendous. They crash and lurch and wail. They pitch him forward into a tunnel that's too small, where his ribs are squeezed. He's drowning in the dark air.

He wakes by hitting his head against the cupboard door. The skin on his legs is creased red with the shape of his shorts. His limbs feel heavy and lazy and one of his feet is paralysed by pins and needles. When he pushes open the door, the bare bulb of the kitchen shines on the patterned linoleum. The fridge must be leaking again because the floor gleams with water. The newspaper taped across the broken window has come loose. Jeremy can only read half of the headline – the first part with big block letters. He tilts his head: 'History in the Making'. The photograph shows three women with grimy faces standing in front of a grey building. Everything that happens is history in the making, really. It hurts his head to think about.

Memories whisper through his mind, of the art room at school: imaginary animals made out of egg cartons; painting his own shape, which had been drawn and cut out, in orange and yellow; finger painting and using potatoes cut in half to make shapes and patterns. It's the smell. Methylated spirits was used to clean the brushes when they ran out of turpentine. Meths would sting the skin on your hands but it could get the paint off easily, whether it was water- or oil-based.

Jeremy climbs slowly out of the cupboard and almost skids on the floor. The smell is everywhere, on the patchy brown cushions in the lounge, across the great sad roses of the carpet, sliding off the kitchen table in slow drops. He can't see his father.

The box of extra-large matches that they use for the pilot light when the hot water goes off is lying on the floor next to the table in a wet puddle. His mother's lighter – that she uses for the Alpines she sometimes smokes with her friend Jean – has been taken. If he was a detective he could call the kitchen the scene of a crime, although the crime hasn't happened yet.

The house is his. Alice and Louise are at the park. His parents are not here. The best magicians can make fire appear and disappear. Illusions are all about making your audience look in the right way at exactly the right moment. His book of card tricks says that most people are so busy keeping the card they chose hidden, tucked unseen into their palms, that they won't notice how you asked them to select it, or if the deck is marked, or that the answer's found by simple deduction. You can distract people with their own expectations: where they think the rabbit will come from, or the hand the coin is meant to be in. He leans over and opens the matchbox.

The matches feel strong in his hand. The box is warm and heavy. He can do anything in the world.

At the crunch of footsteps outside, he jolts. This is a child's game. He is disgusting. He hates his whirring thick mind; it's like a machine you can't switch off. He's a mutant. A retard. A psycho.

No one comes.

He builds patterns with the matches on the floor. A square. A cross. A rectangle. A house.

If you play the danger game you have to do what is dared in twenty seconds.

He can taste sweat like salt on his lips. When he was four and learned to swim he vomited salt water back up. Dad took him to the beach and held him in the water. A wave washed over his face. His dad put his hand under Jeremy's head and tilted him back, saying, 'I've got you. It's all right, I've got you.'

He can still remember the dizziness, the sense of endless falling. Jeremy feels the same now, both heavy and light. Around him the room breathes. It expands and contracts. Whatever he does will change things. He is transforming.

The matches might be too wet. If there isn't enough friction nothing will catch.

Jeremy once kept lots of secrets with his dad. The garden behind the hedge at the park was one. When they played, they pretended the creatures from *Where the Wild Things Are* had come to life.

His dad used to take him to the shop and let him choose any icypole flavour and Jeremy would hope to pick the one his dad thought was best.

The seconds are running out. He sees them fall away, discarded, as if they are real marks or lines. He counts them out of existence, checking them off like squares on a number line. At school if you have to minus negative numbers you take away by counting backwards, on the other side of zero, away from whole numbers.

He takes a match from the dry home of the box. Louise has knocked on the door of the ghostly old man who lives around the corner. She said he was a wizard and that his eyes glowed red when he found her. Alice has walked four blocks on the hot black tarmac of the road in bare feet, without going onto the shady side once. She got blisters on the soles of her feet. They haven't done this.

Hetay angerday amegay.

He tilts the box. His hands shake. He can't.

Back in the cupboard he puts his arms around his knees, hugs the matchbox to him. He can win the danger game.

When he strikes the match, the red tip sparks off. It burns his fingers so he flings it out. It soars in an arc and for a moment it's just a spinning, pretty flash. He sees a streak of orange lagging behind in the shape of a rainbow. Sparklers and Halloween and fairy lights flick on and off in his mind.

He pulls at the cupboard door when he hears the fizzle of the match landing. He waits for a roar, something more definitive. The darkness is soothing. There are three seconds left. He is ten years old and he is magic.

The heat, when it comes, feels like love.

I slept for almost seventeen hours after the visit to our mother's house. I woke at three in the afternoon. Louise was still snoring on the bed beside me, the duvet tossed off her, arms and legs askew. Every so often her limbs twitched. My breath was sour, my throat dry. When I dragged myself to the window and looked out, I saw my downstairs neighbours pegging up washing on the line, sheets billowing around them. People were carrying shopping bags to their cars from the supermarket on the street below. My bedroom was stuffy.

I poured myself a cup of tea and thought of the way my mother had petted the china teapot at her house, as if it were alive and needed comforting. We'd visited Dad on the way home, Louise so tired she'd barely spoken. He was trying to grow seedlings, and showed us the latest wooden model of inner Melbourne, which he was building. Louise had been dark-eyed and tetchy. We played cards with him and Diane who looked at my hand over my shoulder, and called Louise 'Lois' and refused to be corrected. But she'd been disconcertingly articulate, telling us stories of growing up in Nova Scotia. After she left, our dad had said, 'See, when she's on medication . . .' and then let the sentence drift away. When I asked if he knew our mother had spent time as a mental patient he pretended not to hear.

When we left, he stood in the doorway and asked, 'That wasn't so bad, was it?' Louise and I buried ourselves in the noise of the radio on the way home.

I drowsed off in the afternoon sun and dreamed about Sarah. I woke to the sound of thumping techno and realized there was someone knocking at the door and shouting my name.

I opened the door to Sarah, who was carrying a newspaper and some pastries. She looked prim: her hair was held back with a plastic headband; there were tiny silver circles in her ears.

'Are you in exile from the world, Alice? I've been ringing.' Her gaze skittered past my unplugged phone. Sarah placed her offerings on the table, unfolding the newspaper and smoothing it out. She took my face in her hands and looked carefully at me.

'Your hands are cold.'

She rubbed them together, an anticipatory motion that didn't suit her expression, the tightening of her face. '*I* will make coffee. *You* will read the newspapers.'

'Lou's asleep.' I sank ungratefully into a chair.

'Want some bread and cheese?'

'Come and sit for a minute.'

She made a wonky face. 'But I'm trying to make myself indispensable so that you'll think, "That Sarah, she's handy – worth keeping around."'

'We found Mum. We went to her house.'

'Your mum?'

'She calls herself Lucinda Grey. She was incredibly skinny, lonely, marginal.'

Sarah settled into the sofa. 'I hope you never have to sum me up in three words.'

'And an adverb.'

'Did she have anything to say?'

'She was crying pretty much the whole time. She got screwed up because she was cheating with some guy from work.'

'What about Jeremy?'

'She didn't think the fire was at our house. Her story was so confusing I could hardly understand what she was saying. She didn't want to get caught out having an affair with the guy who was waiting out the front. She doesn't know anything else.'

'Did it help? Getting that part of the past back?'

'I wouldn't see her again. Or not unless she found me.'

'But did she tell you why she left?'

'No, she kept talking to me about this fucking birdfeeder she had in the garden.'

'This is big, Alice.'

'Does it have to be?'

'Did you ever really think you'd find her?'

'Nup.' Her sympathy was condemning me. 'Let's leave it for now.'

'*Sorry.*' She pulled her hand back and marched towards the stove, pale summer skirt swishing around her calves. I heard her packing coffee into the percolator.

'When we started having sex,' I began, without looking at her, 'did you expect it?'

She lit the stove. 'Not expect it but I hoped for it, I guess.'

'And what are we now? Friends plus sex, or are you assuming that's it – domestic harmony is declared?'

There was a long silence. I lit a cigarette and played with the silver-foil lining on my pack. Sarah coughed.

'Yeah, I like you – love you – just like I always have.' She turned back to the newspaper. 'Once you read the headline on page eight, you'll want coffee.'

My mother had said that she loved Meredith, that she was putting aside forty dollars a month for her rehabilitation and medical bills. She had told us this without chagrin or hesitation, just as she'd offered to show us photos of them together, and taken me to see the cockatoos feeding in her tiny backyard. The self-deception was monstrous.

The moment before I'd knocked on my mother's front door, when I was still on the threshold of that house, its fragile collection of possessions, its story of a contained life so trimmed and bottled, I had hoped to be angry. Louise, I had expected, would be insane, would spit out the years of longing and spite. Now I wanted to retrieve my mother as furious and whole, frank and unforgiving. Her hope for Meredith brought with it all the symptoms of despair.

And now Sarah was emanating hope, shining with it.

How could she love me just the same way she always had? 'So what is this, just fucking? You're a bit bored, a bit interested, a bit horny?'

'No, Alice. I don't think you're disappointed with me.'

'Oh, stop being so self-satisfied.'

The last time we'd fought like this had been when Sarah was first married.

Sarah walked towards me. 'I'm not Jon. I won't have you self-destructing because of some situation you've engineered.'

'*Right*. So that's what happened with Jon. Thanks for the illumination.'

She came and sat next to me. 'I'm glad we slept together. I want to keep being with you, or learning how to be with you, but I'm too old and too tired and too sensible to let myself get caught up again with someone who's ambivalent. Especially you, Alice.'

'I'm trying to be careful here,' I told her.

'One thing I can promise you: if we try this, I will hurt you.'

I had to laugh. She raised her eyebrows. 'People fuck up when they love each other. You make yourself a soft target. You just have to be prepared to take the risk.'

I couldn't answer.

'Should I go?'

The thin paper bag full of sweet pastry wilted on the table. 'I don't want us to change.'

She tried a smile, a flash of the old Sarah courage. 'It's the weekend. Want to go down the beach and lie around in the sun?'

'I need to find out what's happening with school.'

'I hope it goes well. Sorry for the impassioned pledges. Read the article.'

'So that's it?'

'Up to you, Alice, old girl.'

I joked, 'Old girl makes me sound like a horse,' but she had already closed the door and when I went to the balcony to watch her leave she did so with powerful steps, the wind blowing her faded red skirt around her thighs.

*

Page eight of the paper had a photograph of Sam sniffing some white powder next to a black and white photo of the science building that looked like it had been downloaded from our school website, alongside a random close-up of a needle and the headline: MEET SAM: HE'S 15, HE'S A DRUG ADDICT AND HE GOES TO THIS SCHOOL. His face was disguised, pixelated into a blur, but I recognized him.

Either a member of staff or a parent had leaked the information to the tabloid. The column described Sam as a pupil at 'a trouble-plagued public secondary college.' The education section was titled, OUR SCHOOLS IN CRISIS? and talked about the sale of drugs on the playground, issues of bullying, and violence in the classroom. The text implied that Sam had conducted drug deals just outside the school gates, and reported our 'ongoing struggle to clear "chromers" away from the district'.

I called Anastassia. She answered to a background of cheers and clapping.

'Did you see the paper? What scum.'

'I'm at Caz's netball match. Bear with me.'

'That is so unbelievably cynical of them.'

'Tom's calling the mother in. He confiscated one of the boy's mobiles and that photo was on it.'

'His mum's got cancer, she can't walk.'

'Yes, it's nasty. But good news, Alice. I'm emailing around a proposal from the state executive. The department's talking about working on a middle-school model instead. They want to avoid the community rally, so I've got a motion that we have an in-principle agreement to give the media. "Interested in pursuing discussions" and so on.'

'For a middle school? What about redundancies?'

'No, the organizer reckons they'll stick to voluntaries: transfer or accommodate. Even contracts. *Good girl.* Sorry, it's the semis. We're lucky. A little birdie told me the local rag's keen to run a story about the developers who are greedy for the land if the school closes and sells. I don't think there's any mileage in it but whatever keeps them nervous . . .'

'Can't we get a promise to keep it open?'

'Not going to happen. No way, according to Ned.'

'Have they publicized the rally?'

'For Monday. Say they're going to march and ask the Minister to meet with them and sign off on some agreement to keep the school open until the end of the year.'

'I could organize a teachers' delegation.'

'Well, read the motion I've written. I think it's better to let the parents handle that side. The union will send a statement to be read at the demonstration. But get this . . .' Anastassia trailed off.

'Speak into the phone. I can't hear you.'

'One of the parents said they asked if someone from the state opposition wanted to speak, which is pretty bloody dopey, and the guy's PR manager tells him on the phone, off the record, verbatim: "We're not holding some pity party about a bunch of white trash and immigrants whose parents can't stay off the dole."'

'Oh fuck.'

'Wish she'd had a tape recorder. You know Tom wants to see you.'

'*Me*? Shit. What for?'

'He was poking round the staffroom Friday making a performance out of your sick day. Sounds nasty.'

'Thanks, Anastassia. Who's winning?'

'Can't tell yet. Speak to you soon.'

While Louise slept I put on my sneakers, dusty from lack of use, and went for a run, which became more of a stagger after the first few blocks. In Royal Park at the top of a hill I looked out over acres of bushland and a footy oval, a cricket pitch and the cramped housing created for Commonwealth Games athletes. I crossed the old train line, steered away from the adolescent psychiatric institution and the factory, with its air of chemical secrecy, hemmed by barbed-wire fences and warning signs. Becoming a middle school didn't feel like a victory but it might be the only victory we'd be offered.

People played golf on a small green, families crowded around strings of sausages heaped together in plastic bags near the barbecue, cyclists whirred past in a blurred flash of motion.

Serial joggers overtook me and pounded on, their calves muscular, earphones in, feet hitting the pavement in time to rhythms I couldn't hear.

Anastassia had been so determined but she was already adjusting her expectations, fast and without comment, as if fiddling with the rear-view mirror in a car.

Sarah and I had brought a picnic here to celebrate when I'd first been offered the job. Looking at the horizon, then the mirages of wobbly pools of water on the bike path, shimmering in the blazing sun, I knew I had wanted Sarah to be enthralled by me. I had wanted to be irresistible, for her to need me enough to refuse to give me up.

I was in love with her. I stopped running.

Louise came to school with me, carrying placards and the banner she'd painted. Some of the parents were holding a vigil outside the local members' office in the morning, before the lunchtime rally outside the education department.

'I got a call from my link in the phone tree at *seven* a.m. Alice! These people are cruel and determined.' Louise was trotting along in short steps.

'You'd only had eighteen hours sleep the day before.'

'No dreams.'

I feigned a toast, swung my arm out holding a mimed glass. 'To the end of dreams.'

'I'll drink to that. Speaking of the end of dreams, Dad rang yesterday. He married Diane in a registry office. I guess she's doing it for the money,' her voice rose with sarcasm.

'Bullshit, Louise. You are fucking with my head.'

'Cross my heart.'

'Your black heart indeed.'

'It's true. Romance is not dead, just mentally ill. Can you direct me? I don't know where I'm going.'

'Two doors from the pizza shop once you cross the main road.'

'Why do you think Sarah's using you for sex?'

'Christ, Louise!'

She sped up into a jog. 'You were talking very loudly. And fucking come to the rally.' She sprinted for half a block and then halted when she dropped her signs.

Tom had left a note in my pigeonhole where the notice about our lunchtime union meeting had also been posted. He found me in the staffroom. He liked to wear suits to work but was dressed in beige pants and a faded grey shirt. 'Alice, there's been a complaint about you.'

'Who from?'

He spread his hands on the table. 'This is just an informal chat that we're having. Nothing's on your record and it's not going any further.'

'Is it with Sam? Because I gave him a warning and he was meant to be dropping out.'

'No, it's the Thomases. She rang me. Your private life is your business but she said you were explicitly talking to Chris about how wonderful gay sex is.'

'Does that seem at all likely to you?'

'I vouched for you. I said staff have an obligation to communicate our policy on discrimination and victimisation in the classroom.'

'I promise, it was a bullying incident. Some of the boys were chucking around homophobic drawings.'

'You've got to develop your judgement, Alice. It's an ongoing issue for you with teaching. You want to identify with your students when you need to be the professional, the teacher.'

The energy I'd felt when I woke in the morning drained away from me. 'Maybe you're right but I'm learning, I'm trying.'

'I haven't doubted that, it's just a real shame you didn't return that trust. And for some reason I don't want to know a thing about, a police officer called to say he's coming by at lunchtime to talk to you.' Before I could say anything he held up his hand. 'You don't need to explain, Alice, I'm sure you haven't done anything wrong, I'm just passing on the message.'

Anastassia chaired the school union meeting. She wrote down names as teachers trickled in. 'If we can shift four-point-two up the agenda we'll get through more.'

It was twelve o'clock. 'Are we going to try to get this finished before the rally?'

'From what Ned said, as you can see by the motion, which will go out in the union's name once it's ratified, the department wants to hose things down. We want to release it after all the staff have endorsed it. I don't think the rally's the priority.'

We read the motion. Kirsty cleared her throat. 'Until they're talking formally about something concrete, shouldn't we try and keep the pressure up?'

Anastassia blushed. 'I'm going on what the organizer told me. If we wait and see and then show we're happy with that model, there's a good chance. They wanted to close us quickly, quietly. So we can give ourselves a round of applause that they're back to negotiating.'

I put up my hand to speak. 'I think we should defer the motion until we know what they're proposing.'

Vanessa said, 'I thought there was talk of a legal remedy.'

Anastassia made a face. 'We're getting advice. But this is a smart strategy. We look reasonable, we can secure jobs, do it on our own terms.'

Kirsty was shaking her head. 'The parents really want to keep the school going, the whole curriculum.'

'What about industrial action?' I asked her.

'We're just going all over the place.' She put down her papers with a thump on the table. 'There's no protected action we can take about this. And we'll look like, well, fuckwits, really, if we force kids to miss classes on the basis that we want to keep the school *going*.'

I tried again. 'We can go today and support the rally. That won't look weird. It'll look worse if we don't.'

Kirsty asked what had happened in the past when non-protected industrial action had taken place.

'I don't know. I can't remember it happening since the nineties. That would be totally renegade. Remember, I didn't make the legislation; in fact, I went on strike against it. Can we get back to the agenda?'

Kirsty looked at me and smiled. 'I agree with Alice. I think we should go to the rally.'

Anastassia folded up her union minutes into a tiny square and swore quietly under her breath. 'I'm not trying to *ban* you. If you're on lunch, sure, fine, do it. Just don't expect to be able to call some spontaneous strike.'

Then Deirdre put her head around the door. 'Shutup about your stupid secret union business for a minute. Tom's just resigned.'

'When?'

'Said he's going home on stress leave and can I take over since I'm Deputy Head. He's quitting.'

We scrambled to the window to see a white-faced Tom carrying a cardboard box into the parking lot.

'You know the big cheque for twenty thousand dollars they gave to Brighton High for the swimming pool last week?' Deirdre's eyes were full of joy and malice.

'No,' Kirsty said.

'Well, you know big cheques: they present them at award nights sometimes, they're about three foot high. So the parents holding the vigil made this huge letter, same format, basically promising to keep the school open until the end of the year, and they got the TV news to film them delivering it to the Minister, handing it to him, and he signed it.'

Kirsty asked, 'How come?'

Deirdre shrugged. 'Waiting for a better time, I guess.'

Anastassia took her glasses off and snapped them back in their case. 'So we're not dead yet.'

After I found Louise I called Sarah.

I stood in the classroom. The sun cast dapples of light across the desks. I took in the sounds of students scrambling for their seats, smelled pencil sharpenings and damp erasers. I looked at the floor, at

Doc boots and socks that shrugged down to the ankle, at regulation T-bars adorned with stickers of Japanese cartoon figures.

I held the chug and tremble of Sarah's car humming in my body, from when she had dropped me off in the morning. We'd eaten cornflakes and cheese on toast and she'd kissed me goodbye with a sleep-dry mouth, her nurse's badge digging into me when we embraced.

'*Miss*, she took my pencil case, Miss.'

'Brianna thinks she's the girl in Black Eyed Peas.'

'So *not*.'

For once the chaos and the scramble didn't daunt me. It felt odd, this thrill in my own skin, this sureness and anticipation just because I was with someone who knew the whole story from the very start, or at least the start that mattered, and because, at our school, we'd won back one small thing.

Through the clear windows at the back of the room I saw cars crawl up and down the street, saw the freshly painted lines on the basketball court, white and stark, and I breathed in hope and a beginning.

I turned back to the board. 'Let's start.'

Acknowledgements

I am grateful for the kindness, assistance and insight of Luke Brown, Melissa Rudd and Rikhi Ubhi at Tindal Street Press, Nicola Barr and the Susijn Agency. Special thanks to Louise and Zoe.

About the Author

Kalinda Ashton was born in Melbourne in 1978. She has been involved in student, union and community campaigns. She is an associate editor of *Overland* magazine, and a teacher of writing and editing. *The Danger Game* is her first novel.